## Rebellious Young Ladies

*Finishing school was meant to turn them into perfect aristocratic ladies...but these four friends can never be contained by Society's expectations!*

To conform to what Society deemed correct for females of their class, Amelia Lambourne, Irene Fairfax, Georgina Hayward and Emily Beaumont were sent by their families to Halliwell's Finishing School for Refined Young Ladies—which they soon dubbed "Hell's Final Sentence for Rebellious Young Ladies"!

Instead, the four found strength in their mutual support to become themselves and a lifelong friendship was formed...one they'll need to lean on when each young woman faces the one thing they swore never to succumb to—a good match!

Read Amelia's story in
*Lady Amelia's Scandalous Secret*

Irene's story in
*Miss Fairfax's Notorious Duke*

Georgina's story in
*Miss Georgina's Marriage Dilemma*

And Emily's story in
*Lady Beaumont's Daring Proposition*

All four are available now!

## Author Note

*Lady Beaumont's Daring Proposition* is the final book in the Rebellious Young Ladies series and features Lady Emily Beaumont, the most serious member of the group of four friends who met at Halliwell's Finishing School for Refined Young Ladies, and Jackson Wilde, a man who does his best to never take anything seriously.

The book is partly set in London's East End, which was a deprived, overcrowded area where disease ran rampant during the Victorian period. While the squalid condition in which people were forced to live was often dismissed as being due to laziness and vice, some socially conscious people worked hard to change the conditions of the poor.

I based Emily on these caring people. She works in an imaginary hospital called the Hope Charity Hospital, where Jackson Wilde finds himself after yet another lively night out. What starts out as a mutual dislike doesn't stay that way for long, and this unlikely couple soon embark on an involvement that changes their lives and those of many people around them.

I hope you enjoy reading Jackson and Emily's story, and I love to hear from readers. You can reach me via my Facebook page, Facebook.com/evashepherdromancewriter, or through my website, evashepherd.com.

# LADY BEAUMONT'S DARING PROPOSITION

## EVA SHEPHERD

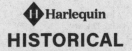

HISTORICAL

# Harlequin®
## HISTORICAL

ISBN-13: 978-1-335-59628-4

Lady Beaumont's Daring Proposition

Recycling programs for this product may not exist in your area.

Harlequin Enterprises ULC
22 Adelaide St. West, 41st Floor
Toronto, Ontario M5H 4E3, Canada
www.Harlequin.com

**Printed in U.S.A.**

After graduating with degrees in history and political science, **Eva Shepherd** worked in journalism and as an advertising copywriter. She began writing historical romances because it combined her love of a happy ending with her passion for history. She lives in Christchurch, New Zealand, but spends her days immersed in the world of late Victorian England. Eva loves hearing from readers and can be reached via her website, evashepherd.com, and her Facebook page, Facebook.com/evashepherdromancewriter.

### Books by Eva Shepherd

### Harlequin Historical

"The Earl's Unexpected Gifts"
in *A Victorian Family Christmas*

#### *Rebellious Young Ladies*

*Lady Amelia's Scandalous Secret*
*Miss Fairfax's Notorious Duke*
*Miss Georgina's Marriage Dilemma*

#### *Young Victorian Ladies*

*Wagering on the Wallflower*
*Stranded with the Reclusive Earl*
*The Duke's Rebellious Lady*

#### *Those Roguish Rosemonts*

*A Dance to Save the Debutante*
*Tempting the Sensible Lady Violet*
*Falling for the Forbidden Duke*

Visit the Author Profile page
at Harlequin.com.

# Chapter One

*London 1895*

The night Jackson Wilde, Viscount Wickford, had his life changed for ever started out like any other. He dined at his London club, played a round or two of snooker. He then proceeded to visit various drinking and gaming establishments throughout the city, deliberately selecting ones his father, the Duke of Greenfeld, would describe as dens of iniquity and lascivious vice.

As the night turned into early morning, the dens became more iniquitous, the vices more lascivious and the décor decidedly seedier. Friends with more refined tastes than Jackson—and you didn't have to be particularly refined to be included in that category—dropped off as the night wore on, until, somehow, he found himself in the dark back alleys of the East End, alone and completely lost.

Well, not completely alone. He'd spotted several large rodents scurrying along the gutters and a few mangy cats out on the prowl, presumably in pursuit of the scurrying rodents. But apart from those undesirable companions the area appeared completely deserted.

He looked up one narrow alleyway, the walls so close they appeared to almost touch. Then he turned and looked back in the direction he had come, taking in the identical red brick walls, appearing black in the light of a half-moon, and the broken cobblestone paths, glistening from a recent rainfall.

'They all look the same,' he said to no one in particular, his voice echoing off the walls.

'And they all smell the same,' he added under his breath, not wanting to offend the rats and cats who called this alleyway home, but unable to ignore the acrid stench of coal smoke, the putrid stink of rotting garbage and rat droppings, and the other less savoury smells whose origin he'd rather not know.

A loud snore drew his attention to a pile of rags in a doorway. It seemed he was not the only human inhabitant after all. He approached the sleeping vagrant but was stopped in his tracks by the overwhelming smell of raw alcohol. This man obviously needed to sleep off whatever demon drink had got him into this state, even more than Jackson did, and was unlikely to provide any useful advice on how Jackson was to wend his way back to his Kensington townhouse.

There was nothing for it. He was going to have to acquire that backbone his father always told him he was severely lacking and work his way methodically through this warren. It shouldn't be too hard. After all, he'd aways managed to find his way out of the maze at the family's Norfolk estate. And had been even better at getting himself lost so his father couldn't find him, and make good on his promise to once again beat some sense into his wastrel excuse of a son.

His not so fond memories of his father were interrupted by a shrill scream, piercing the night air.

'Did you hear that?' He looked towards the sleeping vagrant, who merely snuffled in his sleep and rolled over, as if such sounds merely provided the usual background noise to his slumber.

The woman's scream came again—louder, shriller, more desperate. Orientating himself towards the sound, he sprinted through the labyrinth, hoping and praying he was heading in the right direction.

Another cry ripped through the air, along with the sound of men's laughter.

He was close.

He turned yet another identical corner and found the source of the distress call. A young woman was pinned up against a wall, surrounded by a group of baying males. Her terror delighted the taunting men, whose faces were contorted with looks of cruel pleasure.

'Come on, darling,' one man said, pulling her towards him. 'You promised us a good time. So now deliver on that promise.' He grabbed the front of her dress, her cries for help drowning out the sound of tearing fabric and the accompanying men's laughter.

'Stop,' Jackson called out as he rushed forward, fists raised. Later, when he had time to consider his actions, he would admit it might have been better to take a moment to assess the situation and devise a plan of action. Boxing had been his strongest subject in school. It was, in fact, the only subject he excelled at, but even a man who had shown some prowess in the ring should have known better than to take on five or six assailants all fired up and looking for trouble.

But at the time he didn't have the luxury of hindsight, and thinking things through had never been one of his strong suits. So, instead, he threw a punch at the nearest man, and had the satisfaction of seeing him fall to the ground, before his four or five companions turned in his direction.

'Run,' he yelled to the young woman. She took action immediately, sliding past the distracted men and disappearing around the corner.

As he faced the furious men, it became increasingly clear he should heed his own advice, turn tail and run as fast as he could, but in the time it took to come to that conclusion it was too late. The huddle of men surrounded him, making escape an impossibility. No option was left but to fight.

His fists flew out again, landing with a painful crunch in a second man's face. Jackson smiled as he watched the cur stagger backwards. But it was to be the last time he smiled for some time. Fists continued to fly in every direction, most of them landing on Jackson's face, chest, stomach and anywhere else the men could reach in the ensuing melee.

Somehow, the cobblestones defied gravity and rose up to meet him, smacking him in the face with a powerful force that made the men's punches feel like soft slaps. In the mayhem, self-preservation took over. He rolled into a tight ball, protecting his head, and prayed the men would show some pity and leave him to nurse his injuries.

Sinner that he was, he did not expect his prayers to be answered. They weren't. Boots replaced fists as the men indulged themselves in a kicking contest, treating him like a rugby ball stuck in a scrummage.

'That will teach you for ruining our fun,' one panting man said as he finally ran out of energy. 'Now, where did that little whore go?'

'If we don't find her, we'll be back to finish off the job,' another man added, giving Jackson a final kick in the middle of his back for good measure.

And with that the alleyway fell silent. Jackson could only hope they did come back. That would mean the young woman had managed to escape and her safety would provide some compensation for having the life almost kicked out of him. But if they did return, Jackson did not wish to remain such an easy target. He would at least try and make them work for their sport.

With much wincing, groaning and moaning, he pulled himself along the alleyway, seeking somewhere, anywhere, to hide. At a pace that would put a snail to shame he dragged himself to a corner, hoping the dark night would disguise the tell-tale trail of blood. He wedged himself between the wall and a pile of rotting rubbish, its fetid smell mixing with the metallic scent of his blood. In this uncomfortable refuge he drifted off, not caring if it was to sleep or to death, just wanting to free himself from the unbearable pain wracking every inch of his body.

Jackson forced open his eyes. Through narrow slits, he looked up at the most glorious sight he had ever beheld. He was in heaven and a bewitching angel was watching over him. If he'd realised heaven would be so, well, heavenly, he would have paid more attention during those interminable sermons his father had dragged him to every Sunday.

The old preacher at their local church would have had Jackson's undivided attention if he'd revealed that heaven was populated with chestnut haired beauties, with velvet brown eyes, honey-coloured skin and decidedly kissable red lips. His gaze moved lower. And the preacher most definitely had omitted to mention that angels also had devilishly curvaceous bodies. If he had, Jackson was sure to have remembered.

He tried to smile at the beatific sight, but his swollen lips would not allow it, so instead he contemplated what was potentially a sacrilegious thought. Was it wrong to lust after angels? That was a subject the preacher never raised. But surely, for Jackson, heaven would not consist of cherubs sitting on fluffy clouds and playing harps, but would be full of alluring women, eager to satisfy his every whim.

There was only one way to discover the answer to this deep, theological question. He needed to put it to the test.

'Kiss me, my angel,' he said through thick, swollen lips.

*Thick, swollen lips?*

Wouldn't his suffering be relieved when he reached heaven? He vaguely remembered the preacher mentioning something about that.

The halo of soft light surrounding the celestial being grew brighter, becoming almost painful and forcing him to close his eyes. Excruciating agony ripped through his entire body as he emerged further into consciousness. Even his toes and fingers were screaming out in pain.

He made a concerted effort to sit up, but his angel placed her lovely hand on his shoulder to stop his progress.

'You mustn't move,' she said.

'Aren't you going to kiss me and relieve me of my suffering?' He repeated, more in hope than expectation.

'You will behave yourself while you're here, Jackson Wilde,' she said in a voice that lacked the compassion he would expect from an angel. 'And you will treat the nursing staff with the respect they deserve. No one will tolerate any of your misbehaviour. I can tell you that right now.'

Despite the pain, he forced his eyes open again and attempted to get a better look at his chastising angel. She came fully into focus. With a complaining groan he sunk back down on to the bed, his response more a reaction to his predicament than the state of his body.

Lady Emily Beaumont was frowning down at him. No one, except a man whose mind was groggy with excruciating pain, would ever mistake that strait-laced do-gooder for an angel. He closed his eyes to block out the disapproving sight.

His father had been proven right. Jackson had been sent straight to hell.

Emily could hardly credit it. Even with his face bruised black and blue, his blue eyes almost swollen shut, and his dark blond hair encrusted with blood, Jackson Wilde was still a handsome man.

But good looks such as his had no effect on her whatsoever. Not when she knew exactly what sort of man he really was. She had met men like him before. Men who cared about no one except themselves, and whose only purpose in life was to have a good time.

He was the sort of man any sensible young woman would avoid at all costs. Unfortunately, most young women were not nearly sensible enough and could not see what was patently obvious to Emily. Men like him were not to be taken seriously. They used women for their own amusement and, when they tired of them, they moved onto the next one.

*Kiss me, my angel*, indeed.

Even in this state he could not resist the temptation to flirt and charm. That just showed the man's true character.

And yet, despite his reputation, every debutante seemed

to be under the illusion she would be the one to tame Jackson Wilde. The one he would marry, settle down with—the one to change his ways.

Emily shook her head in disbelief as she looked down at the Viscount as he drifted off to sleep on the hospital bed.

He was not a man she had hitherto shown much attention, but at the few Society balls they had both attended, she had witnessed young women all but throw themselves at him. It was as if he cast some sort of spell over those innocent debutantes and easily had them dancing attendance on him.

They all chose to ignore his reputation and the antics reported about him in the scandal sheets. All because he was good looking, debonaire and would one day inherit a dukedom.

She scanned his face, covered in a mass of cuts and contusions. It was obvious what had happened to him this evening and how he had got into this state. He would have tried out his charms on the wrong woman, and some man had given him his comeuppance. Hopefully this would teach him a valuable lesson, although in reality there was little chance of that. Men like him never changed.

And if he tried to flirt with her again, he would soon discover she was no gullible debutante, or chorus girl impressed by his wealth and status. Nor was she a bored married woman looking for some excitement. She was a woman who would not be toyed with.

Emily would like to think this immunity to men such as him came from innate intelligence and the ability to see through the attractive façade to the real, shallow, selfish man beneath, but she knew this was not so. It was wisdom that had come from bitter experience. A bitter experience she would never repeat. So Jackson Wilde could try all his charming tricks on her, flirt and flatter as much as he liked, he would find it was all simply a complete waste of his time and energy.

He opened his eyes again and once more tried to smile at her, stopping immediately when the crack on his bottom lip parted, causing Emily to join him in wincing.

'So, is this heaven or hell?' he asked, rather nonsensically.

'You're in the Hope Charity Hospital. An institution that treats the deserving poor.'

He attempted a laugh, which quickly turned into a cough. 'And the occasional undeserving rich.'

'You were brought in early this morning by some local men. Matron has assessed you and says you have little more than bruising and cuts, but you were unconscious when you arrived, so they want to keep an eye on you to make sure there is nothing more serious. Once a bed is available, you'll be moved to the ward.'

'In the meantime, can I assume you or one of the other nursing angels will be bathing my fevered brow and tending to my every need?'

Emily stared at him in disbelief as he actually attempted to wink his swollen eye.

'I have already told you, while you are here, you will respect the nursing staff,' she said, enjoying being able to assert her authority and put this self-entitled man in his place. 'You will not charm them, flirt with them, or,' she waved her hand in the air as she attempted to grasp the words, 'do anything else inappropriate.'

His attempt to smile was thwarted when the crack in his lip parted further. 'Believe me, as much as I'd like to do something inappropriate, I don't think I'll be able to for quite some time. So your virtue, and that of the other nurses, will be safe for now.'

'I'm not a nurse.'

He slowly eased his eyes open a little wider, as if assessing her. 'If you're not a nurse what are you doing here, tending to me?'

That was a good question. Matron had informed her, in a rather sniffy tone, that one of *'Emily's people'*, a man dressed in formal evening clothes of white shirt, white bow tie and black swallow tail jacket, had been brought in and she should go and see to him as the nurses were all busy. Emily had resented the implication. The nurses and other staff at the Hope Hospital were *her* people, not this man. She may have been born into the aristocracy, but she much preferred to identify with those who gave their time to helping people less fortunate than themselves, rather than idle, privileged men like the one in the bed who thought of nothing more than endlessly enjoying themselves.

But Matron ran the wards and to have questioned her authority would have only confirmed that ferocious woman's suspicions that Emily was merely a dilettante, passing her time with no real commitment to the hospital. Plus, she had to admit, she was curious to discover the patient's identity. Few of Emily's so-called people would venture into the East End. When they did, it was usually for disreputable reasons.

'Well, I can tell you how I did not end up in here,' she said in her most reproachful voice. 'It wasn't because I got into a brawl and came out the loser.'

'No, I'm sure if you got into a brawl, you'd be the victor, no matter how brawny the opponent.'

Emily straightened her spine, determined to not let this

insult affect her. So what if she had never been the belle of any ball she had reluctantly attended? So what if she was four-and-twenty and still unwed? She had found a place where she was needed, where she felt valued, and she would not let this ne'er do well undermine her confidence or accuse her of being anything less than feminine.

'Well, if you're not going to tell me how *you* got here, can you at least tell me how *I* got here?' he said. 'My last memory is of rotting away in a God-forsaken alley behind a pile of rubbish.'

'You were lucky. Some men found you and carried you into the hospital.'

He spluttered an attempt at a laugh. 'I think we have a different definition of lucky.'

'At least you will now get the treatment you need and will soon be able to leave and be tended at home by your family physician.'

He touched his face and winced. 'I think it might be best if I hide out here until the worst of the damage is healed.'

'What's wrong? Are you worried that your lady friends will be less than impressed by you, now that you've lost your good looks.'

'Why, Lady Emily, I'm flattered that you believe I possess good looks, and that you assume I have more than one lady friend I wish to impress. You make me sound like quite the lothario.'

She didn't have to *make* him sound like a lothario. That was exactly what he was. Jackson Wilde was known to run with a fast set that surrounded the Prince of Wales. The stories of what Queen Victoria's son and his friends got up to were a topic of constant salacious gossip and difficult to ignore.

'Well, perhaps you should take your present condition as a warning,' she said. 'You might not remember how you came to be in Hope Hospital, but you must have some memory of how you came to be in this condition.' It was none of her business, but strangely she wanted to know, if for no other reason than it would confirm all her suspicions about him.

'I'm afraid that will have to remain a secret.'

'I suppose it involves a woman.'

He attempted to laugh again. 'Doesn't everything bad that happens to a man involve a woman, in one way or another?'

It was just as she suspected. 'In that case, you probably got no more than you deserved.' That was a bit harsh, but his smug manner was irritating. He'd been up to no good. That was obvious. And with a woman he should not have been with. He'd taken a beating because of it, and still he acted as if it was all a bit of a lark.

'That's the same thing those men said as they laid into me with their fists and boots.'

'And I don't suppose even that will convince you to change your ways?'

'Never. It will take a lot more than a beating and a stay in a hospital to change the habits of a lifetime.'

Why was she even bothering? If a beating wouldn't change him then he was hardly likely to listen to a lecture from her. Men like him were incorrigible. It didn't matter how many women they hurt, what mayhem they caused— they just went on blithely breaking hearts and destroying lives without a backward glance.

'Are you going to introduce me to this patient?' a voice behind her said.

Emily turned to see that Dr Gideon Pratt had entered

the cubical and was standing just inside the green curtains. She smiled at him in welcome. Gideon was everything she could possibly want in a man and as far removed from the likes of Jackson Wilde as it was possible to get. While Jackson had a reputation as a libertine who spent all his days and nights in pointless pleasure, Gideon was hard working and dedicated to improving the conditions of the less fortunate.

She was so grateful he had come into her life and reminded her that there *were* good men in the world. After her devastating first Season—and the humiliation of falling so hopelessly for that reprobate Randall Cochran—she had thought she would never meet a man she could trust. That was until she met Gideon.

'I didn't realise you were rostered on today,' she said as he approached the bed.

She was always well aware of Gideon's roster and made a point of being on the wards when he was working. She also constantly hoped he would suggest they spend time together on his days off. Something that was yet to happen.

Perhaps that was why he was here, because he was seeking out her company. That could almost be seen as a romantic gesture, something else that Gideon had hitherto not been one to indulge in. Not that she expected it of a man who was both serious and level-headed, but still, it might be nice, just on the odd occasion.

'I'm not rostered on, but I heard that a special patient had been admitted, so I thought it best I come in and offer my services.'

'Yes, you're right,' Emily said, impressed by his dedication. 'There was a rather nasty accident at a local foundry and several men were rushed in with severe burns, but I believe the nursing staff have it under control.'

Gideon tilted his head and nodded it towards the bed.

'Oh, and we've had one man admitted with some relatively minor injuries,' she explained. 'But there's certainly nothing special about him. As soon as there's a bed available he'll be transferred to the ward.'

Gideon gave a small laugh as if she was making a joke, something she certainly was not doing.

'Are you going to introduce me to this patient?' he asked again.

'Why? Shouldn't you try and find the special case you were referring to?'

Gideon actually rolled his eyes at her, as if she was playing some sort of game.

'Oh, I see.' It was apparent that *Jackson Wilde* was the special patient he was referring to, and that *special* label had nothing to do with his medical condition.

Gideon moved closer to the bed and his demeanour as he looked at the Viscount was full of respect and admiration. For a moment Emily wondered if he was impressed because Jackson Wilde was a titled man, then dismissed that as unfair. Gideon was not like that. He had presumably heard a man of substance had been admitted and merely wanted to pay him extra attention, but only in the hope of securing further financing for the hospital. He was always thinking of others.

'It looks like you've been in the wars. How did a man such as yourself end up here?' Gideon asked.

Before Jackson could answer and say something offensive about getting into a brawl over a woman, Emily leapt in. 'He was admitted early this morning. It's obvious he's been in a fight of some kind.'

'Well, you're in the right place,' Gideon said. 'The care you will receive in this hospital will be as good as any you will get anywhere else in London.'

Emily smiled at Gideon. He was right. Gideon *was* a talented doctor, and Emily was constantly heartened to have the affections of such an impressive man. She was also somewhat chastised by her momentary doubt in his inherent goodness. It was shameful that, even for a moment, she had thought him impressed by Jackson Wilde's title. Of course he would be interested in the Viscount, because of the good he could do the hospital. And he was right. She too should be thinking of the financial support he could provide the hospital, rather than lecturing the man on his miscreant behaviour.

'Would you be so kind as to fetch some water, cloths and bandages,' Gideon said, turning to Emily. 'And ask a nurse to come and clean the patient's wounds while I examine him.'

'Matron has already performed an examination and said there's nothing much wrong with him.'

Gideon raised his eyebrows but made no comment.

'Of course, I'll see if I can find an available nurse,' she said, knowing that questioning a doctor was frowned on almost as much as questioning the matron.

'And please inform the nursing staff that we have an important patient who must take priority.' He sent her a smile that suggested he expected her to be in complete agreement.

Emily looked down at Jackson Wilde and wondered whether special treatment would be a waste of effort. Men like Jackson Wilde frittered away their money at the gaming tables or spent it lavishly on chorus girls and actresses. They were not known for being benevolent donors to worthy causes. But if anyone could get this man to change his ways it was Gideon. Even if it was just by setting an example of how a good man behaved.

# Chapter Two

*Well, well, well. The do-gooder was in love with the doctor.*

While it was no concern of Jackson's, watching their courting ritual was at least going to provide him with a much-needed diversion from the pain that was wracking his body.

'I haven't formally introduced myself,' the doctor said, standing stiffly beside the bed and bowing his head. 'I'm Dr Gideon Pratt.'

'I'm pleased to meet you,' Jackson replied, equally formally, and equally ludicrously given the circumstances. 'I'm Jackson Wilde.'

The doctor continued to smile down at him, apparently waiting for more, so Jackson added, 'Viscount Wickford.'

The smile grew wider. 'The eldest son of the Duke of Greenfeld, I believe.'

'The very same.'

'I'm delighted to make your acquaintance and only sorry it is not under better circumstances. But you can rest assured I will inform Matron to treat you with the attention you deserve, and we will endeavour to provide you with as much privacy as possible. Perhaps when you are transferred to the wards the nursing staff can see if a private room is available, and, if not, I will arrange for some screens to surround your bed.'

'Is that usual procedure?'

'No, but we don't usually have men of your stature in this hospital.' He sent Jackson a smile that could best be described as fawning.

'Then I insist you make no special arrangements on my behalf. I'm just pleased that I'm going to get some medical treatment.' At least, I'll be pleased when you stop attempting to ingratiate yourself to me and actually provide said medical treatment.

'That is very gracious of you, my lord,' he said with another bow. 'And I promise you will receive the very best of care. Dare I say it, possibly better than you would get from even the most esteemed physicians.' The smarmy smile turned into a more serious, professional expression, as he finally inspected Jackson's head and neck. 'I believe these injuries are little more than contusions, cuts and scrapes.'

Just as Lady Emily had said, Jackson wanted to add, and just as the matron had observed.

Dr Pratt palpated Jackson's chest and he responded with a loud cry of pain.

'I'm so sorry, my lord, but it does appear you also have a few cracked ribs. Unfortunately, there is not much that can be done, but you will have to remain in the hospital until they start to heal. But once you return to your home, I will be more than happy to continue treating you as your private physician.'

Jackson chose not to respond to that suggestion. 'In the meantime, please do not let me keep you from your other patients,' he said instead. 'Didn't Lady Emily say something about a foundry accident? Perhaps those men need your extra special help as well.'

'A nurse will soon clean up your wounds and bind your ribs,' the doctor continued. 'And, as I say, when you are well enough to be moved home, I am more than willing to accompany you and continue to provide my medical expertise, to you and your family, now, and at any time in the future.'

Once again, Jackson chose to ignore this request, but as the doctor appeared to have no intention of moving from his bedside, he asked a question he really did want an answer to, and it certainly wasn't about anything as boring as his injuries or who would treat them. 'Am I right in assuming you and Lady Emily are more than just colleagues?'

'Yes, Lady Emily and I are courting,' the doctor said, puffing himself up with what looked more like self-importance than admiration for his betrothed. 'She's the daughter of the Duke of Fernwood, you know.'

Jackson nodded. 'The Duke and Duchess must be delighted,' he said, unsure if that would be the case.

The puffing deflated slightly. 'Well, we haven't officially announced our courtship yet, but as Lady Emily is, shall we say, no longer a debutante, they are hardly likely to object.'

Jackson had spent enough time at the gaming tables to know when a man's face shows he is calculating the odds. Dr Pratt would be aware that a duke would want his daughter to marry another titled man, not a doctor, but was apparently hoping her age would mean her parents would be happy to offload their unwed daughter to virtually anyone, including a man with as little status as him.

'So when do you plan to inform them?'

'When the time is right. And I'm sure once we are married her parents will come to see that a marriage to a doctor with a thriving, highly profitable medical practice is an agreeable outcome for all concerned.'

'And you have a highly profitable medical practice, do you?'

'Not yet, but that is my intention, once I have sufficient private patients to set up my own clinic.'

Jackson stifled a sigh. That explained why he had been elevated to the status of a special patient. It wasn't just the usual fawning over an aristocrat. The man was touting for business.

'Does that mean you intend to leave the Hope Charity Hospital once you have established this thriving, highly profitable medical practice?'

'Of course,' the doctor responded with a frown, as if surprised he should even be asked such a question. 'Don't get me wrong, I'm grateful to the hospital. It was thanks to the kind patronage of the hospital board that I was able to undertake my medical training. That is why I work here. I'm bonded until I pay them back for my fees, but obviously I wish to set up on my own, and Lady Emily deserves nothing less than to be the wife of a man who can keep her in the style into which she was born.'

These sounded much more like his ambitions than Lady Emily's. The doctor's calculating expression raised Jackson's suspicions. Was he using Lady Emily to advance his career? Did she know? Did she care?

Lady Emily pushed aside the curtain and came back into the room, now wearing a nurse's apron over her dark blue day dress and carrying a large ceramic bowl, a pile of cloths and several bandages. She placed them on the bedside table and smiled at the doctor.

Their interactions were interesting and diverting, but whatever the true nature of the relationship between the doctor and Lady Emily he had no reason to concern himself with her affairs. She was old enough and certainly assertive enough to not need his help. And if Jackson was foolhardy enough to inform her of his suspicions regarding this Dr Pratt, he was certain his interference would not be welcome.

And surely there were worse men that a woman could marry than one who intended to use his wife as a means to advance his career. A man such as himself, for example. No, he had no need to worry on Lady Emily's account.

'The nurses are busy attending to patients with more serious conditions,' Emily said, drawing Gideon's attention away from the Viscount. 'They said they would get to this patient the moment they had a chance.'

Gideon's eyes grew wide with surprise.

'My apologies, Your Lordship,' he said to the Viscount, causing Emily to swallow a grimace. She knew Gideon was only thinking of the hospital, but she did wish he would not use such a deferential tone of voice. The Viscount's title did not make him the superior man—his behaviour definitely made him inferior to a man as good as Gideon, one who dedicated his time to the care of others. If there was any justice in the world, Jackson Wilde would be deferring to Gideon.

'Then perhaps, on this occasion, you could tend to our patient, Nurse Emily.' Gideon smiled at her as if he had made a joke that would amuse her.

Instead, her teeth gritted together at the condescending way in which he called her Nurse Emily. Gideon knew she would love to be able to train as a nurse, but her parents' objections made that impossible. And the board would never go against the wishes of people of such renown as the Duke and Duchess of Fernwood. Instead she had to help out where she could. But perhaps she should not be so hard on Gideon. He was merely making a joke. Perhaps not the funniest of jokes, but that was of no matter. Gideon had many fine qualities, but an ability to make her laugh was not one of them.

'All you need to do is clean his wounds and tightly bind his ribs,' he explained, despite it being obvious what was required, even to someone with no nursing training.

'Yes, I can do that.' She looked down at Jackson Wilde, who attempted to smile at her and give her another of those salacious winks. Suddenly this did not seem like such a good idea.

'If the patient has no objections, of course,' she said, hoping Jackson Wilde would say yes, he did object. While she loved it when she got the opportunity to help the nursing staff, she would really rather not get that close to this particular patient.

'No objections whatsoever,' he said. 'Providing Lady Emily does not see doing such a menial task as beneath her.'

'Of course I don't,' she shot back, affronted that he would think she was someone that put herself above the dedicated nurses who worked tirelessly on the wards.

His swollen lips curled as much as they could into a smile, and Emily wondered whether she had walked straight into a trap. It was obvious he enjoyed teasing her. In future she would not rise to the bait.

'Good, I will leave you to it, Nurse Emily,' Gideon said, smiling as if he had once again made a delightful joke. 'And I'll come back and check on our patient once he has been cleaned up.' He bowed to Jackson. 'Goodbye for now, my lord. Goodbye, Nurse Emily.'

Gideon departed. Emily continued to stare at the still waving green curtain, uncomfortably conscious that she was once again alone with Jackson Wilde.

'I don't think the doctor will be getting a job as a vaude-villian comedian anytime soon,' Jackson Wilde said. 'Someone should tell him that if a joke isn't funny the first time, it doesn't get any funnier if you repeat it. Don't you agree, *Nurse Emily*?'

Emily dipped the cloth in the warm water and wrung it out tightly, venting her annoyance at both men on the cloth. 'Dr Pratt is an excellent doctor and you are lucky to have him treating you. You wouldn't find a finer doctor anywhere in London.'

'Yes, so he says.'

Emily was tempted to further take out her annoyance on his head, to give it a firm scrubbing to wash away the blood, but that would be appalling behaviour. Worse than that, she did not want him to see how much his criticism of Gideon affected her. Instead, she lightly dabbed at the wounds, slowly removing the encrusted blood.

'So, you and the doctor?' he said, causing her hand to still momentarily.

'I don't know what you are talking about.'

'You seem to have a mutual appreciation for each other.'

'Yes, I admire the doctor immensely,' she said, wringing out the cloth and turning the water pink.

'Perhaps one day he will be one of London's most prominent physicians with a thriving medical practice treating the great and good of the city,' Jackson said, a slight note of derision in his voice.

'Gideon—Dr Pratt is not like that,' she fired back. 'He is a man dedicated to caring for the poor and the needy, not the rich and the privileged. He is a man of high principles. That's something I suppose you would not understand.'

'No, it certainly is not something I understand. I just hope that you do.'

She paused, the flannel suspended above his head, wondering what he meant by that. Deciding it was of no importance she continued cleaning his wounds. He was merely playing a game with her for his own amusement, and she would not let him question her faith in Gideon. He was a good man. Unlike the men she met during the Season, unlike Randall Cochran, that dissolute scoundrel she had once had the misfortune to think herself in love with, and unlike the Viscount. They were all men who cared nothing for anyone else but themselves.

'So do your parents approve—'

'I haven't introduced him yet, but I'm sure they will see just what a wonderful man he is once they get to know him.'

'I was actually going to say, do your parents approve of you working in a charity hospital?'

'Oh.' She dabbed gently at a cut above his eye, annoyed that she had revealed so much. 'Well, they didn't approve at first, but when I informed them that the Queen's daughter, Princess Alice, had been interested in nursing and had been a good friend of Florence Nightingale, and Princess Helena did charity work for the British Nurses Association and the Red Cross, they reluctantly gave their approval. As

I kept reminding them, if it's good enough for Queen Victoria's daughters, surely it's good enough for the daughter of the Duke of Fernwood.'

'Although I suspect the good Queen's daughters are still expected to attend social occasions. I don't believe I've seen you at any balls since your first Season.'

'No, and you won't be seeing me at any more if I can help it.' She bit her lip as if to take those words back. 'I didn't mean I would be avoiding you. I just meant that I would rather not attend any more balls.'

'I took no offence. So, you prefer these, shall we say, somewhat grim surroundings to the glitter of chandeliers and parquet floors?'

He looked around the small cubical, and she could imagine what the stark surroundings looked like through his eyes. She took in the plain, cast-iron bedframe and the white sheets that had been repeatedly boiled until they were threadbare. She was suddenly unable to ignore the strong tar odour of the carbolic soap used to scrub down all surfaces.

She frowned at the apparent criticism. 'Yes, I do,' she stated emphatically.

The hospital might be a bit grim, but it was somewhere she felt she belonged. From the moment she had entered the ballroom, for the first event of her first Season, Emily had known she would never truly fit in. The conversations were superficial, the titled people she mixed with were so self-important, and the other young ladies had made fun of her because she was so hopeless at the required flirtatious behaviour.

And then she had met Randall Cochran and everything had changed. He was so handsome, so charming, and she had loved the attention he had shown her. She had even thought herself in love with him. Until she discovered exactly what sort of man he was.

Her chest tightened and that familiar sense of dizziness swept over her as she remembered that humiliating overheard conversation. She'd gone searching for Randall, knowing he was in the card room, but hoping to lure him back to the ball room for yet another dance.

*'So much for your boasting. You haven't even kissed Lady Emily yet,'* a friend of Randall's had said, stopping Emily in her tracks.

*'The Season is still young,'* Randall had responded. *'The silly chit is already falling in love with me, fluttering those big doe eyes at me every chance she gets. All I have to do is play with her a little longer, charm her, flatter her, and before long I'll have her begging me for it.'*

*'And then you'll be forced to marry her,'* his friend had said.

*'That fate hasn't befallen me yet. That's the beauty of this plan,'* Randall had said. *'I get to take the wench, then I make the family pay me to keep it a secret that I've ruined her.'* He'd laughed loudly. *'Most men have to pay an enormous sum for a virgin. Whereas I'll get a willing virgin for free, and even come out of it all the richer.'*

This had elicited much laughter and back-slapping among his friends, and had sent Emily scurrying back down the corridor. It had all been too humiliating. He had been right. She *had* thought she was falling in love with him, *had* relished every one of his compliments—had even fantasised about him kissing her and caressing her. She had arrogantly considered herself an intelligent woman, but had been revealed to be a gullible half-wit, more naïve than the most credulous debutante, one who is completely susceptible to the charms of a seducer.

After that awakening, she had avoided being in Society whenever she could, and had dedicated herself even further to charity work. And would continue to do so. Discovering the man she thought she loved was a debauched liar had also made her swear off all men. But then she met Gideon, a man she could trust, and with whom she could be content.

'I most certainly prefer these surroundings to even the grandest of ballrooms,' she added, determined not to feel any shame over what had happened between her and Randall Cochran. She had done nothing wrong. It was the rakes of this world who should be ashamed, but she knew they never would be.

He nodded slowly, watching her carefully as she tended his wounds. 'I can't say ballrooms are my favourite place either,' he said gently.

He watched her for a moment. 'You're very good at this. Do you have aspirations of training to become a nurse?'

She looked into his eyes to see if he was teasing, but could see no sign of it.

'Sadly no. While my parents see charitable work as acceptable for a woman of my background, they would never countenance me taking paid employment. I help out on the wards whenever I can but the board members have also made it clear they would prefer it if I focus more on administration work, fundraising, that sort of thing. Activities they consider much more ladylike.'

She looked towards the door, not wanting to mention that nurses were expected to resign if they married. That was something both her mother and Gideon had pointed out to her, but to inform Jackson Wilde of this unfortunate fact would only lead to more questioning about her relationship with Gideon.

'Well, you would make an excellent nurse.'

She could detect no condescension in his voice, but once again she scrutinised his expression for a sign of amusement. 'Thank you,' she finally said, finding no such look.

'So you believe your parents will be happy for you to marry a doctor?'

Emily chose not to answer but to continue with her work, aware that he was watching her carefully. It was not a subject she wished to discuss, and she could not see why it would be of interest to him. Boredom probably.

And she certainly was not going to tell him that Gideon was yet to formally ask for her hand.

'It's quite obvious the doctor is entranced. I'm sure it won't be long before he's down on bended knee, declaring his undying love.'

Once again she chose not to respond. A man like Jackson Wilde would never understand her relationship with Gideon. It was not one based on silly, intangible concepts like love and romance. They had a meeting of minds. They both wanted the same things from life, and she had immense respect for him. That was a much better foundation for a successful marriage than passion and romance ever could be. Wasn't it?

'And once you're married you can continue your life of service to the poor and the needy,' Jackson said, his words suddenly dripping with sarcasm.

She stopped her work and glared at him. 'I don't know why you're being so cynical. I am proud of the work I do at the hospital and proud of Gideon—Dr Pratt. He works long hours at this hospital and is dedicated to providing the highest level of care to his patients.'

'Yes, I've noticed he's been dedicating himself greatly to my care since I was admitted, although I don't believe he's spending quite so much time with the other patients.'

'That's because he's not rostered on today,' she shot back, outraged that he would dare to criticise a man as honourable as Gideon. 'And, well, if you must know, he's hoping you will make a generous donation to the hospital, which will help other people in need who can't afford treatment.'

'There's no denying the man is a saint,' he said.

'Well, compared to some men who think only of themselves and having a good time, yes, he is a saint.'

She expected him to be chastened by her outrage, but he merely continued watching her, assessing her. 'And does the good doctor expect you to continue working here after you're married? Has he told you of his plans for the future?'

'We haven't actually discussed that in any detail, but yes, it is what we both want.'

'Perhaps it is a discussion you should have before you tie the knot, so you are certain you both want to spend your lives working side by side, making the world a better place, curing the sick, helping the needy and all that. You wouldn't want to find yourself married to a man who, say, wants to become rich and successful, tending the wealthy, while his wife stays at home doing whatever it is wives do when they stay at home.'

'Don't be ridiculous,' she fired at him, shocked that he should be trying to plant doubts in her mind about Gideon. 'And who are you to give marriage advice?'

He nodded his head slightly. 'Quite right, Lady Emily, I'm sure you know exactly what you're doing.'

She squeezed out the cloth, wringing out the last of the pink liquid.

'I need to change this water,' she said, picking up the bowl and carrying it out of the ward, fighting to calm herself after that strange, unsettling exchange. Jackson Wilde had tried unnerving her by flirting. Now he was trying another tack, questioning her relationship with Gideon. It was all just mischief-making for his own entertainment. Gideon was a good man. He would make an excellent husband. His dedication was as unquestionable as her own. Jackson Wilde was merely riled at being in the company of a man who was in every way his superior, that was all.

Repeating these words to herself she rushed down the hall, emptied the bowl in the deep concrete sink in the sluice room, pumped out some fresh water and put it on the stove. Watching the water boil she continued to mentally repeat all the things she wanted to say to Jackson Wilde, about how wrong he was, how men like him knew nothing of women like her, or men like Gideon. They were merely wealthy wastrels and she would not let him get under her skin.

Once the water had boiled, and her own mood had cooled down, she picked up some clean cloths and towels and returned to the ward. She gave him her most professional smile, letting him know that she was completely under control, then placed the bowl on the bedside table, sat down and observed her work.

'That looks good, and I don't believe you're going to require sutures,' she said, taking in his skin, which was now free from blood but covered in an array of multicoloured bruises.

'Right, I'm now going to have to remove your jacket and

shirt so I can bind your ribs,' she said, keeping her voice as impassive as possible.

'I'm more than happy for you to undress me.'

She frowned at him, letting him know she would tolerate no more nonsense from him.

'Sorry,' he said with a light laugh. 'You've already told me not to flirt with the nursing staff. But it's what I do in the company of pretty women. I'm afraid I just can't help myself.'

She frowned again, making it clear his flirting and false flattery had no effect on her whatsoever.

She carefully edged his jacket off his shoulders, undid the buttons of his formal white shirt, which was covered in mud and blood. She then slowly slid it off his shoulders and down his arms, taking care not to cause him any discomfort, while fighting to ignore any discomfort of her own.

His chest and back were as bloody and bruised as the rest of him, but even in that state it was impossible to ignore the breadth of his shoulders, the athletic muscles of his chest or the line of dark hairs on the hard ridges of his stomach. Despite his dissolute lifestyle, his physique suggested he also spent time in more physical pursuits—boxing perhaps, or horse riding.

She swallowed, realising that she was staring. What on earth was wrong with her? This was appalling. She should be focusing on tending to his bruises and cuts, not admiring his chest, not speculating on how he got such powerful muscles. And she most certainly should not be thinking about the ultimate destination of that line of dark hairs.

Once more she rang out the cloth, as if trying to wring out her inappropriate thoughts, and took the time to regain her composure. Turning back to him, she adopted the required professional detachment as she gently ran the flannel over his chest, removing the dried blood. She would focus on the job at hand. She would not think about the feel of his muscles under the stroking cloth, nor would she compare them to iron covered in soft leather, and she certainly would not wonder what his naked skin would feel like without the barrier of a damp cloth.

Damn it all, despite her resolve, she knew she was blushing, and that the heat was not confined to her face. With each stroke of her flannel, her body burned hotter, her heartbeat pounded faster, breathing became increasingly difficult.

She had assisted nurses before in cleaning up patients, but never had touching a man caused her to react in this manner. It was all too humiliating, and she just knew that the effect he was having on her would not be lost on the Viscount.

She flicked a glance up to his face, expecting to see a mocking leer, but his expression was far from derisive. Even with his eyes swollen, she could see the intensity in his gaze. It was a look every bit as unsettling as the feel of his chest under her touch.

She swallowed and lowered her gaze.

'That's got you cleaned up,' she said, trying to adopt the brisk, efficient but cheerful tone the nurses used with their patients. Unfortunately, the quivering in her voice sounded neither brisk nor efficient, and certainly not cheerful.

'I'm going to have to bind your chest in bandages now,' she said, wishing it was not so, but unable to think of any way out of this situation that would not make her feel more uncomfortable than she already did.

Not speaking, he merely nodded. It might have been better if he had made some silly, flirtatious quip. A joke, even an inappropriate one, would be far preferable to the way he was looking at her now. A strange feeling shimmered through her as his gaze held hers. It was unlike anything she had felt before—unsettling but strangely exciting.

She blinked rapidly and looked away, trying to regain control of the situation and her absurd reaction. He was merely a patient who needed her care.

'You'll need to sit up so I can wind the bandages around your back,' she said, annoyed that the quivering note in her voice was getting worse.

He did as she asked. Drawing in a slow, steadying breath, she placed the bandage on his chest, leaned over him and rolled it across his front and around his back. Damn it all, this felt even more intimate than stroking his chest with a cloth, but there was no way to complete the task without her body coming dangerously close to his.

She drew in a steadying breath, inadvertently inhaling his intoxicating scent. What was it? Sandalwood, and something else. Something decidedly manly, leather perhaps. Whatever it was, it was causing unsettling reactions deep in her body, as if her heart wasn't just pounding in her chest but had taken her over.

*You don't even like this man*, Emily reminded herself as her inner arm inadvertently brushed against his naked shoulder. *He's everything you despise in a man. Selfish, frivolous and dissolute. He's a womaniser who cares for nothing and no one.*

Forcing herself to focus on the action of tightly binding his chest, she tried to drive all other thoughts out of her mind. She would not think of the touch of his skin, the hardness of his muscles or the way his warm breath gently caressed her neck as she moved in even closer towards him.

'How's the patient doing?'

Emily jumped back at the sound of Gideon's hearty voice behind her, the bandage falling from her fingers.

She had not heard him come into the cubical. The heat on her cheeks burned hotter, as if she had been caught doing something shameful. But she had nothing to be ashamed of. All she was doing was tending to a patient, just as Gideon had asked.

Jackson Wilde's eyes left hers and he looked up at the doctor. 'The nurse is doing an excellent job,' he said, his husky voice presumably the result of her touching his injuries.

'Very good,' Gideon said, still in that hearty manner. 'Let me just inspect your work.'

Gideon leant over her and looked at the bandages, thankfully oblivious to her burning cheeks and awkward manner.

'I'll just finish this off, shall I?' With brisk efficiency he wound the last of the bandage around Jackson Wilde's chest and fixed it in place.

'Excellent job, Nurse Emily,' Gideon said, causing Emily's shame to intensify. He was such a good man, so much better than Jackson Wilde. She should not disparage him just because he was once again making a silly joke that no one laughed at. She sent a castigating frown at Jackson Wilde, so he would know that if he was going to make fun of Gideon she would not countenance it. But he said nothing, merely continued to watch her in that disconcerting manner.

'Right, all that's needed now is for you to get changed into pyjamas and we can put you on the ward,' Gideon said, turning to Emily.

Her stomach clenched and fire burned hotter on her cheeks. She picked up the basin, put it down—gathered up the cloths, put them down—put the cloths into the basin, picked it up.

'I'll just clear this away, and see if I can find someone to help…help do that,' she mumbled, pointing a shaking finger at Jackson Wilde, before turning and rushing out of the cubical.

Once the curtains closed behind her, she paused, shut her eyes briefly and drew in a deep, slow breath. She did not know what had just happened, but it must never happen again. Gideon was the man she wanted to marry. She was not attracted to Jackson Wilde. He was exactly the sort of man she could never be attracted to. She had shown herself up once before over a charming degenerate. It was a mistake she would never make again.

Repeating those commands to herself like a protective prayer, she stood up straighter, then walked briskly down the hallway in her most professional, no-nonsense manner. She was determined to forget all about what had just happened, even though she was unsure exactly what it *was* that had just happened.

# Chapter Three

Jackson had no doubts about what had just happened, but the question foremost in his mind was *why* it had happened. Yes, she was an attractive woman, and yes, she had come intimately close to him, but it was Lady Emily Beaumont for God's sake. Emily 'Do-gooding Moralising' Beaumont. He was not and never would be attracted to a woman such as her. She was everything he avoided—uptight, reproachful and judgemental. And she wouldn't even know the meaning of the word fun, never mind how to have any.

In every conceivable way she was not the sort of woman he had the slightest bit of interest in. The women he liked had a touch of wildness to them. They were women who loved to indulge themselves, who lived for a good time. If he wanted to be with someone whose greatest satisfaction came from lecturing him on his dissolute ways, all he had to do was spend some time in his father's company.

And yet, when she touched him, even through the thickness of a flannel cloth, a strong wave of desire had consumed him. He had wanted her, desperately. Even now he could feel the touch of her gentle stroking hand on his body, smell her enticing natural feminine scent, one unadorned by any artificial perfumes.

It was ridiculous. He must have taken a worse beating

to the head than he had previously realised. He did *not* want Lady Emily Beaumont. And even if he did, which he didn't, he couldn't have her. She was one of those untouchable women who had to save themselves for marriage.

He looked up at the doctor who was prattling on about something, probably himself and what a brilliant physician he was. This was the man she hoped to marry. This was the man she was saving herself for. This cold fish. What a waste. The man was so full of himself he hadn't even noticed what should have been immediately apparent. If he cared as much about Lady Emily as he did about ingratiating himself to Jackson, he would have noticed the obvious signs in his beloved's appearance when he arrived. He would have seen how her cheeks were flushed a bright pink, how her breath was coming in short gasps, how she was unable to make eye contact with the man she professed to want to marry.

This buffoon, who couldn't even see what was right in front of his face, was the one who would take her to his bed on their wedding night, the man who would undress her, would caress and kiss that lovely body, who would—

Jackson released a low grown.

'What is it, my lord?' the doctor said, his face etched with concern. 'Is the pain too great to bear? Do you require laudanum?' He rushed to the curtains and yanked them apart. 'Nurse, laudanum, now,' he shouted down the corridor.

'I don't need laudanum and I don't want it,' Jackson called out. The powerful drug would probably quench his improper desires, which under the circumstances made the offer tempting, but he did not want his brain muddled. He had seen the damage laudanum did, and it was one of the few vices he was determined not to indulge in.

'Are you sure, my lord? There is no need for you to suffer any unnecessary pain.'

If the doctor knew the thoughts that had been going through Jackson's head when Lady Emily had been ministering to him, he was sure he'd be wanting to inflict as much pain on his patient as he possibly could. But, thankfully, the doctor was too blind or too brainless to see what should have been obvious to any man in love.

'Yes, I'm sure. I'm not in any undue pain.'

A nurse came in, carrying a vial of the dreaded drug.

'The patient says he does not need pain relief,' the doctor said, halting the nurse's progress. 'But while you are here you can change him into his pyjamas so he can be admitted to the ward, and please inform Matron that he will require screening from the other patients.'

'Please inform Matron of no such thing,' Jackson interrupted. 'I insist that I be treated exactly like all your other patients.'

'In that case, Matron requires me to help with the men from the foundry,' the nurse said, then caught the doctor's expression. 'But first I'll get the pyjamas.'

She bustled off, and the doctor returned to smiling at Jackson. 'I'll see you again when you are on the ward and we can continue this conversation,' he said, with a bow of his head, before departing.

Jackson had no idea what they had actually been talking about, and had no desire to see the doctor again, but he remained grateful that the man was neither a mind-reader nor particularly perceptive. He could only hope he remained that way.

\* \* \*

Emily emptied the bowl and watched the pink water swirl down the drain. This would not do. Her behaviour was ridiculous. Jackson Wilde meant nothing to her. Nothing. Gideon was the man she cared for.

Despite knowing this, she could make no sense of the effect he had on her, but it was over now, and she would waste no more time thinking of it. He would soon be transferred to the wards. He would be under the care of the nurses and she would not need to see him again.

'I hope I didn't upset you,' Gideon said as he entered the room. 'I forgot myself when I suggested that you help the patient change into his pyjamas. It is something for a nurse to do, not a lady of your delicate sensibilities.'

Emily tensed. She could say that she was not delicate, that she was more than capable of carrying out all the jobs performed by the nurses, but she had just proven that to be incorrect. Although she was sure, if it had been any man other than Jackson Wilde, she would not have flinched. But she could hardly say that to Gideon.

'You'll be pleased to know a nurse has taken over and the Viscount will soon be on the ward.'

Emily forced herself to smile. 'That's good, I'm sure he will get excellent care from the nurses.'

'That is what I wish to talk to you about. I have informed the Viscount that I will be providing him with personal care, and I would like you to tend to his needs when I am absent.'

Emily's eyes grew wide. 'Why?' That one word held so many questions, all of which seemed to be whirling around in Emily's mind, making her confused and somewhat light-headed.

'He is an important patient,' Gideon said, frowning at her, as if such things should not need explaining. 'We need to make a good impression on him. He could be so helpful for our future.'

Emily was unsure if that was the case. Jackson Wilde might donate to the hospital, and possibly even become a patron, but there was no guarantee.

'Don't worry, Emily,' he said, patting her arm. 'I won't be expecting you to undertake any nursing duties. Just keep an eye on him and let me know if his condition changes so I can attend him immediately.'

She continued to stare at him in bafflement.

'All you'll be required to do is talk to him, provide him with an enjoyable diversion while he's here. Perhaps you can read to him on occasion.'

Her already wide eyes grew wider. 'Divert him? Read to him?'

'Yes,' he said, seemingly unaware that the prospect of doing such a thing horrified her.

'And remember, if his condition does change, contact me immediately. Even if I'm not on the ward, send word for me rather than calling for one of the other doctors.'

She looked to him for further explanation. He said nothing, as if no explanation was required.

'Why?' she repeated, as it was seemingly the only word she was capable of forming.

He smiled as if sharing a private joke. 'Let's just say it will be better if he receives care from the same physician. It will be better for the long-term outlook of the patient.'

Emily could not understand his argument. Surely if any patient needed immediate medical attention the nearest doctor would be the best one to summon, but she knew

Gideon always had his patients' best interests at heart, so she did not question this request.

'Right, I'll wish you *adieu*,' he said. 'And remember, contact me if there are any problems with our important patient.'

Emily nodded. On the wards she knew she should do as the doctors requested, but she would not be following that particular command. She would not be providing Jackson Wilde with a diversion. She most certainly would not be reading to him. And if there was any change in his condition, the nurses would be perfectly capable of coping with it. It would be up to them whether they contacted Gideon, or did what is normal procedure and alerted the nearest doctor.

She hated that she would be going against Gideon's wishes, but what option did she have? For some unfathomable reason, Jackson Wilde unsettled her unlike any man had ever done before. She would never be able to explain this to Gideon. It was something she couldn't even explain to herself, but under the circumstances it would make sense to have as little to do with Jackson Wilde as possible.

Emily was still leaning against the sink, contemplating this unsettling situation, when a young woman entered the sluice room looking somewhat lost.

'I'm afraid the public are not supposed to be in here,' Emily said.

'I know, I'm sorry, but can you help me? I've gone and got meself lost.'

'Of course,' Emily said, escorting the young lady back into the corridor. 'Who are you looking for?'

'I don't know his name, but last night some friends of mine brought in a gentleman who had taken a right beat-

ing. He was in ever such a bad way.' She lifted up a battered hat, the rim torn, the crown squashed. 'This here is
his topper. I want to return it to him, and, you know, make
sure he's all right after what happened.'

Emily stiffened. She knew exactly to whom this young
woman was referring. There was only one such patient that
fitted that description.

'Were you present when it happened?' Emily asked,
curiosity getting the better of her.

'Yes, you could say it was my fault and I feel ever so
awful about it.'

A strange sense of satisfaction washed over Emily. She
was right about him. He was a man beneath contempt. He
was just another wealthy man who came down to the East
End in search of a woman desperate for money. It was appalling, and it proved Jackson Wilde was even more de-
spicable than she had previously thought.

Emily clung onto her disapproval with something akin
to pleasure. Disapproving of Jackson Wilde was so much
safer than any of the other turbulent reactions she was
having to him.

'I'll take you to him.' Emily knew she could just as easily give the young woman directions to the ward, but she
was curious to see Jackson Wilde's reaction when he was
confronted with his night-time misbehaviour in the cold
light of day.

They entered the ward, where men dressed in identical blue and white striped pyjamas were either sitting up
or lying down on the rows of white, cast-iron beds. A few
nurses, dressed in their black and white uniforms with
white head-covering, were moving from bed to bed, ad-
ministering to the patients.

They approached Jackson Wilde's bed at the end of the ward. He too was dressed in the same striped, well-worn pyjamas, and the sight of a viscount in such humble clothing was somewhat incongruous, and strangely satisfying.

He attempted to lift himself up to a seated position and tried to smile at his visitors, his strained expression showing both actions were causing him pain.

'The doctor said you are to remain perfectly still while your ribs heal,' Emily commanded. 'You have a visitor.'

She stood back to watch his discomfort. There was not the slightest spark of recognition as the young woman approached the bed. Typical. Men like him used women like her, then returned to their own privileged lives without a backward glance.

'Oh, your poor face,' the young woman said, leaning over him and lightly stroking his cheek. 'I'm Kitty. We didn't have time for no formal introduction last night, what with everything that was happening,' she added with more compassion than he could possibly deserve.

'I'm Jackson Wilde, and I'm very pleased to see that you are looking so well. I was worried about you, Kitty.'

She smiled at him as if he had just bestowed a blessing upon her, and Emily was unable to suppress a rebuking tut.

'Jackson,' Kitty said, her voice soft. 'That's such a lovely name.'

Emily sighed with exasperation. Did this man cast a spell over every woman he encountered? And couldn't women see what sort of man he really was? Thank goodness she was witnessing this exchange. If nothing else, it had brought her back to the reality of the man's true character.

For one, brief, irrational moment she too had almost

succumbed to his charms, but never again. And in the unlikely event she did start to fall for his magic, she would only have to remember this encounter with Kitty to pull herself back from that particular precipice.

'It's just a shame all my customers aren't as much of a gentleman as you,' Kitty continued to coo. 'It would make my life a whole lot easier.'

Emily crossed her arms, her jaw tensing as her teeth clenched tightly together. This conversation was unbelievable, and Jackson Wilde was lapping up the attention as if he was actually a man worthy of adulation.

If she needed any further confirmation on the type of man Jackson Wilde was, which she didn't, Kitty had just provided it. He was indeed a man so base he visited the poverty-stricken prostitutes of the East End to satisfy his craven desires. The depths to which he was capable of sinking was beneath contempt.

Kitty gently stroked that awful man's face again. 'If there's anything I can ever do for you, you know you only have to ask, and I mean anything,' she said with a wink. 'And of course, for you, it will always be free of charge.'

'That's a very kind and generous offer,' his said, his swollen lips moving into what appeared to be a smile. 'But as you can see, I'll be out of action for quite some time.'

'Oh, I don't know. I've had customers in worst condition than you and I've always found ways of giving them satisfaction.' She gave a small laugh. 'But I'll leave you now to get better. When you get out of here, remember— if you want me, just ask on the street for Pretty Kitty, everyone knows me by that name.'

'Pretty Kitty. I will remember and it's a name that suits you perfectly.'

Kitty gave a small, coquettish giggle while Emily shook her head slowly, hardly able to believe the exchange she was witnessing.

'Oh, and here's your topper,' Kitty said, placing the battered top hat she had been clasping in her hands on the bedside cabinet. 'It took a bit of a beating as well.' Then she placed a light kiss on his forehead, careful to avoid the bruises and cuts. 'I'll leave you in this lady's care, but don't forget, when you get out, ask for Pretty Kitty.'

'I won't forget.' He looked up at Emily. 'And if I do, I'm sure Nurse Emily will remember everything we've just said.'

Emily bit down her censorious *hmph*.

'I'll show you out, Kitty,' she said instead.

Once again this was unnecessary, as she was sure Kitty could find her own way out of the hospital, but Emily wanted to let this young woman know she owed Jackson Wilde nothing. If he was degenerate enough to come to the East End in search of women, then a beating was the least he deserved.

'He's such a gentleman,' Kitty said as they walked down the corridor.

Emily merely *hmphed* in response.

'I dare say he saved my life, and I feel so bad about it.'

Emily stopped walking. 'Saved your life? What do you mean?'

'Well, I was set upon by this group of toffs.' Kitty shuddered slightly. 'I should have known better than to go with them. They had that look in their eyes, the one punters get before something bad happens. But I needed the money ever so desperately, so I ignored all the warnings and it didn't take long for things to turn nasty.'

Kitty grimaced, then smiled and pointed back at the ward. 'And then Jackson appeared like a white knight on his charger. Except of course he was running, not on a horse, but he was straight into the fray without a thought for his own safety.'

She beamed a smile at Emily, then frowned. 'I ran off, just like he said for me to do. I was ever so scared. But I came back later with some men from the boarding house where I live. We followed the blood trail and found him in a terrible state. The men brought him in here and I was ever so worried he wouldn't make it. But he looks right chipper today, doesn't he?'

Emily almost wished she had not heard this story. It was so much easier to see Jackson Wilde as the villain not the hero.

'I'm very pleased that you are all right,' Emily said, not wanting to talk about Jackson Wilde any more. 'It must have been a terrible ordeal for you.'

'I'm all right, thanks to him. I just wish there was something more I could do for him than just offer my services for free, but I can't afford no flowers or nothing.' She looked at Emily and blushed slightly. 'Sorry, Nurse.'

'You have nothing to apologise for,' Emily said. She had been involved in the Hope Charity Hospital for long enough to know the desperate circumstances of women like Kitty, and what drove them to this particular work.

'Although in his case it won't be no hardship to offer my services,' Kitty added with a laugh. Seeing Emily's frown, she pulled her face into a more serious expression. 'You will treat him really special, won't you?' she pleaded.

It was the second person today who had made that request, and neither knew just how much they were asking of Emily. 'Yes, he will get the best possible treatment from everyone at the hospital.'

Satisfied with Emily's answer, Kitty said goodbye, leaving Emily to wonder whether she owed an apology to Jackson Wilde.

# Chapter Four

Jackson lay back in the bed, smiling to himself, as Lady Emily approached. He shouldn't take such pleasure in shocking her, but how could he help it? It was what he did best. He'd spent most of his life shocking his father, so such behaviour came naturally to him. And when it came to holier-than-thou types like his father and Lady Emily, he really didn't have to try terribly hard to cause their mouths to curl down in disdain, or their nostrils to flair as if assaulted by an offensive smell.

And that was precisely how Lady Emily had looked at him when hearing of his involvement with Pretty Kitty.

'Have my night-time antics appalled you?' he said once she reached his bed. 'Has my dalliance with Pretty Kitty caused your low opinion of me to descend to even greater depths?'

He waited in anticipation for the inevitable lecture. After many years of being berated by his father, there were few insults or rants about his scurrilous behaviour that riled him, but a telling-off from Lady Emily was likely to be an interesting experience. He was certain she would look simply divine when fired up with self-righteous indignation.

'She told me what happened.' Her ramrod posture and

the downward curl of her lips did not suggest that Kitty's revelation had done anything to improve her opinion of him.

He raised his eyebrows, or at least attempted to, facial movements having become somewhat of a trial. 'I hope she didn't go into too much detail, and, if she did, I hope she praised my performance, deserving or otherwise.'

'She did praise you.'

'Well, I always like to leave the ladies satisfied.'

This comment was rewarded with a delightful blush colouring her cheeks.

'Why did you lead me to believe that you were one of Kitty's clients? And why are you doing so now?'

He attempted to smile at her. He would not apologise for any misunderstanding. She was the one who was so quick to judge and condemn him. Usually she'd be justified in doing so. Fortunately, or unfortunately, in this particular case, he had, for once, done nothing wrong.

'I don't believe I led you anywhere, you went there all by yourself. And as for continuing to do so, well, you wouldn't deny a sick man some entertainment, would you?'

'I am not here for your entertainment.'

'That is a pity. I could do with a bit of a diversion. Perhaps we should call Pretty Kitty back.'

'Stop this now,' she said, her loud voice drawing the attention of the men in the neighbouring beds. 'Stop this,' she repeated, lowering her voice. 'I am sorry I judged you unfairly, but, well, given your reputation you can hardly blame me.'

'You're right, the fault is all mine.'

'I didn't say that. I just mean, well, a lot of men like you do come down to the East End looking for women like Kitty. And those men care not one fig for those women or the desperate circumstances that have led them into that life. Those women often have children to feed, a slumlord demanding rent, debts to money lenders that have to be paid. And their customers are often men who live comfortable lives and could easily free these women from the terrible circumstances in which they find themselves. But they don't. Do they? Instead, they use them to relieve their carnal needs.'

She continued to glare down at him as if expecting him to argue, but she would get no argument from him. He agreed with everything she said, and he hoped that Kitty did find a way out of her unfortunate circumstances. And perhaps Lady Emily was right. Despite his father's disdain for him, the old Duke did provide Jackson with a generous allowance, one that he usually squandered at the gaming tables and on various other forms of entertainment. There was nothing to stop him from contacting Kitty when he left the hospital. Not to claim his reward, but to help her so she, and perhaps all the other women like her, was never placed in such a precarious position again.

'Thank you, Lady Emily, for that enlightening lecture. I'm assuming that moral guidance is provided free of charge, along with the medical treatment.'

'I'm just explaining to you why I was so incensed when I thought you were Kitty's client.' She narrowed her eyes at him, and he suppressed a smile, knowing that yet another blast of moral indignation was coming his way. 'So, what were you doing in the East End if you weren't, you know.' She shrugged, her cheeks turning a slightly darker shade of pink.

'Seeking out female company to relieve my base carnal needs?'

'Yes,' she said, her cheeks darkening further until she resembled a rather pretty beetroot.

'I was lost and, shall we say, slightly under the weather.'

'You were drunk.'

He smiled at the satisfaction evident in her voice, and waited for the next lecture he could see she was itching to give.

'Drunk might be going a bit far, but let's just say I had imbibed a little bit more than was sensible and it had caused me to become somewhat disorientated.'

Her demeanour became amusingly indignant. 'I believe you are splitting hairs. Drunk means you had imbibed too much.'

'Perhaps. But if I hadn't, I wouldn't have got lost and I wouldn't have stumbled across Pretty Kitty and her attackers. So, you could say, in this instance, the demon drink turned me into Pretty Kitty's guardian angel, and I should be encouraged to drink as much and as frequently as possible so I can continue to perform such good works.'

'Your lack of logic is staggering.' She huffed out a sigh, lifted her head and looked straight ahead, as if seeing something of interest on the wall behind his bed. 'But you are right. Kitty was lucky you saved her, and—' she paused '—and I am sorry I jumped to conclusions and judged you so harshly.'

'You've nothing to apologise for. I've been judged harshly before, but never by anyone who looked so delightful when they frowned at me.'

As expected, her lips turned down and her eyebrows drew closer together.

'There it is again, that lovely frown.'

The frown grew deeper and he waited for another lecture on not flirting with the nursing staff. But, instead, she forced her face into an uninterested expression.

'As you are going to be here for a few days, is there anyone you would like me to contact? Your father, or some other relative?'

It was Jackson's turn to frown. While being lectured by Lady Emily was amusing, there was nothing amusing about being castigated by that tyrant. While he was immobilised in this bed he would prove far too easy a target for his father's venom. 'No, I think I will use this time alone for some quiet contemplation.'

'But won't your family and friends be worried?'

'They will all assume, like you, that I have found some female company to while away my frivolous time.'

Her lips pursed tightly together. 'I didn't—' She stopped abruptly. 'Well, hopefully you'll soon be completely better and back to…doing whatever it is you do.'

'Doing whatever you assume I do.'

'Hmm,' was the only response she gave.

Jackson's attention was drawn to the man approaching from the end of the ward—he stifled a groan. 'Oh, look,' he said, not bothering to disguise his irritation, 'it's the good doctor. Again.'

She turned to face the sanctimonious doctor and, to his immense annoyance, sent him a delighted smile. What on earth did she see in that prig? Perhaps it was exactly that. Do-gooders were presumably attracted to sanctimonious prigs.

'How is my patient doing now?' he asked, smiling in that now familiar self-satisfied manner.

*Much the same as I was when you asked me an hour or so ago*, Jackson wanted to say.

'Excellent. I certainly can't complain about the level of care I'm receiving,' he said instead.

The doctor beamed at Lady Emily. 'Yes, I informed Nurse Emily to provide you with extra special personal attention,' he responded, laughing at the repetition of his little joke. His very little joke, a joke that was getting smaller and smaller every time he made it.

Jackson watched with satisfaction as Lady Emily's smile became tense.

'And there is nothing I like more than some extra special personal attention from a lovely young lady,' Jackson added, unable to stop himself from teasing. 'Especially when she offers it so freely.'

The doctor smiled at him as if he had been the one to receive the compliment, although it was apparent his innuendo was not missed on Lady Emily. She was now doing an impression of someone who would rather be anywhere other than standing uncomfortably beside his bed.

'Well, I'll leave you to consult with the patient,' the blushing Lady Emily said before quickly walking away.

Jackson wanted to call out to her, *Please, do not leave me alone with your beau.* There were only so many times he could listen to the doctor telling him what an excellent physician he was. If he was told one more time that Dr Pratt should be treating Jackson's entire family, extending out to the most distant cousin and every titled person of his acquaintance, he would explode and inform the doctor in no uncertain terms that he'd rather take his chances with the least experienced of quacks rather than put up with his fawning presence for a moment longer.

'I'm afraid I am rather tired,' he said instead, doing his

best impression of a waning patient. 'I think I'd like to rest now.'

'Of course, of course, my lord,' the doctor said, backing away from the bed. 'I'll leave you for now and will be back to check on you later.'

Rather than respond, Jackson closed his eyes, and didn't open them again until he was sure he was alone.

# Chapter Five

Jackson Wilde remained on the ward for another month, until the doctor declared he was fit to be moved and could return to his own home. Despite Gideon's imploration for her to spend as much time with the Viscount as possible, Emily did the opposite, and spent as much time off the wards as she possibly could without drawing comment.

Despite that, she couldn't avoid hearing the nurses' gossiping about their favourite patient. Needless to say, those otherwise sensible and professional young women were all entranced by the charming Viscount. With much giggling they would good-naturedly vie to be the one to administer to him, especially when it came time to give him his bed bath. Even Matron, usually such a no-nonsense woman, had made a passing comment about what a personable young man he was.

Kitty visited regularly, and when word got around about his saving her from a band of thugs, the awe in which Jackson Wilde was held only grew among the nursing staff. With each retelling, his role became more heroic, causing the sighing and swooning to increase, along with Emily's exasperation.

She just knew the man was in his element. All those young—and not so young—women thinking him irresistible. Thank goodness she was not one of them. After that one, brief lapse of good judgement she was now completely immune to his allure.

When the day of his discharge arrived, all the nurses, including the ones not on duty, lined up to say goodbye, as if he was some sort of dignitary who required a guard of honour. Unfortunately, Emily had no choice but to attend this shameful act of adoration. The chairman of the board had pointed out that it would be in the hospital's best interest if all members of the board said their farewells to the Viscount, particularly as he had indicated he intended to make a generous contribution to the running of the hospital. While not officially on the board—being a woman excluded her from such a position—her social rank meant Emily was treated as an unofficial member. It had taken a lot of hard work for her to get that recognition, so she wasn't going to jeopardise it by staying away from this irritating send off.

Gideon was also present, which provided some compensation. He had visited Jackson Wilde every day since his admission, sometimes several times a day, even though that particular patient required little further in the way of medical treatment, other than bed rest.

For his departure the Viscount was dressed in a dark grey day suit, having allowed one of the nursing staff to contact his valet the day before his discharge. The man had arrived in a fluster, horrified to see His Lordship in such a place, his snobbery evidently more entrenched in him than in his master.

The valet had attempted to remain at his master's side, so he could provide everything he deemed necessary, but had been sent away by Jackson Wilde, who, so the nurses reported, had told his valet he was receiving excellent care from a team of nurses who tended to his every need like a flock of heaven-sent angels. This had caused further swooning and sighing from the nurses, and teeth grinding from Emily.

According to the nurses' reports, the valet had countered that he should remain so he could dress his master prior to his discharge, but the Viscount had said the nurses were more than capable of doing so. Once this tale had spread there was much teasing among the nurses and friendly arguments over who would be the lucky woman to do so. All Emily could think was thank goodness it was not to be her. The memory of how she had reacted when she had cleaned his injuries was embarrassing enough, she did not want to risk repeating such aberrant behaviour.

And now, finally, he was to depart and life at the Hope Hospital could return to normal. While the nursing staff and board members waited in an excited line, Gideon walked beside the Viscount. Emily hoped she was the only one to notice the irritation on Gideon's face as Jackson Wilde took his time walking around the ward, pausing at each bed and exchanging a few words and lots of laughter with each man.

'Goodbye, Jackson,' one of the men called out, as Gideon finally steered him towards the waiting line of hospital staff and board members. 'Hope all goes well for you.'

'Give my best to your wife,' he responded with a wave. 'And thank her for the cakes. They were delicious.'

Both Gideon and Emily stiffened at this exchange. Emily because it was apparent Jackson Wilde had been charming the female visitors, along with everyone else, while Gideon's reaction, she suspected somewhat unkindly, was because of the informality of this conversation between a workman and a peer of the realm.

Gideon had complained several times to Emily that Jackson Wilde should not have been on the same ward as the other men, and that Matron should have made more effort to either find him a private room or screen off his bed. He'd even bravely suggested this arrangement to Matron and had, not unexpectedly, received a short shrift for his troubles, and been informed in no uncertain terms that she ran the ward and such decisions were hers and hers alone.

Emily should not fault Gideon for this adherence to Society's rigid expectations on how members of the aristocracy should be treated. He was not the only one to think so. Why, even Jackson Wilde's valet had been shocked to see his master in a public ward. She knew Gideon wasn't a snob. How could he be? He worked every day among London's poorest people and had dedicated his life to their welfare.

Matron was first in the line-up and she simpered like a young girl when Jackson picked up her hand and lightly kissed it.

'Thank you so much for your kindness,' he said. 'It has been an honour to meet you and all your hard-working staff.'

Matron blushed slightly, almost causing Emily's mouth to fall open. He had made that stern, somewhat frightening woman actually blush. Unbelievable.

'The honour is all mine,' Matron replied and gave a small curtsey.

Excitement rippled up the line as he thanked each member of the nursing staff in turn, with the women preening and giggling as if this were a social occasion, where harmless flirtation was de rigueur, and not a serious place of work. Emily noted he addressed each nurse by her first name, although this should not really be a surprise. They were women. Of course he'd be on familiar terms with each and every one of them.

As he moved closer to Emily, she forced herself to continue smiling politely for the sake of appearances. It was a smile that should not have to be forced and she *was* pleased he had made such a rapid recovery. She should also be pleased that he was leaving and she was unlikely to ever see him again. And yet, the strange feeling in the pit of her stomach did not feel like pleasure. She wasn't sure what it was, and refused to analyse it, but it was definitely neither happiness nor relief.

'Lady Emily, it has been a pleasure,' he said, finally reaching her in the line-up.

'Viscount Wickford,' she said with a small curtsey, putting her hands behind her back so there was no danger of him repeating the overly familiar gesture he had made with Matron.

She had no need to take such precautions. He merely bowed his head before moving onto the next person in the line-up, giving her even less attention than he had the nursing staff and patients. And that was as it should be.

It was now quite obvious he had forgotten all about their encounter when she was washing his wounds. And thank goodness for that. It was all now in the past and over and done with, and of little consequence to either of them.

Despite Emily thinking about it constantly for the last month, it was apparent he had now completely put it out of his mind, if it had occupied any space in his thoughts in the first place. While it had been a strangely intimate exchange for her, for him it was apparently of no consequence. Good. That was exactly how it would be for her as well, once she was able to shake off the strange heaviness in her chest.

'And thank you, Mr Greaves,' he said, shaking the chairman of the board's hand. 'You should be proud of this hospital and your magnificent staff.'

The chairman returned his hearty shake. 'And I can only thank you again for your pledge of a donation. Very generous. Very generous, indeed.'

Jackson Wilde brushed his hand in front of his face as if it was of no account. 'And have you given any thought to my proposal?'

'I have indeed,' Mr Greaves replied. 'And I think it an excellent idea.'

The Viscount turned to face Emily. 'As it was Lady Emily who gave me the idea, I believe she should be involved in the project from the very start.'

Emily stared from one man to the other. Proposal? Idea? This was all news to her. 'I'm sorry, what are you talking about?'

'The Viscount has made an interesting proposal to the board,' Mr Greaves said, smiling at her like a kindly father. 'He has suggested we extend our services to further help the local community.'

'How?' Emily asked, but what she really wanted to know was why did she have to be involved, or at least why did she have to be involved with Jackson Wilde.

'I believe now is not the time to discuss this in detail,' the Viscount said. 'Perhaps Lady Emily and I can soon meet for afternoon tea, where I can give her the bank draft for my donation and go over the finer points of this new proposal.'

'An excellent idea,' Mr Greaves answered for her.

With that, Jackson Wilde turned and waved his farewell to all the staff. Everyone else waved enthusiastically as if seeing off a loved one on a long sea voyage. All except Emily, who remained somewhat stunned, wondering what on earth Jackson Wilde was up to.

A few days later a note arrived at the hospital, inviting Emily for afternoon tea with Jackson Wilde so they could discuss something of interest to them both. Emily would like to have thrown it away, but the meeting had been arranged with the consent of Mr Greaves. She had no option but to attend.

On the day of the meeting, she resisted the temptation to make an extra special effort with her clothing or hair. Why should she? It was a business meeting, nothing more, and she wanted Jackson Wilde to know that she placed no importance whatsoever on his opinion of her. She had no wish to impress him, and it was essential he realise she was not like virtually every other woman he came into contact with—bedazzled by his good looks and charms, and desperate for his attention.

She was a sensible, serious woman who was being courted by a man of substance, and that was how she expected Jackson Wilde to treat her. She would broker no flirting. This was to be all business.

She arrived at the tea shop slightly before the arranged time, determined to be seated and waiting in a composed manner when he arrived, but found him already waiting for her. It was so incongruous to see him seated among these women dressed in their finery, with their lacy dresses and hats bearing feathers, ribbons and flowers. It was like seeing a lion seated among a flock of exotic birds.

The bell above the door alerted him to her arrival. He stood beside the table and watched as she lingered at the entrance. The image of a lion returned. She couldn't shake off the idea she was approaching a dangerous animal and needed to be on her guard. It was a disturbing concept that wasn't diminished by the way he was watching her, as if he did indeed wish to devour her.

This was simply a business meeting, she reminded herself. To prove that she would not be intimidated, she strode across the room, her head held high, her nose in the air, but the rapid beating of her heart and the jangling of her nerves belied her attempt at aloofness.

'Lady Emily,' he said when she arrived. 'You're looking as lovely as ever.'

She merely nodded her head, reminding herself that flattery and charm were as natural to him as flight was to a bird.

He pulled out a chair for her and she took her seat. As he brushed past her, she inhaled his scent of sandalwood and leather. The uninvited image of his naked chest invaded her mind. She swallowed and pushed it away. That was the last thing she should be thinking about at a business meeting.

As he took his seat across from her, she smoothed out the wrinkle-free white linen tablecloth, moved the rose patterned teacup slightly to the left and then back again. Then, taking a steadying breath, looked at him across the table.

Apart from a bit of tell-tale yellow colouring around his eyes, his face had almost healed up completely. Once again he was that devastatingly handsome man she had met on occasion at Society balls. The man she had hardly spoken to because he was always surrounded by a coterie of twittering debutantes. His dark blond hair was raffishly curly, with one escaped curl teasing his high forehead. Those blue eyes sparkled, as if he was constantly thinking of a joke, or laughing at the world, and those full lips, no longer bearing a painful split, were slightly curled at the edges, as if he was amused by her presence.

Well, handsome is as handsome does, as the wise proverb warns. A man's looks, his charms, his easy smile, these were of no importance. All that really mattered was a man's true character. She had learnt that lesson well in her first Season. It was a lesson she did not need to be taught again. When it came to men, what was in their heart and soul mattered, not superficialities like good looks and charm or a smile that took one's breath away. That was why she hoped to one day marry Gideon, a good man, a man much more worthy than Jackson Wilde could ever be.

With that thought firmly in her mind, her confidence returned and she stared him unflinchingly in the eye.

'Mr Greaves said you have a banker's draft you wished to pass on to the hospital. Have you brought it with you?' Her tone of voice made it clear she would tolerate none of his nonsense. It also signalled she would linger no longer than was entirely necessary.

'Straight to a discussion about money, I see,' he said, those lips quirking further, the edges of his eyes crinkling. 'It seems you and Pretty Kitty have more in common than I would have thought.'

Emily frowned at him and cursed the heat rising on her cheeks.

His smile grew wider. He was obviously enjoying her discomfort.

'Yes, I brought the banker's draft, but I have also discussed with the board another proposal, which I think you might be interested in. I've ordered tea so we can have a nice long discussion about it.'

'That won't be necessary. I'm merely here to pick up the donation. If you've got a proposal it would be best to discuss it with the board.'

'If my proposal is to be a success, it will require some fundraising, for which I will need your help.' He smiled again, that annoyingly slow smile she just knew was designed to unsettle a woman.

'Mr Greaves agreed that you would be perfect for this role, although, may I suggest, it might be a good idea to learn to woo donors a bit first, not ask outright for their money.'

He was teasing her, but Emily was in no mood to be teased, and especially not by him.

'I do not wish to woo you or anyone else. If you don't want to give me the money, then we have nothing else to talk about.'

A woman at the next table looked from her to the Viscount and back again, her lips pulled into a moue of disgust.

This caused him to laugh, and Emily's cheeks to grow even hotter.

'Well, I've ordered tea,' he said. 'You might not want to woo me, but you can at least stay until you've had your tea and heard what I have to say. Then I promise, I will discretely slip the bankers draft to you, so you don't shock the ladies present.'

Emily said nothing, wishing her burning cheeks would calm down.

The waitress placed the teapot on the table, along with a three-tiered stand full of cakes, sandwiches and scones. Emily doubted she would be able to eat anything, not while her stomach remained in such a tangled knot.

'Thank you, Betty,' he said to the waitress, receiving a delighted smile and a small curtsey in response.

'Anything else you want, just let me know,' Betty said.

'You know the waitress?' Emily asked, unsure why she should be surprised. She was a young woman, after all, and a pretty one at that.

'I do now. I introduced myself when I was ordering tea. Do you disapprove?'

'I couldn't care less,' she responded, aware that if she actually didn't care she would not have inquired. 'So what is this proposal?'

He held up one finger as if to still her inquiries. 'Shall I pour?'

She flicked her hand in agreement.

'Before we discuss my proposal, don't you think we should make some polite conversation? I believe that is the usual manner in which business discussions are conducted.'

Emily said nothing, merely sipped her tea.

'For example, you could enquire after my health.'

'How is your health?'

He smiled that annoyingly charming smile. 'Thank you for asking. Yes, I am mending well.'

'And how did your family and friends react when they found out you weren't in the company of a young woman but in fact had taken a rather brutal beating?'

His smile faltered slightly, then returned as bright as before. 'My father was bereft that such a terrible thing had befallen his beloved son.'

She stared back at him, the cup halfway to her lips. Everyone in Society knew how much the Duke of Greenfeld abhorred his son's behaviour. Had that gruff old man actually been concerned for the welfare of his son and heir? It seemed unlikely.

'You had better put that cup down before you drop it,' he said. 'I am of course jesting. My father reacted in the expected manner. I can't remember all that he said, but the gist of it was something about me burning in hell, being a damnable disgrace, a suggestion that I deserve to die among harlots, guttersnipes and beggars.'

'That is so unfair.' Surely if the man knew why he had taken that beating he would not judge him so harshly. Although the Viscount was still smiling, only his lips were doing so. His eyes held no laughter, only a hint of pain.

She placed her cup in its saucer and reached out across the table towards his hand, before realising what she was doing and quickly retracting it.

'But my father is correct. I do want to mix with such types, well, the harlots anyway. And that is why we are here today.'

All pity she might have felt for him instantly evaporated.

'Don't look so shocked, Lady Emily. My proposal has the full backing of Fergus Greaves.'

She doubted that very much. The chairman of the board was an upstanding man of virtue, with impeccable morals.

'Along with giving the hospital a banker's draft, to show my appreciation for the exemplary care I was given during my stay, I also wish to provide some money for Pretty Kitty and her, shall we say, colleagues.'

'And you expect me to pass the money on to them,' she said, her voice growing louder with her outrage. 'And Mr Greaves agrees with this?' Emily was unsure if it was possible to be more offended. 'Well, I will be no party to this.'

She threw her serviette on the table and rose from her chair.

'Please, sit down, Lady Emily. If for no other reason than you are drawing attention to yourself.'

She looked around and saw the ladies had all stopped in their chatter and turned towards her, with a mixture of curiosity, outrage and enthralment.

She sat down, knowing she had already made herself the subject of gossip, and not wishing to give these women any more fodder.

'That's better,' the Viscount said, and Emily scowled at his condescending manner. 'When I was in hospital you mentioned that women like Pretty Kitty often have no option but to ply their particular trade, and I, perhaps more than most men, am now painfully aware of how dangerous that profession can be.' He gently touched the healing bruise beside his eye.

Emily remained poised on the edge of her chair, waiting for him to finish speaking so she could make a quick but discreet exit, one that would not draw the attention of the assembled ladies.

'What I have suggested is working with the hospital board to help these young women find another way of earning a living.'

'You mean, like a training school?' she asked, still wary

that this might simply be another way in which he was teasing her.

'Exactly. One where they can learn different skills.'

'*You* want to set up a school for fallen women? Isn't that a bit like the poacher becoming the game keeper?'

He placed his hands over his heart. 'Lady Emily, you wound me terribly.' Then he smiled at her, that disarming smile she was determined to resist.

'I've talked it over with the board, and Fergus believes it will be just the sort of project you should be involved with.'

'Why me?'

'It was you who gave me the idea.'

She raised her hands, palm upwards in question.

'If I remember correctly, you informed me that men who visited the East End to relieve their carnal needs didn't give a fig about the women they sought out or the terrible lives they lived. They merely used them then return to their comfortable lives and forgot all about them.'

Emily blushed slightly. That sounded exactly like the sort of lecture she would give him.

'Well, this comfortable man agrees with you entirely and he wants to think about more than just his carnal needs for once.'

The heat on her cheeks grew more intense and she wished he'd stop talking about carnal needs.

'At the moment I am dependent on my allowance from my father, and that alone will not be enough to get the school started and pay its ongoing running costs. It will require fundraising, and who better than a woman of your diplomacy, tact and social skills to undertake such a project.'

'I doubt very much if Mr Greaves said any such thing.'

'No, you're right, he didn't. But he agreed with me that

as the daughter of a duke, and someone with friends who are in the highest positions in Society, you will be well placed to host events to help raise the funds we need.'

She stared at him, even more shocked than she was when he first mentioned giving money to Pretty Kitty. 'You want me to take on the role of a Society hostess?'

'Yes, for a good cause. I know you enjoy balls as much as I do, but if the point of the exercise is not to exchange idle chit chat, nor to jostle to make the most advantageous marriage, but to help people who are in desperate circumstances, then it is hardly too great a sacrifice, is it?'

'No, I suppose not,' she said slowly, mulling this over.

'The school will be a project you can commit yourself to entirely from the very start,' he said, his voice full of appeal.

'Hmm,' she said, not entirely convinced.

He shrugged one shoulder and looked uncharacteristically abashed. 'Forgive me if I'm wrong, but I got the impression at the hospital that you sometimes feel a bit surplus to requirements, and that the nursing staff and board treat you as someone merely dabbling in good works.'

She tensed, knowing he was unfortunately correct. Even Gideon on occasion did not appear to take her commitment seriously.

'Well, this will be your idea. You'll be fully involved from its inception and everyone will know it.'

It wasn't actually her idea, but she could see the attraction of being involved in such a worthy project from its beginning.

'Hosting a ball or two might be hard work but you're not afraid of hard work, are you?'

'Of course not,' she said, offended by his words. Then

she saw his smile and knew it had been a deliberate ploy to win her over. But he was right. If hosting a ball was what was required to better the lives of women like Kitty, then she would do it.

'I'd be happy to do whatever it takes to raise the necessary funds.'

'Good. So we host a ball, charge for the tickets and perhaps have an auction to raise even further funds, then use all that money for the school.'

'You want to charge for the invitations? Like a public ball?'

'Yes, exactly, but we make the price so prohibitively high that the great and good of this city feel compelled to buy tickets, just to prove to everyone that they are able to afford them. And as the money is going to charity, they can all feel like worthy people while doing nothing more than enjoying themselves.'

'Yes, I suppose that would work,' she said. 'And I dare say I could get my mother to help. She loves nothing better than organising a ball. And my friends, Irene, the Duchess of Redcliff, and Georgina, the Duchess of Ravenswood, I'm sure would also help.'

She lifted up her tea cup, then placed it back in the saucer. 'And I am good friends with Amelia Devenish. She's the wife of the media magnate Leo Devenish. Their newspapers and magazines are read by all of Society. I'm sure they'll be happy to provide publicity.'

'And if the guests know the ball will be covered in all the Society pages they'll be desperate to attend, all wanting to be seen as bountiful people who are dedicated to helping the less fortunate.'

'Exactly,' Emily said, smiling back at him. 'And maybe

we can ask people to donate goods to be auctioned off. And hopefully, once again, people will be vying to show just how generous they can be.'

'Excellent idea, Lady Emily.'

'No, you were the one with the excellent idea. I'm sure the training school will make a huge difference to women like Kitty.'

'It is all thanks to you,' he said, picking up a cream cake and placing it on her plate. 'I would never have thought of it if you hadn't told me about the plight of such women.'

Emily felt it prudent not to point out that she hadn't just told him about their plight—she had given him a lecture, and all but held him personally responsible. Instead, she took a bite of the delicious cake.

'It will of course mean you and I will have to continue to spend time together while we get the school up and running,' he said, and took a satisfied bite of his scone.

Emily swallowed down her cream cake, her throat suddenly tight. In her excitement for the project, that was one factor she had not considered.

# *Chapter Six*

'A ball. My little girl wants to host a ball, and she wants me to help. I am so happy.' Her mother rushed over to the roll top desk in the corner of her parlour and pushed up the lid. 'Oh, why couldn't you be like this during your previous Seasons, or even earlier in this Season before all the most eligible men were taken?' She pulled out a piece of paper from the drawer. 'But never mind. There's still time, we just have to invite—'

'That's not the point of the ball,' Emily interrupted. 'As I've already said, it's to raise money for a worthy cause.'

'Yes, yes, I know, but it's still a ball, and there's no reason why you can't find a husband while you're doing all your good works.' She opened her ink well, dipped her pen, looked up in thought, then began writing—her pen scratching furiously over the paper.

Emily released a loud sigh, which was ignored by her mother, who was now absorbed by the list she was compiling. There was no point continuing to argue. Her mother would never give up hope in finding her a suitable husband, but she was right, in a way. The ball would be a perfect time to introduce her parents to Gideon. He had been wanting to meet them for some time, and Emily had always hesitated, not wanting to subject him to their scrutiny and possible objections. But the board members would also be present at the ball. They were all eminent men she knew her parents would approve of, and when they saw the high esteem in which they held Gideon, she was sure they would have no objection to him courting their daughter.

Having informed her mother, Emily's second task was to assemble her friends so they too could assist with the organising. To that end, the four women gathered at Amelia's house, anxious to hear why Emily had summoned them. They had been friends since they met at Halliwell's Finishing School for Refined Young Ladies. At that time, they'd been four square pegs expected to fit into unsuitable round holes. It was only the bonds of their friendship that had enabled them to survive the school, which Georgina had renamed Hell's Final Sentence for Rebellious Young Ladies.

They'd remained friends ever since and continued to support each other through the good times and the bad, and there was nothing Emily valued more than their friendship.

'I'm to host a ball and I want your help,' she announced as they took their seats in the drawing room. They all looked at her with surprise, as she knew they would.

'*You* want to host a ball?' Georgina said, eyeing her sideways. 'You? The woman who, if I remember correctly, said at the end of the first Season, *"Absolutely nothing and no one will drag me to another ball,"* and has managed to avoid virtually all of them since.'

'That's right,' she declared. 'But this ball will be different. I'm raising funds for a training school for, well, for fallen women. It was Jackson Wilde's idea.' Damn it all, Emily heard her voice falter at the mention of his name. Something that was not missed by her friends either, who simultaneously raised their eyebrows.

'Yes, I'd heard the Viscount spent some time recovering in the Hope Hospital,' Irene said. 'I'd wondered whether the two of you became acquainted.'

Was it Emily's imagination or did she hear an emphasis on the word *acquainted*?

'Yes, he was a patient for a while,' she said, keeping her voice as neutral as possible. 'I spoke to him on one or two occasions but had little to do with him, really. He was one of Gideon's patients.'

She waited for her friends to excitedly ask questions about the man she had informed them she hoped one day to marry. There was a pause in the conversation.

'More tea?' Amelia asked, signalling to the footman.

'Gideon of course provided him with the best of care and said that the Viscount was so impressed that he will probably ask him to become his private physician. Not that he will, of course. Gideon is dedicated to the work at the hospital.'

'He doesn't want to set up in private practice?' Irene asked, her tone suggesting disbelief. She had met Gideon when she had visited the Hope Hospital to see Emily, and Gideon had actually put aside his work to spend time politely talking to her friend.

'No, of course not,' Emily said. 'He's dedicated to the charitable work at the Hope Hospital.'

The three women nodded, although not as enthusiastically as Emily would have liked. Irene didn't seem to take to Gideon when they met, which was a disappointment, as he was nothing if not completely courteous to her. He had even taken time out of his busy workload to give her a tour of the hospital.

'I'm going to introduce him to my parents at the ball. So it will kill two birds with one stone, as it were.'

She hadn't exactly hoped for squeals of delight from her friends, but a bit more than their muted response would have been nice. After all, introducing a man to one's parents was an important event—one that was a precursor to an official courtship, then an engagement and marriage. Instead, all she got was some polite smiles, a few nods and murmurs of 'that's nice'.

'Well, I wish the two of you every happiness,' Amelia finally said, and the other two raised their tea cups in a toast.

'To Emily's happiness,' Georgina said.

To which Irene gave a, 'Hear, hear.'

'So did you say this was all Jackson Wilde's idea?' Georgina asked, returning to a subject that seemed to animate them more than her coming official courtship.

Emily recounted the tale of Pretty Kitty and the beating he had taken, which, not surprisingly, the three women listened to with wide-eyed interest. Then she explained how this had led to a discussion between her and Jackson on the terrible lives of such women. She used the term discussion, even though she knew that in reality she had harangued the Viscount. Though, on this one occasion, he was actually completely innocent of any wrongdoing.

'And now the two of you are going to raise money for a training school for fallen women,' Georgina said, her hand over her heart and an approving smile on her lips. 'What a wonderful tale.'

Emily was tempted to point out that while, yes, it was good of Jackson Wilde, Gideon gave all his time to the hospital. He worked tirelessly for the poor and never expected any thanks.

'And I suppose it means the two of you will be spending a lot of time together now?' Irene asked.

'Yes, for the fundraising,' she said, adopting a brisk and unemotional tone. 'And we'll be working with the board to find suitable premises. Then I believe the Viscount will be organising tradesmen to turn the premises into a school.'

'It looks like you've transformed him, Emily,' Irene said, beaming with delight. 'You've tamed the rake.'

'Nonsense,' she shot back at this ridiculous suggestion from a woman she had hitherto thought quite sensible. 'He may be giving his time, effort and quite a bit of his allowance to the school, but he's no different to the way he's always been.'

She could hear the disapproval in her voice, but she did disapprove of him and could see no reason to disguise it. The man didn't meet a woman he didn't want to flirt with. He had no doubt left the hospital and gone straight to one of his mistresses. Nothing about this man had really changed.

'Still, what the two of you are doing is admirable, and I will help in any way I can,' Amelia said.

The other two nodded.

'Good,' Emily said, pleased they had got back to the real reason why she was here. And it wasn't to discuss Jackson Wilde. 'Mother has of course leapt into the fray, but it would be good to have your help, otherwise the only people she will invite will be eligible men. And, Amelia, the more publicity your papers are able to give the event the better.' She looked round at her friends, whose expressions were gratifyingly enthusiastic. 'We want people to think this is an event they absolutely must be seen at, and they also must be vying to be seen as the most generous donor present.'

'Leave that to me and Leo,' Amelia said. 'Our newspapers will turn this ball into the event of the Season.'

'Perhaps we should make it fancy dress,' Georgina added. 'Then it will be something quite different for people to get excited about.'

'Excellent idea,' Emily said, as Amelia called for the footman to bring papers and fountain pens so they could begin their organisation in earnest.

'We could also set up a photography studio in one of the side rooms and people could have their portrait taken in their costume,' Amelia said.

'In exchange for a generous donation,' Emily added, which was greeted with a chorus of, 'Yes, absolutely.'

The tea going cold, the four women set about preparing for what they fully intended to be the Season's most memorable ball, one that would have people dipping eagerly into their pocket books, or writing out enormous bank drafts.

Emily smiled to herself as she watched her friends enthusiastically volunteer for the various tasks. Who would have thought, when they first met at Halliwell's Finishing School, that one day they'd all be so respectable?

Now her three friends were all happily married and in love. And she would soon be married as well. Perhaps she wouldn't experience the grand passion that her three friends had, and might not be as besotted with the man she married, but that hardly mattered. In Gideon, she had found the man she wanted. Their relationship might be a tad lacking in romance, but he was a man who made her feel safe, a man whom she could trust, who was honest and reliable.

No woman could ever want more from a man than that. Could she?

# Chapter Seven

On the night of the ball, Emily's nerves were jingling with a mixture of excitement and worry. Would it be a success? Would they raise the money necessary for the school? Would everything go as planned? Would Jackson Wilde dance with her? No, that last one hardly mattered. What she should be thinking about was how her parents would react when she introduced them to Gideon. It was so important that they like him and accept the fact that their daughter would be marrying a doctor.

Strangely, of all the things she should be anxious about, that was the thought causing her the least concern. It must be because she simply knew her parents would admire and respect Gideon for the man he was, despite his lack of title and wealth—just as she did.

'Can you please try to sit still, my lady,' her lady's maid said as she worked on Emily's hair.

Emily had chosen to wear a simple pale gold Regency gown, which she'd had since she was a child, and had often worn when playing dress up. It had belonged to her grandmother. It was hard to believe such a matronly woman had once worn a dress of such fine material that clung to one's curves, emphasising the bustline.

Her lady's maid had spent time analysing family por-

traits painted during the Regency period and was sure she
had perfected the style, with a bun at the top of the head,
and ringlets around the face. She had insisted Emily spend
the night with her hair tied up in strips of cloths to create
the required ringlets, which to Emily's mind was going a
tad too far, but her lady's maid was a perfectionist and it
would have been mean of Emily to deny Mabel her fun,
so she complied.

'Lovely,' Mabel said when she had finished, then frowned.
'But you must leave that alone, my lady.'

Emily realised she was pulling at the low-cut neckline.
Did Grandmama really expose so much cleavage when
she was a young woman? That too was hard to believe.

'Perhaps a simple string of pearls tonight, my lady,'
Mabel said, opening Emily's jewellery box and placing
them around her neck before she had time to answer. Emily
was not so sure. It looked as if she was deliberately drawing attention to her decolletage, and it really wouldn't do
to have anyone think that. After all, she was hosting this
ball for a serious reason, not to flirt or to try and attract
a man's interest.

She gazed at her reflection in the full-length looking
glass and had to admit Mabel had done a wonderful job.
She did look rather splendid. And tonight *was* supposed
to be about having fun. The more fun people had the more
generous they would be, so she really *should* get into the
spirit of the occasion.

She thanked Mabel, pulled on her elbow length gloves,
picked up her matching gold fan and joined her parents
in the ballroom, where her mother was giving last minute instructions to the servants and extra staff who had
been hired for the evening. Not that she needed to, they

all seemed to know exactly what they were doing, but that was what her mother did when she was nervous, so there was no point trying to stop her.

Her father took her hands and smiled at her. 'You look enchanting, my dear,' he said, kissing her on the cheek. 'And what do you think of my costume?'

Emily laughed as he stood back, lifted his head high and placed one hand inside his jacket. 'Well, Napoleon, it looks like tonight you and I will be enemies,' she said.

'Yes, I think we should have had a family discussion about what we were to wear instead of keeping it a surprise,' he said with a laugh. 'Your mother decided to come as Marie Antoinette. Everyone is going to think that it is a sign of marital disharmony.'

She looked over at her mother, who was giving orders to a young maid. She was wearing an ornate costume that could not contrast more dramatically with Emily's simple gown. Her mother's hair was swept up into an enormous bouffant and powdered grey, and she was laden down with what appeared to be every one of the family jewels.

The first guests to arrive were her friends Amelia, Irene and Georgina, and their husbands. The four women spent some time admiring each other's costumes. Amelia and Leo were dressed as Cleopatra and Mark Antony, Georgina and Adam as Romeo and Juliet and Irene and Joshua as Robin Hood and Maid Marion.

It really had been a good idea to have the fancy dress theme. Emily was rather looking forward to the occasion. Usually a sense of dread descended on her when she was forced to attend a ball.

The friends did one last inspection of the room and all agreed that everything looked exactly as it should. The chandeliers with their countless candles sent flickering light around the room. The parquet floor was polished to perfection. The orchestra was seated on the balcony, and servants were waiting to tend to the guests' every need.

'And we were right to go with large bouquets of white and pink lilies,' Georgina declared. 'Their scent is simply divine, and they look magnificent.' That had actually been Georgina's idea, but she was obviously expecting some praise, so the others obliged.

'It is perfect and is sure to be a success,' Irene said, gently patting Emily's arm. 'Amelia's gushing articles in all the ladies' magazines means everyone who is anyone will be here tonight. I'm sure you'll raise even more money than you need for your school.'

Amelia and Georgina both nodded at this comment. Emily smiled at them, knowing they were right. The amount people had paid for the tickets already meant the funds had swollen to a respectable degree, and her friends' husbands had donated significant amounts of money, and pledged to continue supporting the school.

But, strangely, that was not what she was most anxious about. It was seeing Jackson Wilde again. This time she would not be tending to him as a patient, nor would she be in the role of a woman taking part in a serious business meeting or discussing fundraising activities. Tonight she would be a woman dressed in her finery, at a Society ball.

The board members were the next to arrive, and Emily had to supress a giggle. Mr Greaves was dressed as a Roman gladiator, seemingly not worrying that his legs, bearing the blue veins and knots of old age, were on display for all to see. His wife was dressed more sensibly, as a woman from ancient Rome, in a floor-length white gown with a shawl draped over her shoulders.

The room started to fill up with milk maids, Shakespearean characters, pirates, several Henry VIIIs and a surprising number of geisha girls and women in harem costumes.

Gideon arrived dressed as a Roman senator, in a full-length white toga and a laurel wreath in his hair. He greeted Mr Greaves, who good-naturedly joked that tonight Gideon would be the one in charge.

Gideon then bowed formally to Emily. 'You look lovely tonight,' he said. Before she could thank him, he looked around the room. 'I saw you talking to the Duke of Redcliff and the Duke of Ravenswood.'

'Yes, their wives and I are good friends.'

'Excellent. Perhaps you can introduce me to those gentlemen.'

'They have already pledged to donate sizeable amounts to the school,' Emily said, somewhat confused, as Gideon had hitherto shown no interest in the organisation of the ball or the fundraising efforts.

A matching look of confusion crossed his face. 'Nevertheless, I should like to make their acquaintance.'

That did make sense and Emily wondered why she had questioned his motives. Of course Gideon would want to meet her friends and their husbands. She led him across the room to where the Dukes of Redcliff and Ravenswood were in conversation with Amelia's husband, Mr Leo Devenish.

While they made their introductions, Emily looked around at the guests, all chatting and laughing in small groups as they showed off their dazzling costumes. The ball was already a great success and it had hardly begun.

Her gaze was caught by Jackson Wilde, walking towards her from the far side of the room. She quickly suppressed a gasp. Was he dressed as Mr Darcy? Had he known she would come in a Regency gown? She was sure she had mentioned it to no one, not even her friends and family.

And, oh, my, he did look magnificent in his long black jacket, tight leather breeches, tucked into knee-length boots, and a high-collared white shirt with an intricately tied cravat.

The conversation between the four men died away. The sound of the music quietened as he walked towards her. All she could hear was the pounding of her heart. With each step he took, bringing him closer to her, the room became warmer, the air thinner, as she struggled to catch her breath.

The four men all turned in the direction she was staring and it was evident her friends' husbands were pleased to see Jackson Wilde. After greetings were exchanged, he bowed to her. 'May I have the honour of this dance, Lady Emily?'

'Oh,' was the only inarticulate response Emily was capable of giving.

He looked to Gideon. 'I'm sure the senator can spare you for one dance.'

'Yes, of course. Dance with the Viscount,' Gideon said with a wave of his hand. 'While I continue this fascinating conversation with Their Graces.'

Was it a look of irritation she saw cross the two Dukes' faces? She would not have taken them for snobs and could see no other reason why they would object to talking to Gideon. But she had no time to contemplate their reaction as Jackson Wilde linked her arm through his and escorted her out onto the dance floor, where they joined the other couples waiting for the waltz to begin.

When he placed his hand on her waist and took her gloved hand in his, her breath caught in her throat. The warmth of his touch seeped into her body. That was something she had not considered when choosing this costume. The fine muslin material provided little in the way of a barrier between a man's hand and her skin. It was as if he was caressing her naked flesh, sending her temperature soaring.

She placed her hand tentatively on his broad shoulder, feeling the strength under her fingers. A memory of his naked chest flashed into her mind. She fought to drive out the image of those hard muscles, and how they had rippled under the stroking of her flannel as she had cleaned his wounds.

She swallowed, closed her eyes and took in a long, steadying breath. This would not do. It was just a dance. All she had to do was move with him to the music and make some polite conversation.

Conversation. That was it. A bit of mindless chit chat would drive out any further thoughts of his naked body and put a stop to all these disconcerting sensations. She looked up into those blue eyes and anything she might have said disappeared before the words had fully formed. How could she think of idle chatter when he was holding her with that gaze. She stared back, suddenly aware that his eyes weren't just blue, but contained swirls of grey, making them more complex than she had first assumed. Just as she suspected Jackson Wilde contained more complexities than appearances would suggest.

The music started and she surrendered to the grace of his movements as they glided across the parquet floor.

There was no denying that being in his arms felt good. Very good. Too good.

As if drawn by an invisible thread too strong for her to resist, with each step she moved closer and closer to him, until his chest was almost touching hers. Warmth radiated off his body, that scent of sandalwood and leather enveloping her, making her almost giddy.

*Say something, anything,* she commanded her useless brain. *Break this spell.*

Desperate to do so, she attempted a polite smile. The smile quivered and died. The look in his eyes was unlike any she had seen before, and it could never be described as polite. His gaze moved to her lips, which parted on a soft sigh.

Despite what she might think of him, despite how offended she was by the way he lived his life, being in his arms was undeniably an intoxicating experience. And that was how she felt, as if she had imbibed far too much of the punch. It was easy to see how he had gained his reputation as a ladies' man. Surely no woman could remain unaffected when in the arms of such a commanding, desirable man. And the way he was looking at her made *her* feel desirable, like a beautiful woman capable of entrancing a man such as him. She could not be blamed for her reaction. How could she not be dazzled by him? How could any woman not wish for him to do more than just dance with her, more than just look at her? How could any woman resist becoming this man's mistress?

Emily stumbled over her dancing slippers, causing him to wrap his arm around her waist to stop her fall. What on earth had she been thinking? Intoxicated? Becoming his mistress? Where had such a ludicrous idea come from? This was getting out of hand.

*Put an end to this. Now. Do not think of his hand on your waist. Do not think of his strong muscular shoulders or firm chest. And definitely do not think of those dazzling blue eyes or those full lips.*

She coughed to clear her constricted throat. 'The ballroom…' She coughed again. 'The ballroom looks wonderful, don't you think? And I'm so pleased the weather remained fine.'

Emily released a held breath. She had done it. She had made some boring small talk. Perfect. Nothing could bring a person back to reality faster than a dull conversation about the weather.

He smiled down at her, those blue eyes crinkling at the corners, and, damn it all, it gave every appearance of being a knowing smile. Was he aware of the effect he was having on her? Was he laughing at her? She gazed back into his eyes, searching, but could see no hint of mockery in their depths. Instead, she noticed their warmth, like the blue of a summer sky on a languid afternoon, and she felt bathed in their light.

She blinked rapidly to push out that absurd image. He was merely looking at her. There was no summer sky, no bathing in light, no languid afternoons. She needed to take control of this situation. But how? If small talk didn't work, she was completely out of ideas.

He spun her around again and she felt so light in his arms, so feminine. Perhaps she should just surrender to the moment. Enjoy this brief dance and then forget all about it, just as he would surely forget about holding her so close as soon as the music stopped.

And so she did. As one, they swept across the floor and, just as she had completely given herself over to the dance, the music soared up into a crescendo and it was all over.

His hand dropped from her waist and he offered her his arm to escort her off the floor, over to where Gideon was standing, watching them.

Gideon.

While she was in Jackson Wilde's arms she hadn't even thought of Gideon. This was all too, too bad. Had Gideon been shocked by her behaviour? When she arrived at his side she quickly scanned his face, hoping she would not see jealousy or hurt.

He bowed to the Viscount, giving no signs of any such reactions. Perhaps he had nothing to be jealous of. Perhaps those intense looks, the silent exchanges, had all been in her imagination.

'My lord, what a pleasure it is to see you again,' Gideon said to Jackson Wilde. 'And I'm pleased to see you looking so healthy. It's always good to see a patient respond so well to my attentions. And I'm sure I need not remind you that I am more than happy to attend you as a private patient.'

'You're right,' the Viscount said. 'You have no need to remind me.' He bowed to Emily. 'Now if you'll excuse me, I'm sure you will want to dance with Lady Emily.'

'Such a gracious man,' Gideon said, even before Jackson Wilde was out of earshot, seemingly oblivious to the slight, or preferring to ignore it. He turned to Emily and smiled. 'I think now would be a good time to introduce me to your parents.'

'Yes, of course,' Emily said, still feeling somewhat disconcerted by the dance, even though it had been no more than a waltz around a ballroom surrounded by onlookers.

She gazed across the room to where Jackson Wilde was now speaking to a group of men, which included several members of the House of Commons.

Gideon slid her arm through his. 'Emily?'

She turned to face him. 'Yes?'

'You were going to introduce me to your parents.'

'Oh, yes, sorry, of course.'

'Your mother is smiling at us,' Gideon said as they crossed the crowded room. 'That has to be a good sign.'

'Yes,' she agreed, surprised to see he was right. Her mother was smiling at her with approval, something that rarely happened at a ball.

'I see you were dancing with Viscount Wickford,' her mother said before Emily had a chance to introduce Gideon. 'He looks so dashing tonight in that Regency costume. You two looked as if you were made for each other. Is that why you chose that costume? So you would be a match for Viscount Wickford?'

'Of course not,' she said, quickly glancing at Gideon. 'I had no idea what anyone would be wearing tonight.'

'Oh, such a pity,' her mother said, although Emily could not for the life of her think how that should elicit pity.

'But it looks like dancing with the Viscount has put some colour in your cheeks,' her mother added.

Emily cursed her burning cheeks and sent her mother a warning look, letting her know this was neither the time nor place to discuss the Viscount or any reaction she may or may not have had to dancing with him. A look that merely caused her mother to smile back at her, as if unaware she had done or said anything that deserved her daughter's censure.

'Mother, Father, may I introduce you to Dr Gideon Pratt.

He is a doctor at the Hope Hospital. Dr Pratt, my parents, the Duke and Duchess of Fernwood.'

'It's a great honour to meet you, Your Graces,' Gideon said with a low bow.

'Jolly good work you're doing at that hospital,' her father said. 'Well done.'

'And I don't just work at the hospital,' Gideon said. 'I am also setting up my own private practice and intend to soon have a thriving surgery, treating many of the most respected members of London Society.'

Emily frowned. This was the first she had heard of such a plan. 'But he will still continue to provide his excellent level of care to the patients at Hope Hospital,' Emily said, her statement almost a question.

'Perhaps,' Gideon replied, still smiling at her parents. 'Although I will be fully committed to providing the highest level of care to my private patients.'

Emily's mother smiled politely while looking between Emily and Gideon, as if unsure why they were being introduced and why this man was telling her about his profession.

'Well, don't let us keep you young people,' her mother said. 'The orchestra is once again playing. I believe you should be on the dance floor and enjoying yourself, especially after all the hard work you have put into making tonight such a success.'

Gideon bowed again as if her mother had bestowed a compliment on him, when he'd taken no part in organising tonight's ball. Then he took Emily's arm and led her away.

'I believe that went very well,' he said.

'Yes, I suppose so.'

'Once we've had this dance, I believe I should take the

opportunity to circulate with as many of the guests as possible.'

'Oh, yes, of course. That's very good of you. We've already raised a lot of money for the school, but if you circulate and tell them the good work that the hospital does, then hopefully some of the guests will also be willing to act as patrons for the hospital.'

'Yes,' he said distractedly, as they started to move around the dance floor. 'There really is the cream of Society here tonight, all gathered in one spot. It's simply wonderful.'

'Well, if by the cream you mean the richest and the most influential, then yes, you're right.'

He gave a small laugh as if she had made a joke, which she hadn't.

'Yes, the very best people, all in one place, and I simply cannot let this opportunity pass me by.'

Pique rose within her. This was a side of Gideon she had hitherto not seen. Or was she misunderstanding his intentions? She needed to know for sure.

'Did you mean what you said about a private practice, or were you just saying that for my parents' sake?'

'There will be plenty of time to discuss that later,' he said. 'Let's just enjoy this dance.'

They continued to move around the floor in silence. Emily had so many questions circulating in her mind— about Gideon's plans, his ambitions, their future together— and she really did want them answered, sooner rather than later.

'Gideon, before you start circulating again, can we please have a quiet word? Perhaps out on the terrace,' she said the moment the music had finished.

This caused him to smile brightly. He took her arm and

led her towards the French doors at the end of the ballroom and out onto the terrace overlooking the garden.

'So are you going to tell me what you meant when you told my parents about your plans for a private practice?'

He closed the French doors, cutting off the sound of the orchestra and the chattering guests. 'I believe tonight would be the perfect time for me to formally ask your father for your hand in marriage,' he said, as if he hadn't heard her question. 'We could even announce it here tonight, in front of all of Society.'

'Oh,' she said, lowering herself on the cold concrete seat and giving a forced laugh. 'Shouldn't you ask me first?'

He stared at her in confusion. 'Ask? But I thought we had an understanding.'

'Well, yes, perhaps, but it would be nice to actually get a proposal,' she said with a small, somewhat awkward laugh. 'After all, I'll only ever get one.'

He continued to look down at her, his brow furrowed. 'I wasn't aware that you were like that. You're usually such a practical, sensible woman, one who doesn't care for such romantic twaddle.'

Emily shrugged. She thought so too, but, surely, under these circumstances, a bit of romance was called for.

'But if that is what you require,' he said with a condescending smile as he sat down beside her. 'Lady Emily, will you do me the honour of becoming my wife?'

Emily stared at him, willing herself to say yes. Wasn't this what she always wanted, to be married to a sensible, serious man, dedicated to his profession, one who was committed to helping others and making the world a better place? But there were still those unanswered questions. 'Gideon, we need to—'

'Or do you need more romancing?' he asked, once again giving her a somewhat condescending smile. Before she was aware of what was happening, he took hold of her shoulders and smashed his lips against hers. Emily clamped her lips tightly together. She pulled back against his hold as he crushed himself more tightly to her chest.

No, this was definitely not what she wanted. A bolt of realisation hit her. She knew not only did she not want his kisses. She did not want Gideon, did not want to become his wife.

Placing her hands on his shoulders she pushed hard and turned her head, so his lips were no longer on hers.

'Sorry,' he said as he released her, looking more smug than apologetic. 'Although now that we are engaged I believe you can't condemn a man for taking a few liberties. But I appreciate that a chaste woman such as yourself needs a bit more coercing into such intimacies. You need have no fear on that account. I am a gentleman and can wait until our wedding night.'

*Coercion? What did he mean by coercion?*

'Oh, Emily, we are going to be so happy together. Once my practice is established, I'll be able to keep you in the comfort to which you are accustomed. We'll be able to mix with the *crème de la crème* of Society. I promise you, I will make you the very best of husbands.'

'But what of the hospital, the school?'

He smiled and took hold of her hands. 'Once we are married you won't need to fill your time with charity work. You'll be too busy being my wife.'

'I don't want to marry you,' Emily blurted out.

'Don't be silly. We had an agreement. That's why you

held this ball, so you could introduce me to your family, your friends and to Society.'

'I said I don't want to marry you,' she repeated, her voice stronger.

He continued to smile at her as if this was some sort of game.

'You're not the man I thought you were,' she continued. 'I thought you were as dedicated to the hospital as I am, not an ambitious doctor wanting to make money.'

His smile turned into a confused frown. 'What? You expected me to want to spend my life working among the wretched of this great city? I didn't fight my way into medical school and dedicate all those years to study to spend the rest of my life in the East End.'

'That *is* what I expected of you. That is the man I thought you were. I thought you were a better man.'

'I am a better man, and will be an even better man with you at my side. I intend to be one of the most eminent doctors in London. A man you will be proud to call your husband.'

'I would be proud of a man who dedicated his life to those who needed his help, not a man who wants to become rich and well thought of by people whose opinion I care nothing about.'

His eyebrows drew close together, as if he was trying to decipher a language he couldn't quite grasp.

'What are you saying?'

'I'm sorry. I don't want to marry you.'

He continued to stare at her, shaking his head slowly. 'So why did you lead me on? Why did you make me think that we had an understanding? Why did you make me think we were courting? Why did you introduce me to your parents and your friends?'

'I'm sorry,' she repeated, pulling her hands out of his grasp and placing them in her lap.

Emily could not believe she had done it again. She had deluded herself about a man. Again. And she *was* sorry, not just for herself, but for what she had done to Gideon.

'I'm sorry, Gideon. Sorry that I thought you were a man different to the one you really are. Sorry that in my mind I made you into the man I wanted you to be, not the man you really are. None of that is your fault.'

'Is it because I kissed you? I shouldn't have done that,' he said, desperation entering his voice. 'You need not worry about such things. We will need to consummate the marriage to make it legal, but once we've done that we can come to an arrangement. After all, I am a gentleman, I won't force you to do anything you don't want to.'

'I don't want to marry you,' she repeated, her voice rising.

'But—'

'But nothing. I have given my answer. You said you were a gentleman, so just accept that I have turned down your proposal and there is nothing you can do or say to change my mind.'

He frowned at her, as if incapable of understanding this simple declaration.

'I don't want to marry you, Gideon,' she repeated. 'I think you should go now.'

His lips drew into a hard, thin line. 'I cannot believe you have turned down the chance to become the wife of a man who will one day be a successful doctor.'

Emily looked down at her hands clasped in her lap, wishing he would just leave.

'You must know that a woman your age is unlikely to get another offer of marriage.' He stood up and began pacing. 'I had wondered why the daughter of a duke had ended up being left on the shelf. Now I have my answer. All I can say is thank goodness you let me know what you're really like now, before I ended up married to a dried-up old spinster who is terrified of a man's touch.'

Emily clenched her hands tighter and stared straight ahead, out into the dark night, not wanting him to see how deeply his barbed words had pierced her.

'You, madam, are a bitter old maid, who will only become more bitter with each passing year.'

With his cruel words still ringing in her ears, he strode back into the ballroom, leaving Emily shaken and trying to grasp how this had happened. How, for the second time in her life, she had completely misread a man's character, only to discover he was nothing like the person she'd imagined, and had hoped him to be.

# Chapter Eight

$D$r Pratt reappeared in the ballroom, alone, his face like thunder. When he'd departed to the terrace, arm in arm with Lady Emily, shutting the doors firmly behind them, Jackson's heart had sunk. The doctor had looked so pleased with himself after being introduced to the Duke and Duchess of Fernwood, giving Jackson the strong suspicion that he was about to propose.

During the long minutes they had been absent, he had attempted to distract himself with conversation, doing what he was here to do, drumming up support for the school. He had no reason to concern himself with what was happening out on the terrace. Lady Emily was a grown woman capable of making her own choices. Just because Jackson thought the doctor a complete twit did not mean she saw him that way. But, if he had proposed, Dr Pratt's furious expression made it clear what her answer had been.

Satisfaction washed through Jackson. He watched the doors. Lady Emily did not return. The doctor stood against the wall for a moment, as if gathering himself. Then he smiled, strode across the room to a group of men chatting beside the supper table, and bowed politely in introduction.

Jackson's attention turned back to the French doors. She had still not returned. Had the doctor left Lady Emily in a state of distress? There was only one way to find out. He rushed across the dance floor and pulled open the glass doors leading onto the terrace.

She was sitting against the wall, staring into space.

'Is everything all right?' he asked, knowing it wasn't.

She looked towards him. Even in the dim light from the ballroom, he could see tears sparkling on her black eyelashes. 'Oh, yes, perfectly all right, thank you,' she said, sitting up straighter.

'May I join you?'

She shrugged in answer, so he moved from the doorway, closed the doors and took a seat beside her on the stone bench.

'You don't look as if everything is all right,' he said, looking out at the garden, dimly lit from the light spilling out from the ballroom.

She drew in a shuddering breath. 'Gideon proposed,' she said quietly.

He merely nodded.

'I turned him down.'

'I take it he was disappointed that you are not to become his wife.'

She gave a small, humourless laugh. 'Yes, I believe he is disappointed that the Duke of Fernwood's daughter is not to be his wife.'

'I'm sure that's not true. I'm sure he cared about much more than your title,' Jackson said, aiming to comfort her, but suspecting she was correct.

She turned to face him, blinked away her tears, and stared him straight in the eye, her defiant pose contradicted by a slight trembling of her lips. He wanted to take her in his arms and tell her she did not have to be strong, not in front of him, but taking her in his arms was the last thing he should do.

'He actually said that a woman of my age should be grateful he proposed.' The wobble to her voice revealed just how deeply those words had wounded.

*How dare he?*

Jackson's jaw clenched and he exhaled loudly through flared nostrils, then forced himself to rein in his anger. It would do Lady Emily no good if he lost his temper with that craven maggot.

'You shouldn't listen to anything a man with a broken heart says,' he said, fighting to keep his voice even.

She gave another mirthless laugh. 'Broken heart? I doubt that very much. If his heart is broken, it's because he fears losing his dream of owning a private medical practice tending to members of the aristocracy.'

Jackson made no comment, again suspecting that to be the truth.

She bit her lip and looked at him, those liquid brown eyes appealing for his understanding. 'He also said I was a dried-up old spinster who will only get more bitter as I get older.'

'The cad. You mustn't believe a thing that ba—' He swallowed down the word he wanted to use and instead turned on the seat and clasped her hands. 'He is the bitter one. He was just lashing out at you in anger. You are most definitely not bitter. Nor are you old, and you're certainly not a spinster. You're an enchanting young woman and the only reason you are yet to find a husband is because no man is good enough for you.'

She laughed as if his words had been said in jest, but it was no jest. She was indeed a beautiful young woman, one who deserved to be loved and respected by a man much more worthy of her than that Pratt fellow could ever be.

'No, I think he might be right. He tried to kiss me tonight and it was awful. It was my first kiss and I hated it.' Colour exploded on her cheeks. She once again blinked away the tears that were threatening to fall and lowered her head.

He lightly placed one finger under her chin and gently lifted it. A man like Pratt had no right to make this admirable young woman feel bad about herself.

'That's probably because it *was* awful,' he said. 'But it just shows that you either didn't want Dr Pratt to kiss you, or he was a terrible kisser, or both.'

She shrugged one shoulder. 'How would I know if he's a terrible kisser or not?' Her eyes moved to his lips. 'I'm four-and-twenty and no man has kissed me before. All I know is his kiss revolted me so much I couldn't stop myself from pushing him away. He was the man I thought I wanted to marry and I couldn't even bear being in his arms. Perhaps his horrid description of me was right.'

'No, he is wrong.'

Before Jackson had time to consider the wisdom of what he was doing, he took her in his arms and kissed her lovely lips. To his delighted surprised she sunk into his arms and kissed him back.

This was most definitely not the reaction of a spinster, nor of a woman who hated being kissed. This was glorious. Just as he had fantasised. He had wanted to kiss her from the first moment he saw her angelic face looking down at him when he awoke in hospital. And when she had tended his wounds he'd wanted to do a lot more than just kiss her, but he'd had enough sense to know not to. Now it appeared all sense had deserted him.

*Stop. Now*, the small part of his brain still capable of reason told him. *Men like you do not kiss women like her. Not unless you intend to face the consequences.*

He couldn't undo the kiss, but if he had a modicum of decency he would make it a short, light kiss, just to prove to her that she was no dried-up old spinster.

But he didn't stop. Instead he deepened the kiss. His tongue ran along her soft bottom lip. She moaned lightly, her lips parting. She was not objecting to what he was doing, quite the opposite. Her hands wound around the back of his neck, holding him closer as she kissed him back.

His tongue gently entered her mouth, tasting her, savouring her, as she melded in closer to him—her full, soft breasts against his chest. If there was any doubt about the passion of this woman, it had now been firmly stripped away. She was a woman made for the giving and taking of physical pleasure. But he should not be the man either giving or taking. She was a respectable young woman. Respectable young women saved themselves for marriage to respectable men. And no one could ever accuse Jackson of being respectable.

This was wrong. He had gone too far already, and he must not go any further, as damnably tempting as it was to do so.

With the greatest reluctance he withdrew from her lips and, still holding her close, looked down at her lovely face. Her red lips were plump from their kiss, her face flushed a pretty shade of pink, her eyes still closed. Had he ever seen a more tempting woman? If he had, he certainly couldn't remember when, but it was a temptation he should have resisted, and one he must never sample again.

She slowly opened her eyes and gazed at him, her warm brown eyes almost black in the subdued light. Her lips parted and she released a slow sigh, her breath gentle on his cheek.

As if emerging from a trance, she blinked several times, then her hands dropped from behind his neck. She placed them demurely in her lap and once again looked straight ahead, out at the darkened garden.

'I probably shouldn't have done that,' he said, aware of the husky note in his voice. 'But at least we've proven Dr Pratt completely wrong. Whoever you do eventually marry is going to be a very lucky man indeed.'

'Thank you,' she said, causing him to smile. He was unsure whether she was thanking him for the compliment or the kiss, but neither was required.

'You deserve someone much better than Dr Pratt,' he said quietly.

'Maybe,' she responded.

'You do, Lady Emily. You deserve a good man, one who is worthy of your love. I believe that such creatures do exist, although I'm yet to meet one.'

Her small laugh filled him with almost as much satisfaction as that kiss had done. After all the terrible things that cretin Pratt had said to her, it was good to hear her laugh.

'Thank you,' she repeated. 'You are very kind.'

It was his turn to laugh. 'I don't think your parents or Society would see it that way.'

This truly was a peculiar situation in which he found himself. He had just kissed a woman to make her feel better, to make her realise just how attractive she actually was. One could almost see it as a noble, unselfish act.

He smiled at this delusional idea. With her thigh almost

touching his, the taste of her still on his lips, her feminine scent sparking inappropriate reactions deep within him, what he had just done and wanted to do to her right now could never be described as unselfish or noble.

And if they remained out here for much longer, alone on this darkened terrace, she would discover just how ignoble and selfish he really was.

'I believe it might be best if we returned to the ballroom before tongues start to wag.'

*And we should do so while I am still able to exercise some self-control.*

She didn't answer so he forced himself to stand and offer her his hand. It was essential they return to the ballroom, where his behaviour could be modified by the company of others.

'Lady Emily, would you do me the honour of the next dance?'

She looked up at him, nodded and without comment placed her hand in his.

He led her into the centre of the ballroom and quickly looked around, expecting to see no sign of Dr Pratt. But no, there he was, smiling and ingratiating himself to the Earl of Bosworth. Jackson swallowed down his ire. He had insulted this remarkable woman, left her hurt and reeling, and now he didn't even have the decency to leave.

He could only hope that the next man Lady Emily was attracted to was a far better one than Dr Pratt. That of course completely ruled out Jackson.

Despite that kiss, despite discovering there was a sensual woman trapped inside that stern exterior, that sensuality was not his to explore. She was still the moralistic, judgemental Lady Emily, and he was—well, he was Jackson Wilde.

He would enjoy one last waltz and that would be it. They would then go their separate ways. He placed his hand on her slim waist and suppressed a low groan. He could almost feel her skin through the flimsy fabric of her gown. Unlike the usual ornate fashions women wore, clothing seemingly designed to make them inaccessible to men, this gown created little in the way of a barrier. In one quick movement, he was sure he would be able to lift it over her head, exposing her delightful body to his appreciative gaze. He wondered what she was wearing underneath, and if those items would be as easily removed as her gown.

She looked up at him, a question in those deep brown eyes. A question that she would be horrified by if she heard the answer. So he said nothing, instead they moved off in time to the music.

*Do not think of her naked body*, he reminded himself, which of course made him think of her naked body. *Do not think of that kiss*, which made the taste of her suddenly rich on his lips. *Do not think about her scent. Do not inhale and allow that fresh, sweet scent of a woman to send your mind drifting off into inappropriate places. Distract yourself, do something, anything.*

'The ball has been a great success,' he said, wincing at a comment that would be inane at the best of times, but was particularly asinine after what they had just shared.

She smiled up at him, a smile that appeared both amused by his inane attempt at conversation, and somehow knowing, as if she was well aware of the complexity of his feelings.

'Parts of it have been particularly successful,' she said with a little grin.

Was she teasing him? Tonight really was a night full of wonders.

'Why, Lady Emily, whatever do you mean?' he replied, wanting to be the teas*er*, not the teas*ee*, if such a word existed.

'I'm talking about the flower arrangements, of course,' she said with a cheeky smile. 'What did you think I meant?'

'Exactly that. The flower arrangements are indeed tonight's highlight.'

Her smile grew wider as he twirled her around. 'Mmm, the scent of them fills the senses and makes one almost heady with sensual delight.'

He raised a surprised eyebrow. She had moved from teasing to outright flirting. He had assumed she would never do something as frivolous as flirt. Would tonight's surprises never cease?

'Yes, some scents can transport one and arouse one's emotions,' he said, remembering her fresh, womanly scent undisguised by artificial perfumes. He had been consumed by it when he had kissed her, and now he longed to bury himself in that scent once again.

'And the supper was particularly successful as well,' she said, with that teasing smile, as if she knew exactly what affect her words were having on him and was relishing the power it gave her. 'I can almost taste the delicious flavours on my lips,' she added, running her tongue along her bottom lip.

Jackson released a moan, which he covered with a small cough. Was she trying to torture him? If that was the intent, he was prepared to give as good as he got.

'You're right,' he said, preparing for the duel. 'Some tastes are designed to be savoured, to be explored, and delighted in. When something is truly delicious you want to slowly lick it all over, exploring every part of it with your tongue and your lips until you've had your fill.'

That resulted in a satisfying blush colouring her cheeks.

'Don't you agree, Lady Emily?' he asked, unable to disguise his amusement at her discomfort.

She swallowed, drawing his attention to the creamy skin of her neck. 'Yes,' she croaked out, making his smile grow larger. That did the trick. There would be no more teasing, no more torture, no more talk reminding him of the delights of how she tasted on his tongue and lips.

They continued dancing in silence and a tinge of guilt attempted to undermine his sense of self-satisfaction. Perhaps he had been wrong to tease her so. She was new to this game and he was a seasoned campaigner, but, oh, it was good to see her blush, and he couldn't deny he liked seeing a woman who was usually so strong and assertive looking at him in that coy, abashed manner.

The dance came to an end and he took her arm to escort her off the dance floor, where crowds milled at the edges, talking excitedly.

'Oh, and of course your kiss was simply sublime as well,' she whispered with a quick wink as they joined the throng, leaving him no opportunity to retort without being overheard.

He laughed and knew that, despite his best efforts, she had won.

# *Chapter Nine*

As if she'd been drinking champagne, Emily bubbled inside. There were so many emotions she suspected she should be feeling; upset over the collapse of her hoped-for marriage, shock at being kissed by a notorious rake, embarrassment over kissing him back with such unrestrained enthusiasm, but she felt none of these. Instead, gleefulness fluttered through her, making her giddy. And she simply refused to analyse the reasons why. She would just surrender herself to these glorious, unfamiliar sensations.

Like a debutante at her first ball, Emily wanted to twirl around the room, to laugh, flirt, dance and enjoy herself.

It was hard to believe such a transformation could take place, all because of one kiss. But oh, what a kiss. In reality, it was nothing more than the touch of his lips on hers, and yet it had set off such unimaginable reactions within her. It was as if her body had been sleeping until that moment, and he had awakened it. He had given her a small taste of the pleasure a man and woman could give each other and it was delicious. So delicious she longed to feast until she had her fill.

Emily had known such delights existed in theory. Her friends on occasion waxed lyrical about their wonderful husbands and it was obvious even to Emily that they were expressing appreciation for more than just the men's characters. Now she had been given a hint of the decidedly enticing possibilities Jackson Wilde could provide, she knew a hint would never be enough.

The music started up again, and Emily looked up at him expectantly.

'We've already had two dances. I believe if we have another dance, we will set tongues wagging,' he said.

What did Emily care about that? Let them wag.

'Perhaps we should sit this one out,' he continued. 'As committee members we do have to set an example of how respectable people conduct themselves.'

Was he serious? He was Jackson Wilde, what on earth was he talking about, being respectable, setting an example?

'But—'

His laughter cut her off. 'I'm sure you must be in need of refreshments. I know I could do with a drink.'

He linked her arm through his and escorted her over to the supper table, where he poured two glasses of punch from the large bowl and handed one to her. Emily shouldn't have done it, but she couldn't stop herself from lightly stroking her fingers along the back of his hand as he handed her the glass.

His eyes widened, and Emily wondered if she was making a spectacle of herself. Gideon's cruel words crashed in on her. Was she proving to Jackson Wilde that she really was a spinster, just as Gideon had said? One kiss and she was swooning all over him. Was he laughing at her?

But no, she would not think that. She had seen and felt his own reaction when he'd held her close. He had wanted that kiss as much as she did, and he was still at her side.

There was nothing to stop him from dancing with any one of the pretty, single young women present tonight.

Jackson Wilde had kissed her, danced with her, wanted her. He was no gentleman. He had proven that time and time again. If he was still by her side, it was not due to politeness but because that was exactly where he wanted to be.

'Have you had your photograph taken?' a geisha girl asked, breaking in on her thoughts.

'Photograph?' Emily asked.

'Oh, it's such fun, and such a good idea,' Lord Nelson added as he handed the geisha girl a glass of punch. 'And a wonderful memory of such a splendid evening.'

Emily looked to where Lord Nelson was pointing.

'That was Amelia's idea,' she told the Viscount. 'She arranged for a photographer to set up in the morning room as another way to raise money for the school.'

'As it's all in a good cause, shall we?' Jackson suggested, offering her his arm once more. 'An indelible image of tonight is exactly what we need.'

Even greater happiness filled her. He wanted an image to remember this night by. It was a thrilling thought. While having her photograph taken would be fun, Emily knew she did not need a memento to remember what had happened tonight. Nothing could ever make her forget that remarkable kiss. But he was right, it was in a good cause, and it would be lovely to have tonight captured for ever.

They wended their way through the crowd and joined the excited queue.

'Isn't this simply marvellous,' the milkmaid standing in front of them said. 'I had my portrait taken at a studio once, but tonight the photographer has brought all his equipment here to us. Such fun.'

'Indeed, it is, my dear,' the pirate on her arm answered. 'Aren't these modern gadgets just the thing? And I read the other day that some clever chap has even invented a way of filming people while they are actually moving. Marvellous.'

'Oh, yes, we do live in a fabulous time, don't we?' the milkmaid responded, shaking her head in wonderment. 'Maybe one day people will be able to film balls such as this. Won't that be simply wonderful?'

Emily returned her smile, although, considering some of the things that had occurred this evening, she was uncertain whether she would want a complete photographic document available for all to see.

When their turn came, Emily and Jackson entered the adjoining room, which had been transformed into a photography studio, with black curtains obscuring the furniture and creating a booth. They stood in front of the large cardboard backdrop—depicting a pastoral scene of fields and weeping willows—and beside a pedestal bearing a large fern in a porcelain pot.

'Elizabeth Bennet and Mr Darcy, I believe,' the photographer said.

Jackson and Emily exchanged conspiratorial smiles. That had certainly not been her intention when she had dressed this evening. She had merely chosen a costume that was easy to acquire and comfortable to wear. She'd had no idea that Jackson would also be dressed in the Regency style, but it was a lovely coincidence, almost fortuitous, one could say.

'As you are representing a famous couple, perhaps you

could stand a little closer together,' the photographer added, looking at them over his camera and tripod, moving his hands in a manner to suggest the closing of a gap.

Emily and Jackson shuffled nearer to each other. Jackson smiled at her, looking as awkward as Emily felt.

'Now, please turn to face each other, and, Mr Darcy, if you would place your hand on Elizabeth's waist. And, Miss Bennet, if you could put your hand on Mr Darcy's arm. That should capture the romance of their story.'

They exchanged amused looks, but willingly did as instructed.

'And if you could gaze at each other as if you are besotted, just as Miss Austen's famous characters would surely do.'

As one, they rolled their eyes, and despite their laughter did their best impression of two people in love.

'I'm afraid you will not be able to laugh, and it is better if you do not smile,' the photographer said, a small note of impatience entering his voice. It had no doubt been a long night for him and he would be starting to tire of making excitable guests do as they were told. 'You need to remain perfectly still while I capture your image.'

Somewhat chastened, Emily did as instructed and looked up into Jackson Wilde's blue eyes, with what she hoped was an adoring expression. As she held his gaze, this became an increasingly less difficult task. They were such enchanting eyes, she was sure she could stay as she was, staring into them, for an eternity.

He gazed back at her with equal intensity, holding her captive. His gaze moved to her lips. Was he remembering their kiss, just as she was? Were his lips tingling as well?

Was he wishing they were doing more than gazing at each other, that they were once again locked in an embrace?

She closed her eyes and released a sigh of pleasure, imagining his lips on hers. As if conjuring memory to reality, his lips lightly stroked hers.

'I said, don't move,' a voice called out as Jackson's arm slid further around her waist and she was gently pulled up against his body.

'I said...' The photographer's voice faded as she moulded herself into him, loving the feel of his hard muscles against her soft breasts, his strong arms holding her tightly. Gently, she rubbed herself against him, kissing him back, needing to feel him, taste him—to have him.

His hands moved further around her body, capturing her hips and holding her firmly. Heat flooded through her body. Her heart beat fast within her chest, and a deep throbbing pounding within her core. She wrapped her hands around the back of his head and kissed him with a fervour she did not know she possessed.

*'When something is truly delicious you want to slowly lick it all over, exploring every part of it with your tongue and your lips until you've had your fill.'*

His words on the dance floor entered her mind. It was what she wanted him to do now. She wanted to feel his hands, his lips, his tongue on every inch of her body, exploring all those parts his kiss had brought to life.

He pulled back from the kiss and looked down at her, his hooded eyes intense.

She stared up at him, bewildered by what had just happened. Why had he stopped when it was obvious that they both wanted this? Then reality crashed in. The sounds of music, talking and laughing from the adjoining room filled her ears. She was in a public place and had lost all sense of reason and propriety. She continued gazing into his smouldering eyes, and realised she really didn't care. She wanted him to kiss her again and hang propriety, hang reason.

His arms dropped to his side. It seemed he had more sense than her. Damn him, why did he suddenly have to become so sensible?

'You are so beautiful,' he whispered. And she did feel beautiful. Beautiful and desirable, desired by an attractive, virile, breathtaking man. And it felt good. Very good.

'That was splendid,' the photographer said, adjusting his camera.

She turned to face the photographer, as if trying to remember who he was and why he was here.

'I managed to take several shots while you were,' he paused. 'They're perhaps a little bit risqué but have wonderful artistic merit. They should be ready in a week or so and, if they turn out as well as I expect, I'd love to be able to exhibit them. With your permission, of course.'

'No,' Emily and Jackson Wilde said as one, turning to each other with matching looks of disbelief.

'Oh, well, perhaps you'll change your mind when you see them.'

'They will not be for public display,' the Viscount said, his voice firm.

The disappointed photographer nodded and prepared his camera for the next subject, as Jackson Wilde took Emily's arm and led her back to the ballroom.

'How was it?' a waiting Henry VIII asked.

'Words simply can't explain its wonders,' the Viscount said, sending Emily a quick wink and causing her to giggle. Emily couldn't remember the last time she had giggled like a young girl, and it felt rather lovely. In fact, a lot about tonight felt decidedly lovely, at least the bits that had involved her being in Jackson Wilde's arms, either when he kissed her or when they danced together.

'As we have already behaved in a somewhat scandalous manner tonight, I don't think it will do our reputations any more harm if we dance together one more time,' Jackson said, leading her back onto the dance floor.

He was right. Their behaviour tonight *had* been scandalous. It had also been the most fun Emily had had in her life and she did not want the fun to stop. There was no denying Jackson Wilde was a wholly unsuitable man. No respectable woman in her right mind would get involved with such a man. He lived a dissolute life and his salacious antics made him a regular feature in the scandal columns. In so many ways he was exactly the sort of man she should avoid, and yet in so many other ways he was also perfect for what she had in mind.

She wanted him. At least, she wanted his kisses and his caresses. She would be a fool to want more than that, and Emily had made enough of a fool of herself over a man. She shuddered slightly at the memory of Dr Pratt's insulting proposal.

She was not a dried-up old spinster. Jackson Wilde had shown her that. And she wanted him to show her so much more. But, before that happened, she was going to have to have a serious discussion with him to ensure that this time she got it right. Never again would she be duped by a man. Never again would she allow herself to be deluded into thinking he was someone he was not, or that the relationship was anything other than what it appeared to be.

But that was a discussion for another time. The rest of this night would be for enjoying herself. And, as he continued to whirl her around the dance floor, that was exactly what she did.

# *Chapter Ten*

Two days later, Jackson stood in the middle of the drawing room at his Kensington townhouse and stared down at the piece of crisp white paper in his hand.

Lady Emily's feminine handwriting informed him she wished to meet with him to discuss the ball, and intended to visit his home at three o'clock, nothing more. Jackson turned it over, looked at the blank back, then turned back to the written words and read it once again, trying to discern some meaning, any meaning, from the brief letter. Did she want to discuss the kiss—or, to be more accurate, those kisses—and their ramifications?

He blew out a held breath. For Jackson, such a discussion had the potential to be life changing. She could demand a proposal. It was quite within her rights to do so, and he would be honour-bound to accede to her demands and make her his wife. That was something he should have thought about before he kissed her, and it certainly should have occurred to him before he kissed her in front of a witness, and, more than that, he should have taken the time to consider the potential outcome of kissing her while a photograph was being taken. But thinking had been one thing he had done far too little of during the ball.

There was also the possibility he had nothing to worry

about. Perhaps she merely wanted an innocent meeting to discuss the proceeds from the ball, how much money they had raised and how that money could best be used to gain the maximum benefit for the girls and women of the East End.

*Innocent?*

He gave a snort of laughter and shook his head. It was merely a few kisses, but in the eyes of Society there was nothing innocent about a man kissing a young lady. Nor could he use the word innocent to describe the thoughts he'd had about Lady Emily since the ball, all of which had involved sensual antics that were enticingly sinful.

He placed the note on the table and looked at the clock ticking on the mantelpiece. In a few minutes she would arrive and all his questions would be answered. It was best he put aside any thoughts of their kisses, or the fantasies he had harboured in the two days since he had last seen her. Although, to do so demanded a level of mental discipline that was illusive to a man such as himself. Her kisses had been a revelation, nothing less. He had discovered, in the nicest way possible, that the woman he had dismissed as judgemental and preachy was surprisingly sensual, and a rather good kisser.

But that had all happened during a fancy dress ball. People often let their hair down, sometimes literally, at such occasions. The next day they would be back to their highly respectable, buttoned-up selves, and there was a very good chance that Lady Emily would be no different.

Plus, she had just been hurt by Pratt. That could make even the most prudent and restrained woman act out of character. And unfortunately for Lady Emily, she had been in the company of a man who was more than capable of taking advantage of a woman in that state.

Perhaps that was why she wanted to see him. To demand an apology. If that was what she required, she would have it. Not that he was really sorry. How could he ever be sorry to have tasted her kisses? But if it was an apology she demanded, then it was an apology he would give, and he would attempt to make it heartfelt.

He looked over at the abandoned note. Perhaps she wanted to tell him that what happened at the ball was best forgotten. Perhaps she would be back to prim and proper Lady Emily, the woman who thoroughly, and quite rightly, disapproved of him. For one night they had played the roles of Mr Darcy and Miss Elizabeth Bennet, and now it was back to being Jackson Wilde and Lady Emily Beaumont, two people who could barely abide each other. Yes, that also made sense. She wanted to ensure they put what happened firmly in the past and never mentioned it again.

Whatever she wanted, there was no way he could know until the lady herself arrived and enlightened him. In the meantime, he had to exercise some patience and wait. He crossed the room and sat down. Then stood up and returned to leaning on the mantelpiece, looking at the ticking clock.

This was ridiculous. He was nervous. He could tell himself the only thing he had to be nervous about was his dread of being dragged kicking and screaming up the altar, but that was not the only thing causing his agitation.

He was nervous about seeing her again. And that in itself was bizarre. They had shared two kisses, nothing more. Kisses that were quite chaste compared to his usual encounters with young women. And yet, they were kisses that affected him even more than some of his adventurous liaisons with the fairer sex. How was it possible that a woman he hardly knew, a woman he had assumed was nothing more than a moralistic, judgemental do-gooder, could leave him nervous like a schoolboy about to have his first tryst with a girl?

He paced around the room, the clock's ticking growing louder and louder with each passing second. The note said she would arrive at three o'clock. It was now three o'clock. Where was she? He tapped the clock to ensure it was working correctly just as a footman knocked on the door to the drawing room.

'Come,' he called out.

'Lady Emily Beaumont, my lord,' the footman said.

Jackson nodded, and leant against the mantelpiece, adopting his most devil-may-care posture. It would not help his waning masculine pride if he let her see that her visit had flustered him in any way.

She entered and, damn it all, a jolt of raw attraction shot through his body.

Framed by the doorway she looked simply radiant. Dressed in a simple grey skirt with a lacy high-necked white blouse, her hair tied in a neat bun at the back of her head, she looked more attractive than any woman who donned ornate hairstyles, sparkling jewels and lavish clothing designed to attract a man's eye. The skirt nipped in at her small waist and flared out over her rounded hips—the simple blouse clung to those luscious breasts he had felt against his chest when they had kissed. Breasts he had fantasised about ever since.

How could he possibly be blamed for kissing such a woman? What man could resist her? Certainly not a man like him.

He waited for her chaperone to follow her in. No one

else entered. His agitation wrenched up a notch. This would not do. If he couldn't be trusted to keep his hands and his lips to himself when they were in a public place, how was he to be expected to keep his hands and various other body parts to himself when they were alone in the drawing room of his townhouse?

'Please leave the door open, James,' he said to the footman, and saw the man's eyebrows raise almost imperceptibly before he nodded and departed, leaving the door fully ajar.

She turned and looked at the door, then back at him, her head tilted in question.

'You are an unaccompanied young woman alone in a man's home. If the door is closed, and no servants can observe what is happening between us, your reputation could be compromised.'

'I believe that ship has already sailed.'

Was her statement designed to put the fear of God into him? Or, to be more precise, the fear of marriage? Whatever the answer, it still did not mean he would risk a closed door. She may think the worst that could happen between a man and woman when they were alone was that they could exchange kisses. He knew different, and for his own protection, as much as hers, that door had to stay open.

'Despite what took place at the ball, I believe for propriety's sake it best that the door remain open so the servants can see at all times what occurs between us,' he said, sounding like he was the prim and proper one.

She crossed the room and shut the door.

Jackson suppressed a low moan. A shut door when he was alone with a woman sent a signal to his servants that he was not to be disturbed under any circumstances. Did she really care so little for her reputation? And did she really want to put him in this taxing position?

*Well, Jackson,* he told himself. *Now is going to be a test of your mettle.*

Whatever his mettle actually was. His father had always said it was something Jackson did not possess. Somehow, he was going to have to suddenly find it in abundance.

'Won't you please take a seat,' he said, still standing by the mantelpiece and indicating the divan furthest away from him.

Unlike his command to not shut the door, this time she did as he asked. The cotton of her skirt rustled gently as she crossed the room. When she took her seat, he heard that captivating sound of silk stockings rubbing lightly against each other. It was a sound that never failed to entice him. But enticed he could not be, not with a shut door. Not with the guarantee they would not be interrupted by his well-trained servants.

She patted the seat beside her. 'And won't you join me? It's a little hard to talk when you're standing so far away.'

Damn, why didn't he point to one of the wing-backed chairs where she would be carefully contained away from him. Now he would have to sit dangerously close to her, within kissing distance of those lips and caressing distance of that luscious body.

She waited, so he did as she asked, crossing the room and joining her on the divan.

He looked down at her hands, clasped tightly in her lap as if to stop them shaking, while she stared straight ahead into the middle of the drawing room. He wasn't the only nervous one. Of course he wasn't. This must be extremely difficult for her. That would be why she shut the door, so the servants would not overhear this difficult conversation. That would be why she didn't bring a chaperone. His actions had put her in this precarious position, and he needed to put this right.

What would a decent man do in these circumstances? Would he raise the subject of their kisses first or would he wait politely until the young lady mentioned it? He had no idea. He was no gentleman and had never kissed a respectable young woman before. He had no idea what etiquette demanded.

That was a lie. He knew exactly what etiquette demanded. He was supposed to make a proposal of marriage.

Jackson's stomach and heart sank. Oh, God. That *was* why she was here. She was waiting for his proposal. And now he was about to prove everything his father said about him was true. Like the lowlife he knew himself to be, he was going to try and weasel his way out of a situation he should never have got himself into in the first place. He was once again going to fail to take responsibility for his actions.

With his father's glare of distaste in his mind, he braced himself. 'About what happened at the ball,' he said, trying desperately to think *what* he was going to say about it.

'Yes, that's what I've come to talk to you about.'

He swallowed. 'You have?'

'Yes.' She drew in a deep breath. Jackson did the same and waited for his life to be ruined.

'I enjoyed our kisses very much,' she said. 'And I have decided I wish to become your mistress.'

His held breath released from his lungs in a loud exhalation. Had he heard her correctly? 'You what?' he asked, his voice coming out in an unmanly gasp. 'You what?' he repeated in a deeper, more controlled voice.

'I wish to become your mistress.'

He had heard correctly, but it was no less startling on repetition.

'You don't need to look at me like that. You've had mistresses before, haven't you?'

'Ah, yes, one or two.'

'Well, from what I've heard there's been considerably more than that. But that's all for the good.'

'Is it?' He would have thought in Lady Emily's eyes that would be all for the bad.

'Yes, it means you are experienced and know what a woman wants.'

'Well, I suppose—'

'And after what happened between us at the ball, and after all those cruel things that Gideon said, I came to a decision.'

'You did?' he asked, starting to sound like a monosyllabic idiot.

'Yes. I decided Gideon was correct. Or perhaps not correct, not yet anyway, but the way he described me could very well become correct if I don't do something to change my fate.'

'I wouldn't believe a word that man said.' What was he doing? Was he arguing against the idea of them becoming lovers? Was he going mad? Wasn't that what he wanted? Did he not want her in his bed? Hadn't he repeatedly imagined her laying naked beneath him, that long chestnut hair spread over his pillows, her arms reaching out to him. Her legs parted—

He coughed and crossed his legs. Now was certainly not the time to let those images play out in his mind.

'I agree that he was lashing out in anger,' she continued, her voice still matter of fact, as if they were discussing something unimportant, such as a delay in the morning mail delivery, and not a subject of monumental importance. 'But what he said, and those kisses we shared, made me realise that I do not want to become a spinster.'

Jackson could point out that if a woman doesn't marry then she does indeed become a spinster as a matter of course, but suspected now was not the time to point out matters of semantics.

'He also said I would become increasingly bitter, and I admit there is a danger to that,' she nodded to herself. 'I admit I was very imbittered about how he had deceived me into thinking he was a different man just so I would marry him, or, at least, how I had convinced myself he was a different man, and exactly the sort of man I wanted to marry.'

She shrugged as if pushing all those thoughts away. 'But that is not what I'm here to discuss. Realising I had been so wrong about Gideon made my decision clear-cut. It is obvious that I am no judge of men, so it is best I don't marry and risk being stuck in a situation I will live to regret.'

She turned to face him in the seat. 'But I don't wish to remain a virgin for the rest of my life.'

Jackson swallowed. 'You don't?'

'No. And, unlike Gideon, I know exactly what sort of man you are.'

'You do?'

'Yes, you have never tried to hide your true self from me or anyone else. You are a man who drinks too much, who gets into dangerous, sometimes life-threatening situations, one who has had more women in his life than he can probably remember.'

'Hmm.' It was an accurate description, but this was the first time anyone had suggested that these flaws were useful attributes.

'You are most certainly not the sort of man I would ever wish to marry.'

'I'm not?' Wasn't that what he wanted to hear? Yes, of course it was.

'I believe we could come to an arrangement where you are the one to relieve me of my virginal status and show me what it is like when a man makes love to a woman.'

He stared at her, still in a state of disbelief. She had just made an outrageous proposition, and had done so in a completely unemotional manner. This left him stunned.

'I know it is what you want as well,' she continued, while he tried to gather his thoughts.

'From the way you kissed me, and the reaction you had,' she cast a quick glance down at his groin, negating his belief that she was entirely innocent about what could happen between a man and a woman when left alone together behind a closed door. 'I know that you were, well, shall we say, not adverse to the idea of taking things further when you kissed me.'

He still stared at her, trying to come up with reasons why this was not a good idea, while his body was telling him to stop arguing and do exactly what he had been thinking about for the last two days.

'And those kisses made it apparent that you know how to satisfy a woman.'

He'd liked to hope that was correct, and he'd certainly had no complaints. Far from it.

'Well?'

'Believe me, Lady Emily, I would enjoy nothing more, but—'

'Good, that's settled, then.'

'I would enjoy nothing more,' he repeated, hoping this time she would let him finish. 'But have you thought this through? You don't want to marry Dr Pratt, but that does not mean you will never marry.'

He was doing it again. What on earth was wrong with him? Had he suddenly developed a conscience, a sense of morality? And if he had to acquire these undesirable traits, why did he have to do so now?

'As I said, I have also made up my mind about that as well. I shall never marry.'

'You can't say that. You had one bad experience with that Pratt fellow but there are other men.'

'You're right.' She stood up and Jackson quickly did the same, shocked at what he had just turned down.

'I don't wish to argue with you and I'm sorry to have wasted your time.'

'Oh, God, no, you haven't done that. It's just I don't think you had really thought this through, but I'm pleased you have now seen the wisdom of saving yourself until your wedding night.'

She rolled her eyes and he couldn't help but agree that he sounded like some moralistic matron giving advice to a debutante.

'I *have* thought this through and my mind is made up,' she said, picking up her reticule. 'I thought this arrangement would be advantageous for both of us. I thought you'd be agreeable to an involvement with me, one where you taught me about physical love without any expectations of it becoming anything more than a passing involvement, one with no commitments or expectations. But if you are unwilling, I will have to try and find someone else.'

'What? No. Good God, do not do that.' He took hold of her hands and gently pulled her back down onto the divan. Did he see a small smile quiver at the edges of her lips? Had that been a genuine threat? He could not take the risk. The world can be a dangerous place for a woman, and would be lethal to one such as her in search of a lover.

'So you will do it?'

He nodded.

'Then perhaps you should kiss me,' she said. 'To seal the deal, as it were.'

He took her chin in his hand and looked down into those brown eyes. 'Lady Emily, you must be the strangest, most unusual, unique woman there has ever been.'

And then he did what he'd been longing to do since she entered the room. He kissed her. The moment her soft, lush lips were against his any thoughts that this was a bad idea evaporated. It was now a very, very good idea. The best idea anyone had ever had.

But he didn't want to just kiss her lips. He wanted to kiss, caress and explore every inch of her divine body, and, miracle of miracles, she had given him permission to do so.

His lips left hers and he kissed the soft, creamy flesh of her neck, loving the taste of her and the silky feel of her skin.

She let out a gentle sigh as he nuzzled the soft, sensitive skin behind her ears. She was permitting him to strip her naked, to take her, and by God he was desperate to do so.

His fingers moved to the buttons of her lacy blouse, opening the top one at her throat. He kissed the base of her collarbone as he moved to the next ridiculously tiny button. Then he stopped.

It was what he wanted. That was something about which he was certain. She said it was what she wanted as well, but did she really know her own mind? What she said she wanted and what she really wanted could be two different things. He had to take this slowly, very slowly, and see how far she really wanted to go, before her sense of what was proper took over. Then he would have to deal with his own unsated desire for her in the time-honoured fashion of frustrated men.

But there would be no harm in kissing her one more time before she came to her senses. His lips returned to hers and, despite his admonition to take it slowly, he kissed her harder, with more demanding need, just holding back enough to see if she would be frightened by the force of his passionate desire. He detected no fear. Quite the reverse. She kissed him back with matching intensity. Her lips parted. Her tongue stroked his lips. Her breath became small gasps. He could feel her heart pounding against his chest—in desire, not fear.

Could he risk going a bit further? Still kissing her, he undid one more button on her blouse. What he really wanted to do was rip them apart, but he forced himself to move at a speed that gave her ample time to object. No objection came. He moved to the next one, and the next. When the final button was undone, he pushed open her blouse and slid his hand inside, pulling down her cotton chemise.

Unable to resist, he withdrew from her kisses so he could feast his gaze on her breasts. They were just as he had imagined them, full and pert, the nipples pointing at him expectantly as they rose and fell with each quick breath.

Even if she stopped him now, she had given him a glorious sight to fuel his fantasies. The question now was, would she finally object, or could he go even further? He looked from that arousing sight of her breasts and into her eyes. His self-control was becoming seriously undermined. If she was going to stop him, he could only hope she did it soon, before he was completely lost.

She nodded in answer to his unasked question. He cupped her full breasts, loving the feel of their weight in his hands. He kissed her again, expressing his desire for her with his lips and his hands. Her nipples tightened under his touch as he slowly rubbed his thumbs over the hard peaks.

Her moans urging him on, he traced a line of kisses down her neck. She tilted back her head, offering the silky flesh to him. His lips slowly moved lower, kissing across the soft mounds of her breasts still cupped in his hands. Lifting one breast to his lips, his tongue swirled around the edge of the hard, sensitive bud, causing her breathing to come faster and faster, as his thumb continued to stroke its twin. When he took the hard tight nub in his mouth she cried out in ecstasy, and he knew she was now incapable of stopping him. She did want this, of that there could be no question.

'Beautiful,' he whispered, as he shifted to the other nipple, nuzzling and licking.

Any lingering doubts he might have had that he was pushing her too far, too fast, was removed when her hands wove through his hair, holding him to her breast, showing him she had completely surrendered herself to his caresses.

But selfish cad that he was, he still wanted more, much

more. Her breaths became fast gasps as he licked and suck-led. He reached down and pulled at the bottom of her skirt, pushing it up above her knees. His hand slid between her legs, moving up the stockings, past the garters, to the naked skin of her inner thighs.

His body was saying, go on, take what you want—but part of his mind was reminding him she was a virgin. This was all new to her and he might be pushing her further than she was prepared to go.

To his immense satisfaction, her legs parted slightly, giving him easier access. His own breath now came as fast as hers, as his hand moved up her soft skin, under the fabric of her drawers. She put up no objection, even when he reached the cleft between her legs.

But he had to know for certain. His lips released her breast and his hand moved away from her legs. 'Are you sure?'

Her eyes opened slightly. She nodded, then closed them again.

Still watching for the slightest sign that this was not re-ally what she wanted, he lightly ran his hand back up her legs and under her drawers, pausing at the cleft. Her back arched and her body moved to its own rhythm, letting him know that she wanted his touch—more than wanted it, had to have it.

And by God he was more than willing to give it to her.

One arm wrapped around her back, holding her close. He ran his fingers lightly along her feminine folds, parting them gently. Her rapid gasps told him he did not need to hold back. He pushed one finger slowly inside her and gave a low animal growl as the tight sheath closed around him.

What he wanted to do now was throw all decency to the

wind, to wrap her parted legs around him, enter her hard and fast and relieve his own pounding, painful need to be deep inside her. He drew in a long, steadying breath and once again reminded himself she was a virgin. This was her first time and it was his first time with a virgin. He'd heard somewhere it could be painful for a woman on her first time, and the last thing he wanted to do was hurt this lovely, enchanting creature.

Once again nuzzling the soft skin of her neck, he further parted her cleft and pushed a second finger inside her, spreading her wider. As his palm rubbed against her bud, he watched her gorgeous face. Her mouth was open, her head tilted back. Her face, neck and breasts were flushed pink. With each stroke, she gasped louder, faster, until the gasps became deep moans. Her back arched as she rubbed herself against him, her hand over the top of his, urging him to increase the pressure and the pace. He did as she silently commanded, moving faster and faster, pushing harder and harder, until a shiver swept through her body, and her sheath clenched around him tighter. Then she sunk back onto the divan, gasping for breath.

Jackson withdrew his fingers and wrapped her in his arms, her heart pounding against his chest, her head nuzzled against his shoulder, her panting breath warm on his neck.

'Thank you,' she murmured, causing him to smile.

She leant back from him and gazed into his face. 'That was wonderful,' she said. 'But, well, I'm still a virgin. Aren't I? I came here with the intention of losing my virginity and I'm not leaving until I do.'

He had to laugh. She really was the most surprising, captivating, tantalising woman he had ever met.

She looked down towards his groin. 'And we both know it's what you also want.'

'Of course it's what I want,' he said, his husky voice unrecognisable to his ears. 'But once you've lost your virginity there is no getting it back. Are you certain?'

She rolled her eyes as if he was starting to irritate her, reached down and undid the top button of his trousers. He grabbed her hand, pulled it away and lightly kissed her fingers. 'If you really want me to take your virginity, perhaps keep your hands away from that area, or I won't be much use for that purpose.'

'Oh,' she said, narrowing her eyes in question.

'I'll explain later.'

'Good,' she said, lying back on the divan, her skirt still around her waist, her blouse open, her breasts on display for him. Was there ever a more glorious, more sensual, more arousing sight than that? By God, he wanted to do as she asked and take her now, without preamble. But this was her first time. It should be special.

'Would you like to retire to my bedchamber?'

'And risk having you change your mind? I don't think so.'

'Believe me, wild horses couldn't make me change my mind now.'

She smiled at him, the cheekiest, most seductive smile he had ever seen.

'If this is really what you want,' he said, reaching up under her dress, pulling down her lacy drawers and tossing them to the floor. 'Then believe me, I am more than happy to oblige.'

With an unseemly haste he pulled open his buttons and pushed down his trousers. This was not the way a young woman should be deflowered. It should happen in a bed, and it should happen on her wedding night. But, as she was the one to insist, and as he was a mere man, and a randy one at that, there was no point even pretending he would waste any more time debating what should and should not happen.

Wrapping his arms around her, he lowered her back onto the divan and covered her body with his own. Her legs parted. She draped one over the back of the divan while the other wrapped itself around him. He released a deep growl as he positioned himself at her entrance.

Kissing her lips, he slowly eased himself inside her and felt her sheath close tightly around him.

'I promise you, I'll be gentle,' he murmured in her ear, before kissing her neck and easing himself further inside her. Would she tense up? Was that what virgins did? Would she push him away? Would she come to her senses and re-alise what a bad idea this really was? He moved as slowly as his rampaging desire allowed, uncertain as to how she would react.

She did not tense up. She did not push him away. Instead, her legs wrapped around his waist, opening her up further to him. To his surprise her hands cupped his buttocks, pushing him towards where he wanted so desperately to go. He did not need to be asked twice. He pushed himself fully inside her.

She gasped, causing him to quickly withdraw. He lifted himself up, looked down at her face and brushed a loose strand of hair back from her forehead.

'Did I hurt you?'

'No, not really,' she said, opening her eyes. 'Don't stop.'

He entered her again, just as carefully as his pent-up

desire would allow. Her fingers once again dug into his buttocks, and her nails caused a strangely arousing pain. He pushed further inside her, and released a low, primal groan as her wet folds fully encased him. Watching her lovely face, her lips parted wide, her breath coming in loud, insistent pants, he pushed himself even deeper inside her, loving the sensation of her rubbing against every part of his sensitive shaft. No longer thinking, he withdrew and pushed himself into her again and again, faster and faster, deeper and deeper, his arousal growing bigger and harder with each thrust.

Her panting became loud moans, even screams, as she writhed beneath him in time to his thrusting. Using every ounce of self-control he possessed, he held himself back until her core rippled around him and she released a louder cry as she gripped him tightly. Withdrawing from her he reached his own climax, hoping no embarrassing tell-tale sign would be left on her clothing.

Collapsing onto her, Jackson had never felt such euphoria. Sex was always enjoyable, sometimes spectacular, but this had been different. He'd felt such a connection with her, as if they had really been joined, not just physically. Why that should be, he had no idea. It could not be because he was her first. At least, he hoped not. He was not one of those men who saw it as an accomplishment to deflower a virgin, but, he had to admit, he did feel pleased that she had wanted him to be the one to do so.

But whatever had caused it, he had felt something, something different, something more than just the usual sensual gratification, as wonderful as such gratification always was. They continued to lie in each other's arms, breathing heavily, their hearts still pounding against their chests.

Jackson was sure he could stay like this for ever, but when his heartbeat resumed its normal pace, he gently kissed her neck.

'Well, you're no longer a virgin,' he murmured.

She gave his buttocks a playful squeeze. 'And I'm certainly not bitter.'

'No,' he said and lightly kissed her lips. 'You're as sweet as honey.'

'And twice as sticky,' she said, causing him to laugh. 'Nobody ever told me how sticky it all would be.'

Still laughing, he held her close and kissed her again. Now that he had willingly done as she asked, a small part of his mind was asking, what happens now? She had not only said she wanted to lose her virginity, but to become his mistress. After what he had just experienced, he could only hope and pray that she would not change her mind about that either. One taste of the lovely Lady Emily Beaumont was never going to be enough.

# *Chapter Eleven*

She had done it. No one could now accuse her of being a bitter old spinster, because she was no longer a virgin. Not that she would be able to tell anyone about what had happened on the Viscount's divan, but still, she would know. She smiled to herself, a gleeful, mischievous smile, as she basked in her risqué secret. This behaviour was so unlike her, and it felt glorious.

She had made the decision to lose her virginity to the Viscount on the night of the ball, but it had taken two days to work up the courage to ask him. And she almost hadn't come today.

But every time she remembered that kiss and every time she had thought about Gideon's cruel words, her determination had grown. She would not remain a virgin. She would not become a bitter old spinster, and that kiss had proven Jackson Wilde was the perfect man to prevent that happening.

She bit her bottom lip so she wouldn't laugh out loud as she remembered the unemotional way in which she had made her outlandish proposition. He would never know that inside she had been a turmoil of emotions and jangling nerves. Remaining stoic had been the only way she had been able to stop herself from fleeing out the door in mortification at what she was asking. But she had known if she did flee, she would live the rest of her life in regret. And now that she knew what she risked missing out on, she could only say a silent thank you to herself for not letting nerves and emotions win the day.

'I hope I didn't hurt you,' he said, his arms still around her, his glorious weight still on her, his thighs caressing the inside of her legs.

'Not at all,' she said, smiling contentedly.

'I have heard it can be painful for a woman the first time.'

'You've never been with a virgin before?' she asked, somewhat incredulous. The fact that she was offering him the chance to deflower a virgin had been one thing that had given her courage, certain that he would not turn down such an opportunity. Wasn't that what Randall had said?

*'Most men have to pay an enormous sum for a virgin. Whereas I'll get a willing virgin for free, and I even come out of it all the richer.'*

She pushed that painful memory away. She would not let Randall ruin what had been such a wonderful, rapturous experience for her.

'No, never,' he said.

'So this was a first for both of us.'

He smiled and held her closer. 'Yes, I suppose it was. And the first time is never the best.'

'It gets better?' She found that hard to believe. 'In that case, let's do it again.'

He lightly kissed the top of her head. 'If I was eighteen, I'd probably be able to oblige, but I'm afraid I'm an old man of eight-and-twenty, so you're going to have to wait.'

'Oh, all right.' She tried not to sound too disappointed.

He lifted himself off her. 'What excuse have you given your mother for coming to my home without a chaperone?'

'I told her I was attending a board meeting.'

'Then I suspect it best if you return home soon, if you are to avoid arousing your mother's suspicions.'

'Yes, I suppose so,' she said, watching as he stood up, pulled up his trousers and did up the buttons. All the while he watched her in return, and she could see in his eyes that he liked what he was looking at. But he was right. She had got what she came for—to be away from home for too long would cause her mother to ask questions.

She pushed down her skirt and pulled up her chemise.

'So, do you want there to be another time?' he asked, and he almost looked sheepish.

'Yes,' she said, looking back up at him, that one word holding so much expectation. Of course she wanted there to be another time. How could she experience something so divine and not want to go back for more?

'Perhaps next time it should be in a bed, and not quite so furtive,' he said, picking up her lacy drawers from the floor and handing them to her. She stood and wriggled back into them.

'Not that I actually object to furtive,' he said with that sensual smile, reminding her body of all they had just shared. 'But we could take our clothes off next time, not just the essential bits.'

She fumbled with the buttons of her blouse. 'Yes, that would be nice,' she said, her words sounding wholly inadequate.

'Allow me to help.' Before she could answer he lightly pushed aside her hands and slowly did up the buttons at the front of her blouse. Her body instantly reacted to the touch of his hand, the warmth of his body so close to hers, and that masculine scent of leather and sandalwood.

'Next time, we should be a bit more discreet as well,' he added, his fingers lingering on the last button a moment before he stepped back.

'Oh, will the servants gossip?' She looked towards the door.

'No, my servants are used to turning a blind eye to the comings and goings in this house.'

'Good,' she replied, her heart giving an irrational lurch. There was no reason why she should react in such a manner to that statement. His reputation as a womaniser was the very reason why she had come here today. It meant he had experience with women. It meant he was a man who was honest about who he was, and a man with whom she would never be so imprudent as to want anything more from him than what he was prepared to offer. That did not include a commitment of any kind.

No, this all suited her perfectly, and he was perfect for what she wanted. There was no rational reason to care about any other woman he'd had in his life, or would have in his life in the future.

'I also pay my servants handsomely,' he added. 'They know there is no advantage in endangering their position by selling gossip to the gutter press or any other interested parties.'

'Good,' she repeated. This time there was no doubt in her response. As much as she had enjoyed herself, and as much as she refused to believe she had done anything wrong, she would hate for her parents to hear what she had been up to. It was shameful enough for them to have an unmarried daughter with no prospects, but to have one who had all but thrown herself at a man like Jackson Wilde would be a shame they would not be able to bear.

'But I unfortunately do have neighbours, and they *do* take an unhealthy interest in the comings and goings of this house,' he added.

'Oh,' once again she looked towards the door, as if expecting to see these nosy neighbours glaring at her.

'I do, however, have a small set of private rooms located in a shopping arcade that specialises in hats, ribbons, that sort of thing, for young ladies. It is perfect for such liaisons. You will be able to pretend you are on a shopping expedition then discreetly slip down the alleyway that leads to my rooms.'

Emily listened as if merely taking an interest in this plan. She ignored the tightening in her stomach and refused to speculate as to how many other young ladies he had entertained at his private rooms, rooms chosen exclusively for such liaisons.

'If you wish we could meet there on occasion,' he said.

Oh, yes, she wished, she wished a great deal.

'I believe that would be a satisfactory arrangement,' she said, once again using that detached voice to cover a turmoil of confusing emotions. She moved to the looking glass over the mantelpiece to fix her hair.

He stood behind her, smoothing the loose strands back into the bun at the back of her neck. She watched him in the looking glass. He really was devastatingly handsome. His dark blond hair had fallen over his high forehead and she was itching to push it back, to run her fingers through his tousled locks. His blue eyes had narrowed as he concentrated on his task, the laughter lines visible at the edges. Her gaze moved down to his full lips. Lips that had kissed her lips, and her body, and sent waves of ecstasy coursing through her. She could hardly wait until they were kissing her again.

As if hearing her thoughts, he leant down and kissed her neck. She closed her eyes and sighed.

'Until next time,' he murmured and took a step backwards.

She blinked several times to pull herself back into reality.

'Yes, until then.' She quickly scanned the room to ensure she had not left behind any items of clothing, then walked out the drawing room, her head held high as if they had merely just concluded another meeting about the school.

The footman was waiting at the front door. He escorted her down the steps to her waiting carriage, held out his hand and helped her in. The Viscount was correct. The man was the very soul of discretion, and she could read not a trace of judgement in his impassive expression. But why should he react in any other way? This was no doubt a regular event for him, as it was for the Viscount.

She looked back towards the three-storey cream townhouse, at its black railings leading up to the portico and oak door.

Did every young lady who entered that house to spend time with the Viscount experience what she had just experienced? Did he turn each and every one of them into a woman desperate for his touch, aching to have him inside her again, filling her up, making her his? And afterwards, did they all feel as if the earth had been somehow tipped off its axis? Did they all feel as if they had been changed in some fundamental way? She suspected they did, that he was an expert at making them feel that way, and she was not special at all.

That was why he was such a successful womaniser. And that was why she had chosen him, so she had no right to judge him or to expect any more from him than what he had just given her.

She would not think about those other women. She would just be content at how wonderful it had all been. And it was going to happen again. A little shiver ran through her at the thought of his hands, lips and tongue on her once again, of him taking her again, bringing her up to that soaring height and sending her crashing over into that blissful state.

As the carriage took Emily home, she couldn't stop herself from smiling. It was so hard to believe. She, Lady Emily Beaumont, was now Viscount Wickford's mistress. Or, at least, one of his mistresses. Her smile quivered slightly, before she forced it to return, just as brightly.

She would not allow herself any regrets. It had taken too much internal debate to come to this decision for her to let any doubts creep in now. But the Viscount was right. Now that she had lost her virginity there was no going back. Men from her social class wanted women who were chaste, and should she actually meet a man she wanted to marry, she would not lie to him.

She released a huff of exasperation. It was all so unfair.

Gideon's revelations as to his true character had left her with two choices; marry a man she neither loved nor respected, or remain on the shelf and become a woman pitied by all. Neither of those choices appealed.

She sat up straighter in the carriage. But she had boldly taken a third option, one forbidden by Society's rules. And for that defiance she could not help but harbour a secret pride.

She nodded, as if to underline her conviction. No, this was the best solution. She would officially remain a spinster, but she would experience pleasures that would otherwise be denied her.

She sighed, long and slow, and closed her eyes.

And oh, what pleasure she had had experienced. His kisses had been sublime, but making love to him was more than she could possibly have imagined. And she would soon be making love to him again. It made the sacrifice of never marrying worth it.

Didn't it?

Of course it did.

On arrival at her family's Belgrave home, Emily quickly checked herself in the hall looking glass. Her cheeks were still a little flushed, but that could be explained by the wind. As could her hair, still slightly dishevelled despite the Viscount's attentions. She pushed a few stray locks back into her bun. Her finger slowly moved down her neck as she remembered his farewell kiss.

She wasn't sure how she would explain her lips, which appeared somewhat plumper than usual. If asked, perhaps she could say she was doing something risqué like trying on lip rouge. Her mother would be shocked, but it would be nothing compared to how shocked she would be if she knew the real reason for her changed appearance.

She inspected herself one more time, looked down at her blouse and skirt to ensure all buttons were in the correct buttonholes, and, satisfied that all was as it should be, entered the drawing room, where her mother was taking tea and working on her embroidery.

'You're looking rather pleased with yourself,' her mother said, signalling to the maid to pour Emily a cup. 'Did the meeting about the school go well?'

'Oh, yes, very well.'

'The results were as good as you expected?'

'They certainly were, much better than I could ever imagine.' Emily said with a nod of thanks as she took the cup from the maid.

Her mother gave her a long, appraising look, the tea cup poised in her hand. 'You're looking rather, I don't know, different. Did you see Viscount Wickford at your meeting?'

'What? No. Well, yes, he was there, I suppose, but, no I didn't see him.' Heat rose on Emily's cheeks. That was something she was going to have to get under control if she was to conduct a clandestine relationship. She could not blush, stammer or act in a generally awkward manner every time the Viscount's name was mentioned.

'Hmm, I see,' her mother said, causing Emily's cheeks to burn brighter. 'I had noticed you spent rather a lot of time with him at that fundraising ball of yours.'

Emily fought to maintain a calm demeanour, determined to prove to herself she really was up to the task of subterfuge. 'Yes, well, he was part of the organising committee. It's only natural that we would spend time together. We had much to discuss.'

'Hmm, I see,' her mother repeated in that annoying manner. 'Only natural, indeed. Perhaps we should host another ball before the Season is over so the two of you can continue your...' She paused and waved her hand in a circle. 'Your discussions.'

'No need. I'll be seeing him at the board meeting tomorrow,' Emily said, pleased that her voice remained even and her cheeks were now cooling. She could do this after all. To the rest of the world she would continue to be the same sensible woman everyone expected her to be, while maintaining a secret life that would shock Society to its very core if they ever found out. She took a sip of her tea, rather liking this new, decidedly naughty side of herself.

'Hmm, I see,' her mother said yet again. 'Another meeting so soon. Did you not get everything discussed today that you needed to talk about?'

'Obviously not,' Emily answered and waited for her mother's inevitable response.

'Hmm, I see,' she said, causing Emily to smile.

Emily had not been lying to her mother. Not entirely. She did have a meeting the next day with the board, and Jackson Wilde would be there. This was going to be a test for both of them, but Emily in particular.

The meeting was to discuss the purchase of an abandoned warehouse, which Mr Greaves believed would be perfect for conversion into a school. The board members had been invited to inspect the premises, along with the primary fundraisers, Emily and the Viscount.

When her carriage arrived outside the warehouse, she paused and took a few deep breaths before alighting. At all times she would have to act as if the Viscount was nothing to her. She would continue to see him as merely a man she didn't entirely approve of, a man about whom she was putting aside her objections regarding the way in which he lived his life, for a greater good; that is, a school for disadvantaged women.

Too much was riding on her ability to remain dispassionate when dealing with the Viscount in public. While she would be publicly shamed if Society knew she was yet another woman that Jackson Wilde had taken as his mistress, there was more at stake than just her embarrassment.

Her parents would be mortified. The board would be scandalised. It might even put the future of the school in jeopardy. Knowing this was about more than just herself, she stepped down from the carriage, lifted her head high and strode into the warehouse.

The Viscount and the board members had already assembled. They were standing in the middle of the immense building, with its towering ceiling showing exposed wooden beams, brick walls and large dust-covered leadlight windows.

It was hard to see how this building could possibly be transformed into a school suitable for female students learning skills such as cooking and needlepoint.

Emily greeted each man in turn with a polite nod, and made a point of not holding the Viscount's gaze for any longer than that of the other men present.

'I was just telling everyone that the ball was a resounding success,' Mr Greaves said. 'Lady Emily, Viscount Wickford, you are to be congratulated.'

This was greeted with 'hear hears' from the other board members, and the Viscount received several pats on the back, while Emily merely tilted her head slightly in acceptance of the praise. But what they had achieved did feel good, very good. This was what she wanted to do with her life. She wanted to make a difference and improve the lives of others, and the school would do that.

'Thanks to your efforts,' Mr Greaves continued, 'we have more than sufficient funds from the tickets, the donations and the pledges of patronage to purchase these

premises outright without a bank loan, to pay for the con-
versions, hire tutors and for the school to continue for the
foreseeable future.'

This earned the Viscount some more back-patting and
nods of approval in Emily's direction. Mr Greaves led the
party around the warehouse, pointing out features and
where partitions could be placed for school rooms, and
how, once cleaned, the windows would provide ample
lighting for all the classrooms. Offices already existed on
the mezzanine floor. They would require nothing more
than clearing out and appropriate furniture being installed
for them to be converted to a board room, offices for senior
staff members and a staff room for the tutors.

The board members and the Viscount discussed the
premises as they walked around the building. But, despite
the talk she had given herself before she entered the warehouse, Emily could not quite forget she was in the presence
of her lover and felt it best to keep quiet, in case her voice
inadvertently revealed her inner turmoil.

The Viscount, on the other hand, had no such problems.
He was chatting away to Mr Greaves and the other board
members, making suggestions and comments, and even the
occasional joke, which everyone except Emily laughed at.

But what else did she expect? That he would fall apart
just because he was in the company of his latest mistress?
While this was all new to her, it was far from new to Jackson. He'd had countless illicit affairs and would be a master at living a double life.

And if she was being painfully honest with herself,
what happened between them probably meant little to him.
It had been her first time, and its significance could not

be greater, but for the Viscount she was merely one more woman in a long line.

The tour came to an end. The board members said their goodbyes and climbed into the row of black carriages lined up outside the warehouse. Emily released a sigh of relief as she headed to her own waiting carriage. She had done it. She had got through her first public meeting with the Viscount and she had revealed nothing. It seemed she could do this after all.

'Lady Emily,' that familiar deep voice called out, just as the footman was about to help her into her carriage.

She turned around and saw the Viscount approaching. Her ordeal was not yet over. Despite her pounding heart, she adopted what she hoped was a nonchalant expression.

'What is it?' In her determination to prove this man meant nothing to her, it came out perhaps more sternly than intended.

'At some time in the near future it would be a good idea if we met to discuss securing future patronage for the ongoing funding of the school.'

'But I thought Mr Greaves said we had—'

His eyebrows arched, halting her words.

'Oh, yes, of course. That would be an excellent idea. When do you have in mind?'

'Tomorrow afternoon, if that suits you.'

'Yes, I believe it does.'

*It suits me more than you could possibly imagine.*

Jackson held out his hand to help her into the carriage. As he did so he passed her a note, which she quickly closed her hand around.

'Until then, Lady Emily,' he said with a formal bow.

'Yes, goodbye.' She took her seat and Jackson closed

the door. The moment the carriage drove off she opened the letter, then stared at it in disappointment. It was an address. What had she expected? A declaration of love? He had merely given her instructions on where they were to meet. And that was as it should be. She did not need a declaration of love, nor did she want such a thing, and she'd be horrified if she actually received one. This was not about love. This was merely an adventure, an exciting adventure, but nothing more than that.

She looked back down at his handwriting. Her disappointment was chased away as a delicious thrill coursed through her. Tomorrow that adventure would continue. He wanted to see her again. He had written this note before he came to the meeting, ensuring he would see her again as soon as possible. While he was talking to the board members, pretending there was nothing between them, this note had been in his pocket and he had been waiting for an opportunity to pass it to her.

Did that mean he was thinking of her throughout the meeting, just as she was thinking about him?

A frivolous side of her nature, which she hadn't known existed, hoped this was the case, while her more sensible side knew it was unlikely. This would not be affecting him the way it was affecting her. If she was to keep that frivolous side of herself in check, her sensible nature needed to never, ever forget that.

She placed the note in her reticule and reminded herself to stop being so flighty and emotional. This was an arrangement that suited them both. It was a chance to have some fun, to experience something wonderful and forbidden, but it meant no more than that. To think anything else was an absurdity.

## Chapter Twelve

The next day at the arranged time Emily found herself wandering around the Tanner Street Shopping Arcade, pretending to admire the hats, gloves and ribbons on display in the shop windows. As if admiring the ornate fixtures and fittings, she looked around, taking in the high arched-glassed ceiling, the faux marble columns, and the brown and white tiled floor. In reality, rather than admiring the modern shopping area designed to attract discerning women with plenty of money to spend, she was looking for the small passageway that led to the door of the Viscount's private rooms.

She spotted it between a glove shop and a hat shop, exactly as his note had described, and made her way along the arcade acting as innocently as every other woman out for a day's shopping. A pretence that would be easier to achieve if every nerve in her body was not alive, her stomach wasn't rolling, her heart beating so loudly in her chest it was hard to think above its pounding.

As surreptitiously as possible, she looked around to see if anyone was observing her. No one was paying her the slightest bit of attention. Instead, elegant women, moving in groups, pairs or alone, were looking in shop windows, chatting, entering and leaving shops to the sound of tinkling bells.

With as much boldness as she possessed, she walked down the short alleyway to the black door at the end. Unable to stop herself, she took a quick, furtive look over her shoulder before she opened the door and slipped inside. When the door closed behind her, she leant against it and released her held breath.

She had met no one she knew, and was sure if anyone did see her, they would never suspect that well-behaved Lady Emily Beaumont would be up to anything other than a bit of shopping.

No one would ever suspect she, of all women, was about to make love to one of London's most notorious philanderers. Still leaning against the door, that guilty thought sent a delightful shiver coursing through her.

She was Viscount Wickford's mistress and would soon be making love to him. It was unbelievable, even to her, so it was sure to be unbelievable to anyone who did happen to see her at the shopping arcade.

She entered the living area, to find him waiting for her while holding two champagne flutes, the bubbly liquid resembling her own fizzing emotions.

Her heart pounded faster in her chest as she took the glass from his outstretched hand. 'I see you were confident I would come,' she said and took a sip, the bubbles tickling her nose.

'If you hadn't, I would have drunk all the champagne myself to drown my sorrows.'

*Or shared it with one of your other women*, a killjoy voice murmured.

But Emily would not think like that. She would not be possessive. She would not be jealous. That was not what this was about.

'I'm afraid I don't have that much time. I told Mother I needed to shop for some gloves.'

He removed the champagne flute from her hand and placed it on the small table beside the settee. 'You're going to have to tell your mother it took a long time to decide on the perfect gloves, because I don't intend to rush this.'

'Oh,' she gasped, loving that idea.

'Last time was somewhat hurried. This time I want to enjoy you fully. Last time I was so desperate to have you we didn't even disrobe properly. This time I want to undress you, entirely.' He smiled at her, that slow, sensual smile that made her legs turn to jelly. 'Will you let me do that?'

Emily could only nod, excitement and nerves jangling within her, making her almost weak. He was desperate for her. He wanted to take her slowly. She definitely liked the sound of both those concepts.

'We best get started,' he said, his smile becoming decidedly devilish, driving her longing for his touch to fever pitch.

He reached up and removed the clips holding her hair in place. Her hair tumbled around her shoulders. He ran his hands through the locks, combing it out so it curled freely and naturally.

It was a small gesture, but it sent Emily's pulse racing in expectation of what was to come.

That wicked smile still curving his full lips, he slowly undid the buttons at the front of her blouse, then frowned. 'I believe these tiny buttons are designed to drive a man insane, or perhaps they're a devious way to increase my expectation and make my desire for you even more fierce than it already is.' He smiled at her. 'If that was the intent, it's working.'

Emily silently cursed herself. Why had she not chosen a blouse that could be removed more easily? She had taken so much time selecting her clothing, picking the pale lemon blouse because she thought it flattered her complexion.

But he *was* right. As each button was slowly undone, her desire for him did grow increasingly fierce. His hands lightly swept across her hard nipples and she moaned lightly, wishing he would just be done with it and rip the cursed thing off her.

The buttons finally undone, he slipped the blouse off her shoulders, pausing to kiss each shoulder. She closed her eyes and all but purred at the touch of his lips on her skin. This was what she wanted. This was what she was risking her reputation for.

He dropped the blouse onto a nearby armchair, and undid the buttons of her matching skirt, pushing it down over her hips. She was standing before him dressed only in her underwear. She should be feeling awkward, nervous, embarrassed, something she would expect a well brought-up young lady to feel, but all she felt was deliciously wanton and burning with expectation.

'Turn around,' he commanded, his voice thick with desire for her. She did as he asked and released a sigh of pleasure when he lifted her hair and kissed her neck. His hands moved to her corset, unhooking it with more expertise than her lady's maid had ever shown.

*He's probably had more experience in doing so*, Emily thought, then pushed it out of her mind.

It mattered not how many other women he had stripped naked. He was with her now. Now was all that mattered, and now was wonderful, exciting, intoxicating.

He placed her corset on the chair on top of her blouse

and skirt, reached up under her chemise and pulled down her drawers. When they reached the ground, she stepped out of them.

With his hands on her shoulders, he turned her around.

'Raise your arms above your head,' he ordered, his voice thick and husky. She did as asked and her chemise was quickly skimmed off her body, leaving her standing in front of him wearing only her silk stockings, held up by garter belts. The cool air caressed her naked skin but could do nothing to relieve the soaring heat of her body.

He stepped back. His gaze swept over her, slowly, appreciatively.

'My God, you are perfect, Lady Emily.' His gaze slowly moved up and down her naked body, his eyes dark and hooded.

She bit her bottom lip, her teeth running across the sensitive skin, her body throbbing for his touch.

'Emily. Call me Emily,' she said, her husky voice unrecognisable.

'Emily,' he repeated, his voice soft and soothing. 'My beautiful Emily. And you of course must call me Jackson.'

'Jackson,' she repeated, loving the sound of his name on her lips.

He stepped towards her, his gaze returning to her face, and cupped both breasts, his thumbs rubbing over the hard nubs as he watched her reaction, his eyes sparking with desire. She clasped the material of his shirt, holding onto it to steady herself as her body became a deep throbbing want.

Her lips parted and her eyes closed as she surrendered to his touch. When he kissed her—deep, hard and slow— she sank into his arms, her sensitive skin rubbing against the fabric of his shirt and trousers. His kisses moved slowly down her neck and traced a line over the top of her breasts.

Was he teasing her, playing with her? If he was, it was a delicious cruelty. His kisses inched closer to her waiting nipples. When he took a tight bud in his mouth, she released a deep sigh of gratitude, which soon turned to gasps of ecstasy as his tongue moved in circles while his lips suckled, driving her wild with need.

With each stroke of his tongue that need grew fiercer, more demanding. Her heart beating faster, pounding through her entire body, she moaned her mounting desire for him so loudly a small part of her worried she might be heard over the noise of the shoppers.

Taking his hand, she placed it between her legs. No longer thinking, just reacting, her body moved against his rubbing hand, her back arching back and forth, needing the release only he could give her. Her gasps growing louder, the pounding between her legs mounting, she took hold of his shoulders, her fingers gripping the material of his shirt.

'Jackson,' she cried out as the cresting wave took her up to a peak and crashed over her, leaving her gasping in its wake.

He stood back and gazed down at her, desire radiating from his face.

'You are even more beautiful when you climax. And I want to see that sight again and again.'

She gasped in a few breaths, that insistent pounding once again resuming in response to his words.

'First, I want to see you naked as well,' she said, surprised her voice sounded so in control given the torrent of desire raging inside her. But she did want to see his body, and to feel his naked skin under her fingers and lips.

He smiled at her and spread his arms wide as if his body was hers for the taking. With surprisingly steady fingers she undid the buttons of his shirt. Unlike him, she was not able to go slowly, but quickly undid each button and pushed the garment off his shoulders so she could feast her eyes. His chest was just as she remembered it when she had bathed him in hospital, minus the bruises and cuts. The muscles were as sculptured, the stomach as hard and firm, and that line of hair was just where she remembered it.

Unable to resist the temptation to do so, she kissed his chest, his skin warm under her lips. Her fingers moved down to the buttons of his trousers. She could feel him hard inside, telling her just how much he wanted her. In the same way that his hands had lightly brushed against her breasts under the guise of undoing her buttons, she lightly brushed her fingers over his arousal. He gasped, grabbed her hands and took them up to his lips.

'If you want me to be good for what is to come, I would advise against that,' he said, taking her hand and lightly kissing her fingers. 'I want you so much, Emily,' he said, looking down into her eyes. 'But I want to take things slowly, so I better call a halt to this before I lose the ability to do so.' With that, he scooped her up into his arms and kissed her, his lips hot and insistent.

Still kissing her, he carried her through to the adjoining room and placed her down gently on the large bed. His eyes never leaving her, he quickly discarded his trousers and boots.

'Stop,' she called out as he was about to join her on the bed. The surprised look on his face under any other circumstances might have made her laugh, but instead she couldn't take his eyes off him.

'You took your time to look at me, you can at least allow me the same enjoyment.'

The surprised look turned to one of amusement as he stood in front of her completely naked. Her gaze moved slowly up and down his body, taking in every glorious inch of his masculinity. He really was magnificent. Like a statue of an athletic Greek god, each muscle was sculptured and delineated and packed with explosive power. Her eyes moved down his slim hips, to those long lean legs and back up again, pausing at his arousal, loving the knowledge that it was a reaction she had caused.

'Turn around,' she commanded. And he did so, giving her a glorious view of his round, tight buttocks. She had felt them under her fingers when they had last made love. She knew they were hard and muscular, and the sight of them sent a delicious thrill ripping through her. Soon she would be feeling them again as he moved between her thighs, bringing her to that delicious state of abandonment.

'Now you can join me,' she said, loving the way she was in charge.

'Thank you, my lady,' he said, that seductive smile once again returning.

His hard body stretched out beside her, warm naked skin against warm naked skin. He took one curl of her hair and wrapped it around his fingers, his blue eyes gazing into hers with something that resembled love but she knew to be lust—wonderful, marvellous lust.

'What do you want me to do now, my lady?' he asked with that slow, cheeky smile that promised delightfully wicked things to come.

'Kiss me,' she ordered. The words had barely left her lips and she was in his arms. His lips were hard against hers, taking her with a force that would have been overwhelming if her desire had not been as strong as his. She melted against him, seemingly turning to liquid in his arms, as his tongue entered her mouth. Her need for him was almost painful. She had to feel him inside her. Now. She needed him to relieve her deep, pulsating desire for him.

Unable to speak, she wrapped her legs around him, telling him with her body what she needed.

'God, I want you, Emily, but I wanted this time to take you slowly.'

'I don't want slow,' she gasped out. 'I want you inside me. Now.'

Responding immediately to her command, he placed himself between her legs, hips against hips, thighs against thighs. She lifted her legs and wrapped them around his waist, opening herself up for him, showing him what she wanted, what she had to have, what only he could give her.

'Emily, you really are ready for me, aren't you?' he murmured close to her ear as he pushed himself deep inside her. She released a long sigh, finally getting what she wanted so badly, what she had been constantly thinking about since she was last with him.

She cupped his buttocks, loving the feel of those taut muscles under her hands, flexing as he pulled out of her and pushed in again, harder and deeper. With each thrust her pounding need intensified, her moans coming louder and louder in time with his rhythm.

'I want to watch you,' he whispered in her ear. His chest lifted off hers. She opened her eyes and looked up at him. He was staring down at her with such adoration, such passion. Her gasps still matched his thrusting as they held each other's eyes. Emily felt so beautiful as he gazed down at her with such intensity—beautiful, wanton and desired.

As the fire within her burned more fiercely, she reached up to him, wrapping her hands around the back of his neck. His eyes holding hers, he thrust into her, again and again, until the fire became an inferno, flashing through her body, and she cried out his name then collapsed back onto the bed, exhausted and fulfilled.

Kissing her panting lips, she felt him pull out of her and release his own pleasure, then he lay on top of her, his heart pounding furiously against her chest, his body slick with perspiration.

Through the fog of her desire, Emily knew she must not see this for anything more than what it was. It was just a physical act, a glorious, sensational physical act, but nothing more. Despite knowing that, right now it did feel like so much more than just physical. She felt so close to him, felt adored by him, even loved by him.

It was all so confusing. But, right now, Emily refused to let that confusion undo this wonderful sensation. She would just lie here, with this magnificent man still so close, and enjoy the feeling of his weight on her and his arms holding her. All thinking, all reasoning, all introspection could be left for another time.

His pounding heartbeat slowed. He lifted himself off her and laid down by her side. 'I didn't take it slowly the way I had planned, but at least we managed to get our clothes off this time,' he said, amusement in his voice. 'But next time we must make sure we have even more time. There is so much more we could do.'

*More?* Emily liked the sound of that.

He brushed a lock of hair back from her cheek. 'Do you

think you can get away again soon? Maybe you could tell your mother you need to visit your dressmaker, or something that will take all afternoon and we can spend hours and hours in bed together.'

'Oh, no, my mother.' She sat up suddenly. 'Mother thinks I'm shopping for gloves. She'll be wondering where I am. Especially as I told her it was merely a quick visit to a shopping arcade and I would not need a chaperone.'

'Quick,' he said with a laugh. 'You know how to wound a man, don't you?'

Emily had no time to ask him what he meant by that—she had to leave, immediately.

She jumped out of bed and rushed back to the adjoining room, followed by Jackson. In a rapid reversal to her slow undressing, Jackson quickly helped her into her chemise, laced up her corset and, with two sets of fingers working together, they buttoned up her skirt and blouse.

'Here, let me fix your hair,' he said, turning her around and lifting up her locks. To her immense amazement, he brushed out her hair with his fingers, expertly twirled it into a bun at the nape of her neck and secured it with clips.

*How had he learnt to do that?*

Perhaps she'd rather not know.

Once he was finished, he quickly turned her around, did a quick inspection and kissed her lightly on the lips. 'You're the very picture of innocence and propriety,' he said. 'No one will have the slightest inkling that you haven't been out on an innocent shopping expedition.'

Emily hoped so.

'Until next time,' he said.

Next time? Could she actually wait until next time? Her eyes raked over his still naked body. It was a wonderful body, one capable of making her feel things, want things, need things that a few days ago she had not even known it was possible to feel.

Could she stay? Just a bit longer? No, of course she couldn't. She had to go.

'Yes, until next time,' she said and rushed out of the door.

She entered the shopping arcade where women continued to wander from shop to shop. It was difficult to believe the world had carried on as normal outside his flat, while inside she was being transported to a place of ecstasy. But there was no time to dwell on that. She raced into the shop that sold gloves. Grabbing the first pair she saw, she thrust some money into the shopkeeper's hand.

'Don't bother to wrap them and keep the change,' she called out as she raced towards the door.

'Thank you, miss. Thank you very much indeed,' the man said as the door closed behind her.

As quickly as she could without drawing attention to herself, she rushed out the arcade and climbed into a waiting hansom cab. Then she drew in and slowly released a deep breath. She looked down at the new gloves clasped in her hands.

She closed her eyes as if to block out the shocking sight, then opened them and looked again at the gloves she was holding. The second glance was no better.

They were red, fingerless and lacy. It was a brazen style she would never be seen dead wearing. This peculiar purchase was going to take some explaining when she got home.

Emily was far from being the first woman Jackson had entertained in his private flat, nor was she the first woman who had been forced to rush away due to commitments in her other life. Even though he had not acknowledged it before, it had always been a relief when that happened. They had both got what they wanted, gone their separate ways, and he could move onto the next source of fun without a backwards glance.

It should be the same with Emily. But it wasn't.

He pulled on his trousers, contemplating this strange reaction, which almost felt like loss. Could it be because making love to her once again was so unexpectedly passionate it had left him wanting so much more of her? But that would not fully explain these odd sensations gripping him.

It wasn't just that he wanted to make love to her again, although he certainly wanted that. He wanted her, here, with him.

After they had made love, he'd wanted to continue to lie in bed with her in his arms, talking and discovering all there was to discover about this complex, unusual and delightful woman.

He huffed out a laugh of disbelief and pulled on his shirt. That too was a first and something he struggled to understand. His ethos when it came to women was always: keep it light, keep it fun, keep it uncomplicated. Any other approach was far too dangerous. That could lead to women expecting more from him than he was prepared to give, more than he was capable of giving.

And yet, somehow, this time it was different. He slowly buttoned up his shirt. Perhaps it was simply that she was his first virgin. He exhaled a long breath. Had it given him some strange sense of responsibility? He hoped not. Responsibility had never been something that sat easily with him.

He also hoped it was not something he was going to live to regret. Emily had been his first virgin and he had been her first lover.

He stared at his reflection in the looking glass as he tied his cravat. Didn't virgins become attached to their first? Hadn't he heard that somewhere? Hopefully, it was a fallacy. He did not need any woman becoming attached to him, nor would it be wise for Emily to waste time and emotion on a man such as him.

To avoid such a possibility, perhaps the kindest thing to do was end it now.

He sat on the still warm bed and pulled on his boots. Yes, that was what he should do, end it now. Their love making was already far too intense. While that was immeasurably pleasurable, it was causing him to react in an unfamiliar manner and that was something he did not like.

He turned and looked at the tousled sheets and inhaled deeply. Her unadorned scent still lingered on the linen.

Yes, he should end this now. He should not have taken her virginity and he should not have compounded that wrong by inviting her to his rooms, further corrupting that innocent woman by making her his mistress.

He closed his eyes and inhaled her scent, taking it deeply into himself. And yet, while he knew what he had done was wrong, he was also completely aware of what a weak man he was. He would not be ending this. Not yet. He would go against everything he knew to be right so he could indulge himself in something he knew to be wrong, at least one more time.

He shook his head and stood up. Once again, his father had proven himself to be correct. He was a no-good scoundrel who thought only of his own selfish needs. A better man would have resisted. A better man would not have taken her virginity. And if a better man did transgress, he would immediately be down on bended knee proposing marriage to make right his appalling behaviour. But as everyone knew, including himself, he was not a better man.

Yes, he definitely was a no-good scoundrel. Even though he knew this to be wrong, all he could think about now was the next time he would have her in his arms, in his bed, her glorious, curvaceous body beneath his. He groaned as the memory of how she looked when they made love consumed him—her eyes closed, her lips panting and calling out his name. God, that image was going to haunt him until he did have her back in his bed. Yes, he was indeed a weak man. A man who would not be able to resist her until he was completely sated. And he suspected, given the strength of his desire for her, that was going to take longer than it had with most of his mistresses.

Hopefully, by the time he did finally satisfy his lust for her, she wouldn't have done something silly like think she had fallen in love with him.

He sighed loudly, stood up and moved away from the bed. Without her scent distracting him, he might be able to think more clearly.

If he had stuck to his type of woman, he would not be facing this dilemma. He would have just made love to a woman and would not be wracked with all these conflicting emotions and arguments.

Why hadn't he just stuck to his type of woman? The ones who lived outside of Society, who could weather the ignominy if the affair became public, or were well-versed in burying scandal before it did become public.

Emily was not that type of woman and he knew the

price of getting involved with a woman such as she. If they were discovered, to avoid a scandal, to stop her from being ruined, he would have to marry her. Neither wanted that. For both their sakes he should stop thinking of his carnal desires and end this now.

He looked back at the bed, still bearing the imprint of her body, and released another deep moan. But perhaps not quite yet. One more time would surely not be too much of a risk. One more time and maybe, just maybe, he'd have got her out of his system. One more time and he could inform her that the most sensible thing for both of them would be to never meet again and forget it had ever happened.

He snorted a laugh. Or, in his case, *pretend* it had never happened, because he doubted he would ever forget what had happened this afternoon.

He pulled his fob watch out of his jacket pocket and flicked it open. By now Emily would be far away from the shopping area and it would be safe for him to leave. But what was he to do with his time until he saw her again?

That too should not be a problem. It had never been so before. One thing he never lacked for was entertaining ways to fritter away his time, but right now he could not think of a single way to occupy himself until Emily was once again his.

# Chapter Thirteen

Days, weeks, months passed, and Jackson was no closer to ending his involvement with Emily. He was seemingly caught up in a never-ending circle of lust, regret, determination to end it, then lust consuming him yet again the moment he saw her.

He had hoped he would soon tire of her, as he had with every other mistress, making ending things so much easier. But instead of his desire waning, it increased with each meeting. It was as if he was in her thrall, under some sort of spell she had innocently cast over him and he was powerless to break free.

This was a situation he had hitherto never encountered. As was his difficulty in faking his indifference to her each time he saw her in public.

That too had never been a problem with any of his previous mistresses. He was well practised at living a double life. Making polite conversation with a woman he had just bedded, acting as if they were merely passing acquaintances, it was all second nature to him. But every time he saw Emily, no matter where they were, he wanted to touch her, to kiss her, to let the world know they were lovers.

He had to constantly remind himself to be on his guard when in public. No one could ever know of their involvement. If anyone found out it would cause such a scandal she might never recover and it would send deep shame crushing down on her parents. A shame that could only be mitigated by a proposal of marriage.

It was with that in mind he stood at the entrance of The Women's Education Institute, composing himself before he attended yet another meeting. One where Emily would be present, one where he would have to watch everything he said, every gesture he made, every look he gave her so no one would ever suspect the truth of their relationship.

He could do this. He had done it before over the preceding months, many times. He had held in his inclinations through all those other meetings, when they'd been called to inspect the renovations of the school, and through the official opening. Now he could do the same for this meeting, to show off the school to a group of local dignitaries and an assortment of other interested worthies.

Mr Greaves had been so excited about this tour, which would provide an opportunity to display the accomplishments the school was already achieving. Mr Greaves expected Emily and Jackson to be equally as proud and enthusiastic. And Jackson was. It would just be a lot easier to concentrate on being enthusiastic if he wasn't constantly thinking about Emily and how much he wanted to be alone with her so he could drop all this pretence.

He entered the now bustling school. Local tradesmen had placed dividers to create classrooms in the previously cavernous building, and it all now looked highly professional. Even before the official opening, a large number of girls and women of all ages had signed up for the courses. The school had a lively energy about it, with students and tutors buzzing about, laughing and chatting.

He joined Emily and the board members in the reception area, where a tour group had assembled. He nodded his greetings to each man and made certain his eyes did not linger on Emily. A command made especially difficult as she was looking particularly pretty today, in a cream and gold striped dress and wearing a simple straw hat adorned with a few roses perched on her lustrous chestnut hair. Thick hair that was held back with a few clips. The temptation to remove those clips so her locks flowed over her shoulders was all but overwhelming, so he placed his itching hands in his pockets.

'Welcome to The Women's Education Institute,' Mr Greaves said to those assembled, and sent a smile in Emily's direction.

The board had wanted to call the school The Women's Reform School or The Refuge for Fallen Women, but Emily had insisted they avoid anything that sounded judgemental. She had convinced the board it was essential the school be open to all women, and they should not have to feel they had to have fallen or were in need of reform in order to take advantage of the opportunities offered.

'The school has been a great success,' Mr Greaves continued. 'Already most of our classes are full. Many of our students come from desperate circumstances and have had little opportunity to improve their unfortunate lot in life.'

With a sweep of his hand, Mr Greaves indicated Jackson, standing at the back of the group. 'And we have to thank Viscount Wickford for spreading the word among some of London's more unfortunate women, so they would know that the education institute is open to all, no matter how far they have fallen from grace.'

As one, the members of the tour party turned to face

him, some, but by no means all, were smiling at him with approval.

'Kitty, I mean Miss Kathryn Trotter, one of the inaugural students, played a large part in publicising the school,' Emily said quickly. She'd have realised that anyone who read the scandal sheets would see no advantage in having a known reprobate involved in a school for fallen women. 'She recruited her friends and asked them to tell everyone they knew. She is already one of the highest achieving pupils and has provided an invaluable service to the school.'

Most of the tour party had turned to Emily and were smiling, although those who had been scowling at Jackson continued to look at him as if their delicate sensibilities had been offended by his mere presence.

Jackson shrugged it off. Yes, he was a man with a reputation that shocked the sanctimonious, but he was proud of the work he had achieved at the school. It was possibly—probably, well, definitely—the first time he had been proud of any achievement, and he would not let a few judgemental old fogies dampen his spirits. If they wanted to upset him, they'd have to do more than just turn up their noses. He'd had enough experience ignoring his father's disparaging looks to be disturbed by a few scowls.

'Now, if you'd all please follow me, you'll be able to see first-hand the good that we are achieving and meet some of our students,' Mr Greaves said, and led the worthies into a classroom where a group of women were being instructed in dressmaking, Pretty Kitty sitting among them. She beamed at Jackson, filling his heart with joy and driving out the sour taste left by those few disagreeable visitors.

'And this is the student Lady Emily mentioned,' Mr Greaves said, indicating Kitty. 'Miss Kathryn Trotter was the first student to join the school and has made sterling progress already.'

Kitty stood up and made a small curtsey to the group. 'I'm pleased to meet you,' she said in a demure voice. She had also signed up for the speech and deportment classes and was apparently a star pupil, although Jackson hoped that didn't mean she would lose her delightfully cheeky spirit.

While the party moved around the room, Emily and Jackson stood at Kitty's desk, admiring her work.

'This is really lovely needlework,' Emily said, running her fingers along the stitches.

'Thank you, my lady,' Kitty said, beaming fit to burst.

'I'm sure it won't be long before you are able to get work as a seamstress,' she added.

Kitty's large smile grew wider, something Jackson would not have thought possible if he hadn't witnessed it himself.

'I already have,' Kitty said. 'The broker I used to pawn me clothes to—I mean, my clothes to when I was really down on my luck has given me a job doing repairs. But I don't want to be stuck there repairing all those old rags. I hope to get a job with a real dressmaker and make lovely outfits like the one you're wearing.'

They both looked at Emily's gown, and under the circumstances Jackson could see no reason why he couldn't sweep his gaze over her luscious figure. After all, he was doing nothing more than admiring the work of her seamstress.

'That's wonderful news, Kitty,' Emily said, picking up her embroidery sampler.

'Yes, wonderful,' Jackson added, returning his gaze to the material in Emily's hands. 'What do you call these stitches,' he said, running his finger along the embroidery and lightly stroking the tips of Emily's fingers. He smiled to himself as she gave a little gasp, which she covered up with a cough.

'That's back stitch and those little ones there are French knots,' Kitty said proudly, her smile moving between Jackson and Emily. 'Who would have thought when I met His Lordship in that dirty alleyway that I'd be soon learning how to do all these fancy stitches.'

One of the women on the tour group turned and sent Jackson her most accusatory glare, causing Kitty to give a small harumph, hold up her sampler and wave it in the disapproving woman's direction.

'It's French knots and back stitch,' she called out. 'It makes a nice change from French letters in back alleys.'

'Kitty,' Emily gasped out while Jackson laughed at the look of horror that crossed the old shrew's face. Kitty hadn't lost her fighting spirit. Thank God for that.

'As you can see,' Emily said, with a conciliatory smile directed at the outraged woman, 'the school plays an important role in providing young women such as Miss Trotter with alternative sources of employment.'

The woman merely sniffed and walked away to join the group, which was moving off to another schoolroom.

'Sorry about that,' Kitty said, not looking particularly sorry. 'But old cows like that really get my goat.'

Jackson laughed at the bizarre animal imagery.

'I'd like to see her find herself without a penny to her name, debts mounting up, kids to feed and no decent jobs available and see what she has to do to try and make ends meet,' Kitty said, her fists firmly on her hips.

'But that life is now in your past,' Emily said, causing Kitty to smile again.

'Yes, and I'm ever so grateful to the two of you. I've told everyone I know that they must join up. In no time at all there's bound to be a long waiting list of girls wanting to get into the school. You're going to have to have another one of those fancy balls and raise more money for a string of schools.'

Jackson and Emily exchanged a smile. Another one of those fancy balls didn't sound like a bad idea. Then there would be no reason why he couldn't dance with Emily, holding her in public instead of constantly having to hide away, as if they were doing something shameful.

'Yes,' Emily said. 'And why stop at one more school or restrict ourselves to London? Why not schools of this sort all over England?'

'I'm up for it if you are.'

They continued smiling at each other until Kitty coughed, drawing their attention back to her. 'Um, I think you've lost your friends and I need to get back to perfecting these French knots.'

'Yes, yes, of course,' Jackson said. 'Goodbye, Kitty,' he added then placed his hand on the small of Emily's back to escort her out the room. It was perhaps a bit overfamiliar, but the desire to touch her again was more than he could bear. And surely it would only be interpreted as a polite gesture.

'I have to see you again,' he whispered in her ear as soon as they left the classroom. 'Can you meet me this afternoon?'

She nodded and an erotic charge of lust rushed through him. All he had to do now was get through the rest of this tour, act normally for another hour or so, and he would have her back in his bed. He swallowed and dropped his hand, which had unaccountably moved from the small of her back to her rounded buttocks.

He was surely capable of acting normally and keeping his desire under control until this interminable tour was over. Forcing a smile onto his face he joined the group and commenced nodding at everything Mr Greaves said. He also took the sensible course of not looking at Emily again so his act of normality would not slip, and his thoughts would not drift off to the exquisite pleasure to come.

The moment he was free, Jackson rushed back to his private rooms to ready them for Emily's visit. He wanted to make sure the flat looked inviting. That too was something he had never worried about before. A servant regularly visited and did whatever servants did, but Jackson always felt the need to inspect the rooms before she arrived. He had also instructed his staff to make sure there were always fresh flowers in each room.

Another first, and sometimes he wondered why he made such an effort. Their time together was always far too short and they certainly did not waste a second of it admiring the large bouquets the servants arranged. But he wanted it to be perfect for her, because in so many ways *she* was perfect.

He moved the vase of flowers onto the main table, then moved it back to its original position, then laughed to himself at his odd behaviour. He took yet another look around the room, flicked open his pocket watch and frowned. What was keeping her?

He looked at the champagne bottle sitting in the melting ice. That was something else he insisted on, although more often than not the bottle remained unopened as they had no time to waste on drinking anything other than each other.

He paced around in circles, his agitation growing with each passing second. The door opened. She entered and rushed into his waiting arms.

'I am so sorry. I don't have much time,' she said, pulling at the buttons of his shirt. 'Mother says she wants to discuss my wardrobe for next Season. She's curious about all these visits I'm making to the shops and to my dressmaker. She wants to know when she's going to see some of these new gowns and dresses I'm having made.'

'What are you going to say?' he asked, his own fingers frantically undoing the line of buttons down the front of her dress.

'I don't know, but I'll think of something.'

Freeing her of her interminable clothing he took her hand and they rushed through to the bedroom. He so wished this did not have to be so hurried. It would be wonderful if they could spend entire days together, nights together, entire weeks, an entire life.

*An entire life?*

He paused. His lips withdrew from hers.

'What's wrong?' she asked, lightly stroking his jawline.

'Nothing, absolutely nothing,' he replied, scooping her up into his arms as he tried to digest what he had just thought. Would it be so bad to spend an entire life with this glorious woman? He placed her on the bed and joined her, his lips exploring her glorious body.

No, it would not be bad at all, he thought as he kissed, licked and nuzzled every inch of her. Then he could take all the time he needed to really get to know everything about her.

Each time they made love they learnt new things about each other's bodies, but Jackson was sure there was so much more to learn it could take a lifetime, and he was a more than willing student.

When she reached another shuddering climax and he found his own relief, he encased her in his arms and held her tightly against him. This too was what he lived for, this closeness, this feeling that they were one.

'Well, that was a nice way to end a frightful day,' she said.

'Nice?' he asked with mock offence. 'Is that how you describe what we just did?'

She playfully poked him in the ribs. 'Very nice, then.'

'I think my performance is being damned by faint praise.'

'And I think you're fishing for compliments. You know how good it was for me, how good it always is. And you were right, it does get better and better the more we know each other.'

He stroked back a damp lock of hair from her forehead. 'That's better. As long as it was more than just nice. So why was your day so frightful?'

'That woman at the school, the one that kept giving you those terrible looks. She was so rude and it was so unfair.'

'Oh, that. I'd forgotten all about her. I'm used to disparaging looks. I don't believe my father has looked at me any other way from the moment I was born.'

She turned onto her side, lifted herself up onto one elbow and looked down at him. He wrapped a lock of her hair around his finger then released it, watching it drop down and curl around her glorious full breasts.

'You never talk about your father or your family.'

'What? That's because there's not much to say.'

She raised her eyebrows and he knew she wanted more.

And whatever she wanted, he was prepared to give, especially after what they had just exchanged.

'What can I say? My parents were like so many other couples. Their marriage was arranged by their parents. They were completely unsuited to each other. My mother did her duty and produced the required heir, then they barely spoke to each other again.' He paused briefly, pain starting to push through his flippant manner. 'My mother died when I was thirteen. I was away at school at the time and my father didn't bother to inform me until I came home for the holidays.'

Her eyes grew enormous and she lightly stroked his cheek. 'That's terrible. You must have been devastated.'

The memory of that day crashed in on him, causing his chest to tighten, his stomach to clench. It was a reaction that talking of his mother always caused, a reaction he had learnt to push away with fun and frivolity. But for some reason he wanted to talk about her with Emily.

'I was devastated, unlike my father who remained unaffected by her passing. After telling me of her death he said we were better off without her.'

'The brute,' she gasped. 'Did you miss her terribly?'

'Yes,' he said, that one word holding a wealth of distress. 'She was so lively, kind and loving, or at least she was when I was a small child. I remember the two of us running together around the estate, playing games in the maze, picking apples, having picnics.'

He smiled at the memory. 'But eventually being married to my father seemed to sap the life out of her and she became a shadow of her former self. He was such a misery and expected everyone around him to be just as miserable.'

'I'm so sorry,' she said, her hand running gently over his chest and helping to relieve the tightness.

'He ruined my mother's life and he tried to ruin mine. That's why I'm determined to never let him, or people like him, affect me, including that old bag in the tour group.'

'Your father can't possibly disapprove of you now? You've founded a school for disadvantaged women. That is surely something that has made him see what a good man you really are.'

Jackson huffed out a mirthless laugh. 'I believe when he found out he said something along the lines of, *"I see you've found a way to corral all your whores in one place so you can have your pick."*'

'That's appalling.'

'That's to be expected. He would never think I'd done something for altruistic purposes.' Guilt surged through him, and he wondered if his father might be right. Had his intentions been entirely altruistic, or had he made the proposal to start the school because he was looking for a way to spend more time with Emily?

'Well, he's wrong about you, and that woman in the tour group was wrong about you as well,' she stated emphatically.

Jackson chose not to answer, suspecting that those two had a more realistic understanding of his true character than the lovely, forgiving Emily did.

She sunk back onto the bed and stared up at the ceiling. 'I'm surprised your brute of a father hasn't insisted you marry. After all, you will be the Duke one day. You are expected to produce your own heir.'

He gave another laugh containing no humour. 'That's one of the reasons I avoid him as much as possible. He never stops going on about it being time I married and produced an heir. That and ranting on about what he's read about me in the scandal sheets. One of his favourite speeches is that I'll never find a decent wife if I continue to carry on the way I am, which of course only encourages me to do everything I can to prove him right.'

'I see,' she said quietly.

He cringed at what he had just said. Right now, he was holding a young lady who was eminently respectable, exactly the sort of woman any man would be happy to take as his wife. At least she would have been until he ruined her. *That* was precisely the sort of debased behaviour his father would expect from him.

'I'm sorry, Emily,' he whispered.

'Sorry for what?' She lifted herself back up onto one elbow and gazed down at him.

'For this.' He waved his hand around, encompassing their naked bodies, the tousled sheets and the flat where they had to meet in secret. 'I have never wished to marry, if for no other reason than to spite my father, but I'm sure, despite what you said, one day, when you meet the right man, you will want to wed. If any of this gets out it will—'

'Oh, that.' She dropped back down onto her side. 'I told you I have no wish to marry. Gideon finally opened my eyes to that realisation.'

'But won't your parents insist you do so, eventually? Isn't that what parents always do? It's what my grandparents did with my parents, and what my father wishes he could do with me. I'm surprised they haven't already found a suitable man for their lovely, well-connected, clever, delightful daughter. One certainly more suitable for you than Gideon Pratt.'

'My parents married for love and they want me to do the same. They have always said I should make my own choice. They encourage me, and they live in hope, but that's all. They have never put any pressure on me the way some parents do with their daughters.' She sighed lightly. 'And yes, I did once hope to marry, but unfortunately I have a terrible habit of falling for completely unsuitable men.'

'Like me?'

She sat up quickly, a hand on her chest, covering her heart, while her eyes grew enormous. 'No, I didn't mean that. Not that I mean you're unsuitable. I mean, you are suitable, and I'm not intending to marry you. And I haven't fallen for you, so I suppose you are unsuitable.'

She collapsed back onto the bed. 'It's different with you. It's not serious. We're not going to marry.'

Jackson refused to let that hurt. After all, she was saying nothing he didn't already know.

They remained silent for a few breaths.

'Well, you did make a rather unfortunate choice with Pratt,' he said, moving the subject away from him. 'But you said men. Were there more unsuitable men, other than me and Pratt?'

She sighed deeply. 'Yes, Gideon was my latest mistake, but not my first.'

He rolled over to look at her. 'I thought I was your first.'

She pushed him playfully in the chest. 'I mean the first man I thought I was in love with. The first man I wanted to marry.'

Love? Marriage? Neither of which applied to Jackson. Again, he would not let that affect him.

'So, who was your first love then?'

Why was he asking this? Did he want to torment himself?

'Randall Cochran.'

He collapsed onto his back beside her and stared at the ceiling. 'I see what you mean. They don't come much less suitable than Cocky Cochran.' That is if you exclude Jackson from the list of potentially unsuitable husbands.

She gave a small laugh and rolled onto her side to look at him. 'Is that what you call him? If I'd known that was his nickname, I wouldn't have fallen for his tricks.'

'That man almost makes me look like a saint.' *Almost.*

'I know. My parents didn't approve of him either, which, being an eighteen-year-old girl, made him seem even more attractive, as if he was a bit wild and exciting. Fortunately, I found out before it was too late that he was merely a cruel man who treated women like they were commodities, things he could play with for his own amusement.'

She sighed lightly as Jackson's chest tightened with guilt. No, he was not that bad. He had always been honest with the women he was involved with. He had never used any woman and never deceived them. That had to count for something. Didn't it?

'That was why I was so keen to marry Gideon,' she continued. 'He was everything Randall was not, except he was deceiving me just as much as Randall was. Or at least, I'd been deceiving myself as to the sort of man he was, trying to make him fit into an image of my perfect husband. On the night he proposed, when I couldn't delude myself any longer, I realised that despite thinking of myself as an intelligent woman, when it comes to men I am completely gullible.'

She shook her head and gave another sigh. 'Mother didn't appear to approve of Gideon either. At the time I thought it was just snobbery, but perhaps she could see something I couldn't.'

'Or perhaps he tried to solicit her into becoming his private patient, as he'd done with me and every other titled person he came into contact with.'

'Yes, perhaps.'

'Well, at least you'll never have to see him again.'

'Thank goodness. It's strange how he suddenly resigned, but I must say I'm very pleased that he did.'

Jackson wondered whether he should inform Emily that there was nothing strange about it at all. It had merely taken a quiet word with Mr Greaves. Once the board chairman had been informed that the good doctor had chosen to treat a member of the aristocracy with minor injuries ahead of men who had been seriously burned in a foundry explosion, Mr Greaves had lost all confidence in the doctor and had suggested he tender his resignation before he was dismissed.

Jackson had said nothing that wasn't the truth, but had done so to ensure Emily never again had to be in that odious man's presence.

'Mother said it was good to see the last of him. I suspect she knew I was hoping to marry him.' She rolled over onto her stomach, and ran her finger gently along his jawline. 'Strangely enough, my mother thoroughly approves of you.'

'Well, that just shows she has no insight into a man's true nature. If she could see us now, I don't think she'd be approving of me one little bit.'

'I suppose not,' she softened this with a smile. 'But unlike those other men, you have never tried to pretend you are anyone other than exactly who you are.'

Jackson doubted that was a compliment and chose to

laugh it off. 'No, with me, what you see is exactly what you get.'

She ran a finger down his neck, and across his chest, her gaze following her finger. 'And what I see I like. Rather a lot.'

He took that as a signal that their conversation had now come to an end, slid his arm underneath her and rolled her on top of him.

'Do you have enough time?' he asked, looking up at the glorious body straddling his and praying she would say yes.

'I suppose I could tell Mother the seamstress made a complete mess of my dress and I insisted she start all over again, right back to taking my measurements.'

His prayers were answered.

She leant down and kissed his lips, her breasts skimming his chest. He groaned with expectation as her kisses moved down his neck, across his chest and trailed a line down his stomach.

All thoughts of the future and the past, all questions about what others would think about what they were doing, all of it left his head. Right now, he was exactly where he wanted to be, with the woman he wanted to be with, doing what felt so right it could not possibly be wrong.

# Chapter Fourteen

A few days after her last meeting with Jackson a letter arrived for Emily in the morning post that sent shivers of anxiety charging through her. She had been summoned to a meeting with Mr Greaves to discuss a very serious matter. Emily folded up the letter, pushed it back into the envelope and placed it beside her plate.

'Is something wrong, dear?' her mother asked, pausing in the buttering of her toast.

'No, not at all,' Emily said with a forced smile, and poured herself another cup of tea, the tremor in her hands causing her mother's eyebrows to raise further up her forehead in question.

'The board have asked me to attend a meeting. I'm just a bit worried that it might be bad news,' she said. 'About the school I mean.'

'Oh, I see,' her mother said, her voice suggesting that she had no real interest in the goings on at the school. 'Will Viscount Wickford be there?' she asked, her voice perking up with interest.

'I have no idea.' Emily took a sip of tea, wanting this discussion to come to an end. She could only hope the meeting was to be about the school and that it would be a problem that could easily be put to rights. If word had got back to

Mr Greaves about her clandestine meetings with Jackson then the outcome for her could be catastrophic. She would no longer be welcome at the school or in the hospital. Mr Greaves might feel honour-bound to inform her parents what she had been up to. They would be deeply ashamed of their daughter. Exposure had always been a danger, and yet she had willingly put herself in peril, had even, dare she admit it, enjoyed taking such a risk, seeing it as wickedly exciting. She had also enjoyed having such a salacious secret that she'd not even shared it with her closest friends.

And now she was to pay the price for throwing good sense to the wind and going against how Society demanded a respectable young woman conduct herself.

Breakfast over, Emily took the family carriage to the school. Her heart a dull thud in her chest, her stomach a tight, churning knot, she entered the school and took the curved wrought iron stairs up to the board room to find only Mr Greaves and Jackson waiting.

Both men stood as she took her seat, Mr Greaves's face was mournful, while Jackson sent her a small, supportive smile, although he couldn't disguise the anxiety gripping his usually relaxed body, or those two lines that appeared between his eyes whenever he was worried.

'Thank you for coming, Lady Emily,' Mr Greaves said. 'I'm afraid I have received some rather disturbing news.'

Emily took her seat, gripped her hands tightly in her lap and prepared for the worst as the two men also took their seats.

'I've received a rather disturbing letter from a Mrs Turnbull,' Mr Greaves said, holding a letter in his hand. 'She is the chairwoman of a group called the Ladies for the Promotion of High Moral Standards.'

'Oh,' Emily said, her voice coming out as a small squeak. Jackson placed his hand lightly on her knee under the table and patted it in reassurance.

'Rather disturbing, indeed,' Mr Greaves said, looking back down at the letter. 'They're calling for the closure of the school as they believe it is encouraging moral laxity. Unfortunately, it mentions you, Lady Emily, and you, Viscount Wickford, by name as encouraging such abominable vices.'

Mr Greaves coughed lightly, placed his spectacles on the end of his nose and held the letter close to his face as he read.

*"'A student encountered by one of our members while inspecting the school was undeniably a woman of ill repute. This student made a lascivious and repugnant comment that shocked the esteemed gentlewoman, leaving her shaken and insulted. Rather than rebuke the offender and expel her from the school immediately, Lady Emily Beaumont and Viscount Wickford encouraged her disrespectful and offensive behaviour by laughing."'*

Emily placed her hand on her stomach as relief swept through her. They were objecting to Kitty's joke about French letters and back alleys. Thank goodness for that.

'I believe I was the only one to laugh,' Jackson said. 'Lady Emily was not amused.'

'It goes on,' Mr Greaves said frowning. *"'This incident proved to our members that there is no moral guidance being provided by the organisers of The Women's Education Institute. Unless it is closed immediately our group will be forced to mount a sustained campaign until we bring an end to this debased institution."'*

Jackson gave a dismissive snort of laughter.

'I'm afraid this is no laughing matter,' Mr Greaves said,

placing the letter down on the table and removing his spectacles. 'The school does not need such bad publicity. There is a danger that our patrons will withdraw their support, not only from the school but possibly from the hospital as well.'

'They wouldn't do that, surely,' Emily gasped out, suddenly aware of the full impact of the letter. 'These women wouldn't ruin all those people's lives just because Kitty made a silly joke and upset one woman?'

'I have no doubt that they will. We need to do something before this gets out of hand,' Mr Greaves said, tapping the letter. 'That is why I called you here today.'

'Do we know who is in this group?' Jackson asked, his slow drawl suggesting he could see an easy solution to the problem.

'Yes, I had my assistant make some inquiries and he has compiled a list. They are mainly middle-class women whose husbands are businessmen, lawyers, bankers and so forth.'

Mr Greaves rustled through the papers in front of him, found the one he was looking for and handed it to Jackson.

Jackson scanned down the list and scoffed. 'I know several of these men, including John Turnbull, the husband of the esteemed and outraged leader of the moral guardians. They are members of some of the somewhat less than reputable gentlemen's clubs I have also been known to frequent.'

Mr Greaves frowned, as did Emily. They both knew what sort of clubs he was referring to, and neither wished to be reminded that Jackson visited such places. Although Emily suspected Mr Greaves had a different reason to object than Emily did, thinking only of the reputation of the school. But she had always known what sort of man Jackson was. That was why she had chosen him. There was no point being upset about it now.

'Or, should I say, places I used to frequent.' He handed back the list to Mr Greaves. 'So I believe that is your answer.'

Mr Greaves and Emily both shook their heads, waiting for him to explain.

'It means, shall we say, they are men who use the services of women such as Kitty.'

Mr Greaves looked in Emily's direction, his face pained. 'I don't think it is appropriate to—'

'It is all right,' she reassured him. 'Let's just hear what Jack…what the Viscount has to say.'

'They're threatening us, so why not threaten them?'

'I don't think—'

Jackson held up his hand, interrupting Mr Greaves. 'If I make it clear to those men that their less than moral behaviours will be exposed to their morally upright wives if they don't nip this immediately in the bud, or if I inform a few of the more influential women, such as this Mrs Turnbull, that their husband's less than virtuous behaviour will be made public, I am confident this campaign will die an immediate death.'

'You want to blackmail them?' Emily was hardly able to believe what he had said. Randall Cochran had told his friends he intended to take Emily's virginity then blackmail her parents under the threat of making it public. Such behaviour was beneath contempt.

'Yes, all in a good cause.'

'Good cause or not, I cannot countenance that,' Emily said.

'I'm afraid I must agree with Lady Emily,' Mr Greaves

said. 'It would do the school's reputation no good if such an action became public.'

'Then we make sure it doesn't become public,' Jackson said, his nonchalant manner making it clear he could see no moral dilemma in such an action. 'And the ladies and their husbands would have a vested interest in making sure no one ever does find out. That is the beauty of blackmail.'

'No,' Emily repeated. 'That's wrong. Perhaps if Kitty apologises?'

'I did write to Mrs Turnbull and suggest that,' Mr Greaves said. 'She replied that under no circumstances did she want to come into contact with a woman such as Miss Kathryn Trotter.'

Jackson sent Emily a wide-eyed look as if to say, *'See, that is the sort of person we're dealing with.'*

'Perhaps if the Viscount and I apologised and explained that it was merely a joke, a bad joke at that, the likes of which will never happen again,' Emily suggested to Mr Greaves.

'That is a kind offer, but I doubt if even that would assuage this woman. I even suggested in my letter that we expel Miss Trotter to make an example of her.'

'No,' Jackson and Emily said at the same time.

'But even that would not satisfy Mrs Turnbull,' Mr Greaves continued with a shake of his head. 'She said all she would countenance was the expulsion of every woman of lax morals.'

*Which would include me*, Emily thought dolefully.

'That would effectively cause the demise of the school and everything it is trying to do,' she said instead.

'Well, if they want lax morals exposed,' Jackson said, raising his hands, palm upwards, as if he had won the argument, 'then threatening to expose the lax morals of their husbands should do the trick.'

'No,' Emily shot back. That was a level of hypocrisy she would not countenance. While she did not approve of men who used the services of women like Kitty, she would not stoop to the level of blackmail. And if she was being completely honest, her own secrets would make her a good target for a blackmailer. It was a dangerous path to go down, one over which they could easily lose control.

'I have another idea,' she said, looking from one man to the other. 'Let me invite the Ladies for the Promotion of High Moral Standards to an afternoon tea and try and persuade them the school is committed to reforming women and taking them off the street. I am confident I can make them see the school is a force for moral good and something that all upstanding women should support.'

Both men looked at her dubiously, Jackson in particular.

'If you think that will work,' Mr Greaves said uncertainly.

'I'm sure it will,' Emily said, not sure in the slightest, but determined to try.

'Well, I suppose we have nothing to lose by you attempting to change their minds,' Mr Greaves added.

'And if scones and jam don't work, I can always blackmail them,' Jackson said. Emily sent him a stern look, which merely caused him to smile back at her.

Mr Greaves stood up to signal the end of the meeting. They exchanged their goodbyes and Jackson escorted her out of the office, down the staircase and towards her waiting carriage.

'So do we have enough time for a bit of outrageous, immoral and lascivious behaviour of our own? Before you mount your campaign to convince the Ladies for the Promotion of High Moral Standards just how moral and high standing you are,' Jackson said as he took her hand to help her into her carriage.

'Yes, I believe we need a further meeting to discuss our strategy,' Emily replied, the pleasure of anticipation erupting inside her.

'Charles,' she called out to the driver, 'I wish to do a spot of shopping before I return home.'

'Very good, my lady. Would you like to go to the usual shopping arcade?'

'Yes, thank you. I always find their service so satisfying.'

As the door closed she heard Jackson's low chuckle and smiled to herself.

Driving through the busy streets, she reminded herself that this time she really must buy something other than gloves as evidence that she had been on another impromptu shopping excursion. The pile of multi-coloured gloves taking over several shelves in her bedroom cupboard was starting to look a tad questionable. And, after this morning's scare, the last thing she wanted was anyone, including her mother, to start asking questions.

# *Chapter Fifteen*

It was just an afternoon tea, but so much was riding on its success and that was making Emily nervous. She had gathered her friends together, hoping the members of the Ladies for the Promotion of High Moral Standards would be snobs, and the presence of the Duchess of Ravenswood, the Duchess of Redwood and Lady Amelia would impress them and make them forget all about their campaign.

Gilded invitations on the stationer's most expensive card had been sent out, informing each lady by name that Lady Emily Beaumont invited her to afternoon tea at the Belgrave residence of the Duke and Duchess of Fernwood.

When the women started to arrive Emily could see immediately that such a ploy was having the desired effect. The women were all dressed in their finery of silk, satin and chenille gowns in a bright array of colours. Elaborate hats bedecked with ostrich feathers, lace and ribbons sat proudly on their heads, and Emily could only wonder at the expertise of the milliners who had created these fantastical concoctions.

The women entered the drawing room and were conspicuously on their best behaviour. Tea was sipped with pinkies extended as far as it was possible for fingers to go, backs remained ramrod straight, noses were held firmly in the air and pretentious smiles adorned every lip.

Emily was sure some had even adopted contrived aristocratic accents for the occasion.

Irene, Georgina and Amelia were also on their best behaviour, taking their role of gracious aristocrats seriously, and chatting and laughing with each and every woman. Emily was heartened to see the women were finding this attention flattering.

It was perfect, and she was determined to prove Jackson wrong. When they'd been lying in each other's arms he had still maintained that blackmail could achieve so much more and a lot faster than fancy cakes and cucumber sandwiches ever could. She had responded that the diplomatic approach might take longer but it resulted in everyone being pleased with the outcome, and no one got hurt.

He had wished her good luck but had remained unconvinced.

Now all she had to do was prove that she was indeed capable of diplomacy.

Several maids circled the room, making sure each woman had everything she needed, that her cup was filled and her plate overflowing with an array of delicious treats.

'You are so lucky to have such attentive and polite staff,' Mrs Turnbull said to Emily as she smothered more cream on her scone. 'The servant problem is really becoming something of a trial.'

This elicited nods of agreement from the assembled ladies.

'And your cook is simply marvellous,' another woman added. 'My cook makes scones that would be better used as door stops.'

The women all tittered their agreement.

'Yes, I had heard there was a servant shortage,' Emily said, shaking her head in sympathy. She could have added that if the women were prepared to pay decent wages and provide good working conditions they might not struggle to find staff, but this afternoon was about diplomacy, not lecturing.

'Oh, indeed there is,' Mrs Turnbull added, shaking her head mournfully. 'A terrible shortage. Something really needs to be done about it.'

'That is why The Women's Education Institute includes lessons on an array of domestic skills,' Emily said, pleased that Mrs Turnbull had provided her with the perfect opportunity to discuss the reason for the afternoon tea.

Mrs Turnbull's lips grew thin, but before she could speak Emily rushed on.

'I'm sure you'll be interested to know the afternoon tea you have just enjoyed was prepared by young ladies from our cooking, baking and pastry courses.'

The women all looked at the scones, pastries and sandwiches they were eating and frowned, their looks suggesting they were wondering whether eating such light and fluffy delicacies meant they were now morally contaminated.

Emily forced herself to keep smiling in her most benign manner. 'I know what you are all thinking,' she said, knowing no such thing. 'You're all wishing you could hire the pastry cook and have her create such impressive fare when you host your own afternoon teas.'

No one agreed with her, but no one disagreed either, which had to be a good sign.

'But I'm afraid I have to disappoint you. The young

woman who made the pastries has been offered a job at the estate of the Duchess of Redcliff, so you won't be able to poach her for your own staff,' Emily added with a small laugh as if she had made a joke.

'I'm so sorry, ladies,' Irene said. 'I'm afraid I have a terrible sweet tooth and once I tasted the cook's Victoria sponge I just had to hire her.'

This caused renewed twittering from the ladies. Emily nodded to the maid, to indicate she should serve each woman more cakes and pastries. They immediately commenced eating, presumably under the assumption that if a duchess could trust the cook, then the cakes were probably safe to eat.

'And the maids who are doing such a marvellous job today are all students in our domestic science classes at the training school.'

The women looked at the young ladies moving unobtrusively among the guests, dressed in black gowns and perfectly starched white aprons and caps. There was not a hair out of place among them and certainly not a painted face to be seen anywhere.

'You have done an admirable job,' Mrs Turnbull said to Emily, but her tight-lipped expression contradicted her compliment and indicated a threat to come. 'But I for one would not give house room to a woman who had proven herself to be of low moral character.'

Taking their lead from Mrs Turnbull, the other women nodded their agreement and several placed their now empty plates on a side table, as if in protest.

Emily forced herself not to react but to continue smiling, all the while wondering whether Jackson might be correct.

Perhaps now might be a good time to drop a hint or two regarding Mr Turnbull's night-time excursions.

'I agree,' another of the moral guardians said. 'Men can be led astray so easily by a wanton woman. Such women should be punished for the harm they cause to men who would otherwise not fall from the path of morality, and for the harm those women cause to their families.'

Emily swallowed her annoyance and tilted her head as if listening to the woman's outrage with interest.

'Yes,' another moral lady added. 'Such women need to be made to see the error of their ways, not rewarded for their moral turpitude with training and jobs in fancy country estates.' This was greeted by another round of nodding from the women.

Mrs Turnbull sent Emily a condescending smile. 'I know you mean well, but it is essential that such women are provided with strict moral guidance. They need to be taught the difference between right and wrong, and need to be made aware it is essential they repent and pay the wages of their sins.'

The nodding continued.

'I agree entirely,' Emily said, causing her friends to send her surprised looks. 'That is why we have several clergymen on the board of directors for the school. They also provide religious instructions and guidance for the students.'

Emily saw no need to add that all these clergymen were compassionate and non-judgemental. Like Emily, they saw no need to punish women who had already suffered so much, and they only had the students' well-being at heart.

'I am pleased to hear that,' Mrs Turnbull said. 'And that is no less than I would expect. Someone needs to address these women's lack of moral rectitude and ensure they are redressing their sinful pasts.'

She looked down at the fluffy scone on her plate, and her expression softened slightly, before once again becoming stern. 'Lady Emily, your promises that the school will take a high moral stance at all times and that any straying from the path of righteousness will in future be severely dealt with has provided me with some reassurance.'

Emily hadn't quite given that assurance, but now was no time to quibble over details, not when victory appeared to be at hand.

'Therefore, I believe the Ladies for the Promotion of High Moral Standards can find other areas in this sinful city on which to focus our good and essential work.'

Emily released a held breath and smiled at Mrs Turnbull.

'But rest assured,' Mrs Turnbull continued, raising one finger and pointing it at Emily, 'I personally will be monitoring the school. At the first sign of any moral lapses, my ladies and I will resume our campaign to have the school closed with renewed vigour.'

'Thank you. That of course is to be expected,' Emily said.

'So, now that that is settled,' one of the moral guardians said, 'are any of these young women looking for work?' She eyed the young maids lined up against the serving table, who all stared straight ahead, their bodies rigid, as if to say, *Please do not pick me*.

'Unfortunately, these young women are still receiving training,' Emily said and could see the young maids' shoulders relax as they drew in relieved breaths. 'But if you wish you can make inquiries at the school.'

Inquiries that will be ignored, as none of the students

deserve to be subjected to such intolerance and harsh judgement from their future employers.

The woman smiled at Emily, thinking all her servant problems had been solved.

The afternoon tea continued in a congenial manner, with the moral guardians taking every opportunity to inform Emily and her friends just how sinful London was, and how easy it was to slip off the pathway of righteousness. Emily continued to nod and smile, and resisted the temptation to mention the decidedly unrighteous gentlemen's clubs that their husbands were reputed to frequent.

When the afternoon tea came to an end, and the footman finally showed the ladies out and into their waiting carriages, Emily and her friends slumped back into their chairs, exhausted from so much false smiling and forced civility.

'You were all marvellous,' Emily said to her friends and the maids. 'I believe we've just saved the school.'

Maids and friends joined in a rousing cheer.

'And after all your hard work, I believe you deserve your own afternoon tea,' she said to the maids. 'I've asked the cook to make sure there are plenty of treats left over and they're waiting for you down in the kitchen.'

The maids wasted no time clearing away the tea service and departing. As the door closed behind them, giggling erupted along with much joking and teasing about which one of them was the biggest sinner and who was destined for the worst type of damnation.

'I don't know about you ladies, but I for one need a stiff drink after that,' Georgina said, rising from her chair and pouring four glasses of brandy before anyone had answered.

She handed the glasses to her friends, then raised hers above her head. 'Here's to slipping off the path of righteousness and falling into a world of vice and sin.' She took a deep swig of her brandy, sighed, then refilled her glass. 'Long may it continue.'

'Speaking of sin and vice, how is Jackson Wilde?' Irene asked.

Emily almost spluttered on her brandy. 'Jackson Wilde?' she asked, as if unsure who they were talking about.

'We've seen so little of you recently and we've all been dying to ask,' Georgina added. 'We had been hoping you would reveal all before now, but you've been playing your cards rather close to your chest.'

Emily stared at her friends, who were smiling back at her as if all party to the same secret.

'You all know?'

'Well, we don't know the details,' Amelia said. 'But we all saw the two of you together at the fundraising ball. And you have been decidedly conspicuous in your absence over the last—what would it be since the ball, six months?'

The other women nodded.

'I've called at your house a number of times over the last few months and your mother always says you're in a meeting with the Viscount, either that or shopping for gloves,' Amelia added.

'Gloves,' Georgina said with a laugh. 'That's an interesting name for it.'

'And you bounced back remarkably quickly from the end of your involvement with Gideon Pratt,' Amelia added. 'To my mind that usually means there's another man involved.'

As one, her three friends leant forward, all looking at Emily in expectation.

'So, are you going to tell us what's happening, or are we going to have to drag it out of you?' Georgina said, looking as if that was exactly what she wanted to do.

'Oh, all right, I'll tell you the whole story, and thank goodness the Ladies for the Promotion of High Moral Standards have left, otherwise they would be scandalised.'

'Oh, goody,' Georgina said, topping up everyone's brandy glasses. 'There's nothing I enjoy more than a good scandal, so don't leave out a single detail.'

# Chapter Sixteen

Jackson waited in his carriage, discreetly parked up the street from Emily's parents' home, anxious to hear how the meeting went. He watched those self-righteous old dragons leave the house, smiling and simpering as they chatted on the doorstep, their extravagant hats perched like exotic birds on the top of their heads, bobbing along with the conversation. Then, with repeated calls of goodbye and much waving of gloved hands, they climbed into their carriages and drove away.

He was unsure whether smiling and simpering was a good or bad thing when it came to dragons. Did that mean they were joyfully preparing for battle and the destruction of the school? Or did it mean Emily had managed to negotiate a diplomatic solution and they had happily driven away never to be seen again?

As much as he liked the thought of indulging in a bit of well-placed blackmail and threatening to expose the level of their hypocrisy, he hoped it was the latter, and Emily's scones and cream had worked their magic.

Once the street was clear of carriages, he waited a few moments longer in case there was a straggler or two. No one else emerged from the house, so he knocked on the door and informed the footman he wished to see Lady

Emily. It was his first visit to her parents' house since the ball, which did go against his strict rule of never ever meeting his mistresses outside of his rooms, but today he would make an exception. This was about the school, and he knew he wouldn't rest until he heard the outcome of her meeting.

'Lady Emily is in the drawing room,' the footman said. 'Please wait here and I will announce you.'

'No need to trouble yourself,' Jackson said. 'I'll find my own way.' He looked up the black and white tiled entranceway with its array of doors and frowned.

'It is the fourth door on the right,' the footman said, seeing his predicament. 'The one that has been left ajar.'

Jackson nodded his thanks and approached the door. His progress was stopped by the sound of female voices. Damn, not all the moralistic viragos had left. A few must have found some remaining fire and brimstone that they still had to cast far and wide.

It was time for Jackson to make a quick and tactical retreat before his presence reinforced for the remaining harridans that the school was a den of vice, and only they could save the world from its corrupting influence.

His shoes squeaked on the highly polished tiles and he froze, his breath held. No incensed crones came rushing out armed with pitchforks and burning torches, so he released his held breath and took another quieter step forward.

'We just knew there was something going on between you and Jackson Wilde,' an unfamiliar woman's voice said, halting his progress and causing his breath to once more catch in his throat. 'But we didn't know things had gone quite so far.'

This was a disaster. It would take a lot more than a few

diplomatic scones to save the school now. He waited for the remaining vipers to start convulsing with paroxysms of moral outrage over their relationship, then threaten to burn down the school, with Emily and Jackson in it.

'You really are a dark horse, aren't you?' another woman said, the amusement in her voice sounding anything but outraged. 'And I must admit, Jackson Wilde is, how shall we say?'

Jackson quietly moved closer to the door, wondering what Jackson Wilde was.

'A bit more exciting than Dr Gideon Pratt,' the woman added.

This caused the other women to laugh. It was a compliment, but not much of one. You didn't have to be particularly exciting to be more exciting than Pratt. Nor was it a conversation that Emily was likely to have with the moralising women. It was evident she was chatting to her friends. About him. He should leave. Even though he was the one under discussion, it was a private conversation and to eavesdrop would be an invasion of her privacy, the height of bad manners.

He leant in closer towards the open door.

'I must admit, I had my doubts about you marrying Dr Pratt,' a woman said. Jackson nodded at the astute woman's comment. 'I know you thought him upstanding, dedicated and all that, but well.' She paused. Jackson could have added, *'But the man was a social climbing bore and his treatment of Emily was beneath contempt.'*

'He was a little *too* upstanding,' she added. It seemed Emily wasn't the only one dedicated to diplomacy.

'So how is, you know, with Jackson Wilde?' another female voice asked. This was a question to which Jackson would also be interested in hearing the answer, assuming he and the woman speaking meant the same thing by 'you know'.

'It's good.'

Then again, perhaps he'd rather not hear Emily's answer.

'Oh, all right, it's very good.'

That was better he supposed, but still, not exactly a ringing endorsement.

'Oh, all right, yes, it's wonderful. He makes me feel things I did not know it was possible to feel. Sometimes I just have to think about him and my body starts to react as if I can feel his touch. It's as if I can't get enough of him. He really is the most magnificent lover.'

A chorus of female voices sighed.

That was more like it. Jackson would like to believe his pleasure in hearing those words was because it was further confirmation that he was satisfying Emily, but he knew his smugness was simply due to his prowess in the bedroom being admired.

'So where to now with Jackson Wilde?' another voice asked.

That too was a question Jackson was also interested in having answered.

'Nowhere,' Emily stated emphatically. 'It's just some harmless fun. It means nothing to either of us.'

Those words should have held no surprise for Jackson. Emily was saying nothing he didn't already know. That had been the agreement when they first became involved. She had promised to make no demands on him, to have no expectations. So why did hearing her repeat it now in such a dispassionate manner make him feel like he had just been punched in the stomach?

'Are you sure?' the interrogator asked. 'It's not like you to be so cavalier. You've always been, shall we say, somewhat intense.'

'Well, people can change,' Emily stated. 'I've changed. Haven't I? No one, including the three of you, who know me so well, would have thought I could ever become the lover of a man like Jackson Wilde.'

This drew murmurs of agreement, and Jackson was hoping they would ask what she meant by 'a man like Jackson Wilde', even though he suspected he already knew what the answer would be. No one asked that question.

'After I realised what Gideon was really like, how he was using me, and how he was more interested in my connections than he ever was in me, I decided I was done with men and marriage,' Emily continued. 'No more looking for the right man. That was why I became involved with Jackson.'

Because he was not the right man? So if he wasn't right what was he? Wrong?

'Was it because Dr Pratt hurt you so badly?' a woman asked quietly. 'Did you take up with Jackson Wilde so you could get over him?'

Jackson's mood sunk even lower. Surely he was not merely a sop for her to recover from Pratt. His previously puffed-up masculine pride could not have deflated further if Emily had taken to it with a hat pin.

'No, not really,' Emily said, giving him some hope. 'My feelings for Gideon were deluded. It was such a shock to discover I had done it again. I had once again been deluded into thinking a man was the person he pretended to be, just as I did with Randall Cochran, only this time it was worse. The signs were all there showing me what Gideon was really like, but I'd convinced myself they weren't, because I wanted him to be the perfect husband for me. He wasn't lying to me. I was lying to myself. What happened with Gideon merely reinforced the lesson I should have learnt with Randall. I am a terrible judge of character when it comes to men. But at least with Jackson I know exactly what he is like.'

Jackson held his breath, sure that what he was about to hear would not be something he would like.

'He's a philanderer, a man incapable of committing to one woman,' Emily said, confirming his suspicions. 'He's the sort of man no sensible woman would ever think of marrying.'

'But if you changed, can't he change as well?' a woman asked.

Emily laughed as if someone had made a joke. 'Not Jackson Wilde. That man will never change.'

The room went quiet, then a woman asked. 'Emily, are you sure about this? Isn't there a danger that you might fall in love with him, despite what you say?'

'No, never,' she stated, her voice loud. 'That is why I picked him, because I knew I could never fall in love with such a man. In choosing Jackson I could, well, to not put too fine a point on it, I could enjoy all the pleasures a woman can experience with a man without risking my heart.'

Jackson slumped back against the wall. Everything she was saying was the truth. He was the sort of man no sensible woman should fall in love with, and women didn't get much more sensible than Emily. But that did not make the words any less painful to hear.

'But do be careful,' the same woman added, her voice

full of concern. 'We all know how easy it is to fall hopelessly for a man you think is wrong for you.'

This caused a murmur of agreement from all present. All, he assumed, except Emily.

'We all saw how upset you were over Randall Cochran,' the woman continued. 'We'd hate to see you have your heart broken again.'

Emily laughed dismissively. 'I had hoped to marry Randall, and yes I was hurt when I discovered he had no feelings for me. But I have no such aspirations with Jackson.'

'But that doesn't mean you can't have your heart broken. We're pleased that you're having fun, but we just don't want Jackson Wilde to hurt you.'

Jackson wanted to burst into the room and inform these women that he would move heaven and earth to ensure Emily was never hurt. How could he possibly hurt the woman he loved?

He placed his hands against the wall to steady himself as the full implication of that thought crashed down on him.

Love?

He was in love with Emily Beaumont.

That was what he was feeling. That was why he thought about her constantly. That was why he missed her so intensely, even when they were only apart for a short time. That was why everything about her delighted and entranced him.

He loved her.

And that was why her words cut through him like a rapier.

He was in love and suspected he had always been in love with her. For him, what had happened between them had never been just fun. From the first time he had made love to her it had been something much deeper, much more profound. It had been love. He just hadn't realised it.

He had fallen in love with a woman who saw him as a man not worth loving, a man no sensible woman marries, a man who was only good for having fun with. Once that was how he would have described himself as well. Once he would have hoped that any woman he took as his mistress would see him that way. But not now. Not when it came to Emily.

'Jackson won't hurt me,' Emily stated, and Jackson was relieved that at least she saw him as possessing one virtue. 'Nor will he break my heart,' she added. 'For the simple reason that I am not in love with Jackson Wilde and never will be. As soon as this relationship has run its course I will leave it in my past where it belongs. As I said, it's just nothing more than a bit of fun that means nothing.'

With as much dignity as he possessed, Jackson quietly retraced his steps back down the hallway and out into the street where his carriage was waiting. Hardly aware of anything around him, he told the carriage driver to go, not caring where it took him, just knowing he had to escape.

Emily was unsure who she was trying to convince more, herself or her friends. Whichever it was, it wasn't working. Her friends' concerned expressions made it clear they didn't believe a word she was saying, and her aching heart made it abundantly clear *she* did not believe a word she was saying either.

'None of that is true,' she whispered, pleased to be finally speaking the truth despite the pain gripping her heart.

'Oh, Emily,' her friends said as one and quickly gathered around her on the settee.

'My relationship with Jackson means more to me than just some harmless fun, so much more. I am such a fool. I've done it again. I've fallen for a completely inappropriate man and this time I knew he was inappropriate, but I fell in love with him anyway.'

Arms wrapped around her as her friends tried to reassure her that she was not a fool.

'I promised myself, and I promised him, that this would mean nothing,' she said, taking a handkerchief from Georgina's outstretched hand and wiping her eyes. 'I said all it would be was fun, and it *has* been fun, but it has also been so much more than that. For me at least.'

'You can't help what your heart does,' Irene said. 'Is that why you fell in love with him, because being with him was so much fun?'

Emily smiled and nodded through her tears. 'When we're together he makes me laugh so much. It's wonderful. Never before have I felt so carefree and joyful as when I'm with him.' She swallowed a sob that was neither joyful nor carefree. 'But that's not why I fell in love with him.'

The three women tilted their heads, as if asking the same question.

'He's so surprisingly kind. I hadn't thought a man with his reputation could be so kind to everyone he meets, no matter who they are. He was so popular with the other patients in the hospital, and he never treats anyone as if they're beneath him. And he's so brave. Look how he saved Kitty.'

She placed her hand over her heart and looked from one friend to another, each of whom was nodding in agreement.

'And he respects me and what I do.' She shook her head in wonderment. 'That too was a surprise. The school was really his idea, but he involved me right from its inception.' She looked at her friends in question and continued to slowly shake her head. 'How did he know that I would find establishing the school so fulfilling? It's as if he knows me better than I know myself. He could see that I wasn't really needed at the hospital, and was searching for something that would fully engage me. How did he know that?'

She looked from friend to friend, who were all bearing the same knowing look.

'Perhaps he feels the same way about you,' Amelia said. 'Have you asked Jackson how he feels?'

'No,' Emily responded immediately, 'I haven't said anything to him. He knows nothing of any of this, and that is the way I'm going to have to keep it.'

'Is that wise?' Amelia asked, her voice gentle.

Emily nodded, wiped her eyes again, then crumpled the damp handkerchief into a small ball. 'Yes. I don't want to look like a complete idiot in front of him. I've already done that in front of two men and I never want to do that again.' She squeezed the ball tighter. 'I decided to become involved with Jackson because I thought there was no danger of falling in love with him and no danger of making an ass of myself again, because I knew exactly what sort of man he was, and that he was a man I would never want to marry.'

'But things change, people change, feelings change,' Irene said, handing her another dry handkerchief. 'Your feelings for Jackson Wilde have changed. Perhaps his feelings for you have also changed.'

Emily looked at Irene through her damp eyes and wondered whether this could be true.

'And you're never going to know unless you ask him,' Irene added.

'It will take courage,' Georgina said. 'But you've always had plenty of courage.'

Emily was not entirely convinced by that.

'It took a lot of courage to suggest to him that you become lovers, didn't it?' Georgina asked in a soothing voice.

Emily could only nod. It *had* taken an enormous amount of courage, more than she thought she possessed, but that was nothing compared to the amount of courage it would take to expose her feelings to a man who had the power to break her heart.

'And you can be courageous again and find out how he is really feeling,' Georgina added, as if it was all that easy.

'And you're not going to know for certain how he does feel until you do ask,' Irene said, stroking Emily's hand. 'All you're going to do is assume he wants nothing more from your relationship.'

'But if I do tell him how I'm feeling and he's horrified by me wanting more, I might lose him completely.' The thought of that caused the tears to once again well up in her eyes, but she blinked them away. 'Although, I suppose if he doesn't want anything more from me, then I'm going to lose him eventually anyway, when he finally loses interest in me and moves on to the next woman.'

Emily gripped the sodden handkerchiefs tighter, her nails digging into her palms at the thought of Jackson with another woman.

Irene continued to gently stroke her hands until she released their tight clench, while Georgina and Irene once again wrapped their arms around her shoulders. As sad as she felt, she was grateful to have such close friends to share this with.

'I do want to know how he feels,' she confessed. 'But I don't want the pain of finding out he cares nothing for me.' She gave a small, humourless laugh at her predicament. 'I want to know but only if he tells me exactly what I want to hear.'

She looked down at her hands. 'But I supposed one way or another I'm going to find out eventually. By not asking him then I'm only delaying the inevitable. If he leaves it will be heartbreaking, but I've got over heartbreak before, I can do it again. And perhaps it will be better to find out now rather than wait until I'm even more hopelessly in love with him.'

Emily was unsure whether any of that was really true. Yes, she had recovered from finding out that Randall Cochran was not the man she thought he was, but her heartbreak had been over a man who did not really exist, and a disappointment that she would not have a successful first Season that would end in her becoming a bride. With Jackson she knew exactly what he was like. She was in love with the real Jackson Wilde, with all his faults and flaws. And was it really possible to be even more in love with him than she was now? She doubted that.

'Or you might discover that he is in love with you as well,' Georgina said, always the optimist.

She smiled at her well-meaning friend. 'Perhaps. But you're right. I'm never going to know until I ask him. So I'll do it. I will ask him how he feels about me, whether we have a future together and what that future will entail.'

Her smile started to quiver as her friends held her closely, and she wondered whether she would actually be able to be true to those brave words.

# Chapter Seventeen

The letter from Mr Greaves requesting Jackson's presence at a meeting at the school could only be about one thing; the outcome of Emily's attempt to cajole the Ladies for the Promotion of High Moral Standards into dropping their ridiculous campaign. He still didn't know whether she had succeeded or not, and he wanted to find out what, if anything, the ladies had planned. He just wished he did not need to see Emily again in order to do so.

It was ironic that only a day ago he lived to be with her again, but one day could change everything. One day ago, he didn't realise what he was feeling was love. One day ago, he did not know that the woman he was in love with did not feel the same way about him. He did not know that he was of so little importance to her. He did not know he was nothing more than a passing diversion.

If he'd heard any of his previous mistresses talking in such a manner he would have been relieved that they wanted no more from the relationship than he did.

But Emily was different. How he felt about her was different.

Now he was going to see her again, knowing the truth about how she felt about him and aware of the depth of his feelings for her. Feelings that were not reciprocated.

This was going to require a level of fortitude he was unsure he possessed.

He arrived at the board room slightly later than the time Mr Greaves had arranged, finding endless reasons to delay his arrival. He entered to find Emily and Mr Greaves waiting for him. Mr Greaves was smiling, fit to burst, making it obvious what he was going to say. Emily's expression was less easy to read. Nothing should have changed for her, and yet her expression was, what? Tentative? Shy? Whatever it was, it was not his place to try and analyse what was going through her mind about the meeting with the moral ladies. He knew her mind when it came to him, and that was all that concerned him.

He made his greetings and sat down.

'I was just telling Lady Emily the wonderful news,' Mr Greaves said, holding up a letter and waving it in the air triumphantly. 'We had another note from Mrs Turnbull, this time singing the praises of the school.'

'That's excellent news,' he said with as much enthusiasm as he could muster. And it *was* excellent news. The school was safe. Kitty and all the other girls and women attending the school could continue to pursue new lives. They wouldn't be stuck in the dire circumstances that had been forced on them by lack of opportunity.

'Congratulations, Lady Emily,' Jackson said with a polite nod. 'Your approach has proven to be the correct one and you are to be commended.'

'Hear, hear,' Mr Greaves added, smiling at Emily, before his expression turned more serious. 'But we're not entirely out of the woods,' he continued. 'Mrs Turnbull does say that she and her ladies will be monitoring the school and, should they detect any sign of scandal, inappropriate or immoral behaviour from anyone at the school—students, teachers and board members included—they will not hesitate to mount a campaign to have the school closed.'

Jackson made a point of not looking in Emily's direction and hoped she was doing the same. If those moralistic ladies got even a hint of what had been occurring between them it would be the end of the school, not to mention the destruction of Emily's reputation. They were risking so much, and all for what she described as meaningless fun.

'I believe in that case it might be wisest if I tender my resignation from the fundraising committee,' Jackson said, surprising himself.

'Why?' Emily said, rising slightly from her chair.

'That is most unfortunate,' Mr Greaves said with a frown. 'And I don't believe it is necessary.'

Mr Greaves obviously did not read the scandal sheets, or perhaps he did and had noticed Jackson's absence from them over the last six or so months and erroneously thought him a reformed man.

'Be that as it may, I still wish to resign.'

'I am so disappointed to hear that,' Mr Greaves said, shaking his head. 'You have been a marvellous asset to the school, simply marvellous. The school owes its very existence to you. It was your idea and you and Lady Emily have been the driving force to get it started.'

Jackson smoothed down a non-existent wrinkle in his trousers, being unfamiliar with such adulation and not sure how one was supposed to react.

'Is there anything I can do or say to make you change your mind?' Mr Greaves continued. 'You will be such a great loss to the school.'

It was kind of the elderly gentleman, but if he knew

Jackson's real character he would not be so quick to praise him, and would be enthusiastically welcoming Jackson's resignation.

'No, I'm afraid my mind is made up,' Jackson said.

'Lady Emily, perhaps you can change his mind,' Mr Greaves said, looking at Emily in appeal.

'Nothing can change my mind,' he interjected before she could say anything. 'I am afraid there are things in my past that the ladies could use to damage the school's reputation.'

'But that's all in the past,' Emily said. 'They can hardly fault anyone for what they did in the past. And isn't that what this school is all about, giving people a fresh start, letting them put past mistakes behind them?' She looked from him to Mr Greaves, who nodded his agreement.

'I doubt if the moralising ladies would see it that way.' Jackson countered.

*And it's not exactly in the past, is it?* he could have added.

'So you're going to let *them* blackmail *you*?' Emily said, looking somewhat irate.

'I'm going to make sure they're not in a position to blackmail the school,' he said, not wishing to argue about this, particularly here in this office. 'My mind is made up,' he said, turning back to Mr Greaves.

'As you wish,' the older man said. 'It is very disappointing, of course, but I can see you have done so for the highest motives.'

Jackson winced. He had done so because he did not wish to spend time with a woman he loved, a woman who saw him as nothing more than someone to pass the occasional enjoyable afternoon with, not a man she could ever take seriously.

The meeting over, he escorted Emily out to her carriage,

knowing he not only had to cut ties with the school, but also with her, if he was to ever shake off the despondency that had possessed him since he overheard that conversation.

'I believe we should have our own meeting so we can further discuss your resignation,' she said, as he helped her into her carriage.

Instead of giving his usual enthusiastic response, he climbed into the carriage beside her. 'We can have that discussion here and now,' he said.

'Oh, yes, well, I suppose we could,' she said, looking around at the interior of the carriage, her brow furrowed.

Jackson drew in a deep breath and tried to compose the words he planned to say to her, words he both wanted and didn't want to say.

She waited. He prevaricated. If he said nothing, if he pretended he had not overheard what she had said to her friends, would that be so bad?

If he ignored what he'd heard, if he ignored how he felt, they could go straight to his rooms. He could have her naked, in his bed, writhing under him, giving him the exquisite pleasure only she could provide. But then she would leave, and he would have to continue dealing with the truth. He would not be able to ignore that the woman he loved would never see the time they were together as anything more than an enjoyable past-time. And every time he thought of that, the pain he would feel would only intensify. No, he had to be strong and end this. Now.

'I also believe it would be best if we no longer see each other.'

Her eyes grew enormous and her mouth opened in an unspoken *'oh'*. He was tempted to retract that statement, to tell her he did not mean it, that he wanted her, wanted her desperately. But he would not be a coward.

'It has been fun, Emily,' he said, cringing at that word, a word that had wounded him so deeply. A word that summed up all that their relationship had ever been for her. 'But I believe it has run its course.'

Wasn't that what she had said to her friends, that it would eventually run its course and it would be over?

'Oh, I see,' she said, staring straight ahead.

'We both knew this would happen eventually, didn't we?'

'Yes, we did.'

'And we've had our fun, haven't we?'

'Yes,' she responded, not looking at him.

'So, what with everything that has happened at the school, and the moralistic women's threats, now is probably a good time to end things.'

'Yes.'

'We both agreed this would only ever be a dalliance and that neither of us would take it seriously.' *An agreement I broke.* 'So I believe it is time we gave each other the freedom to pursue other relationships.'

She took a quick look in his direction, then resumed staring straight ahead. 'Is there another relationship you wish to pursue?' she asked.

'What? No, not at the moment. No.'

'I see,' she said, looking down at her hands clasped tightly in her lap. 'Not at the moment, but you hope to pursue another relationship sometime soon?'

'I haven't really thought about it.'

*And doubt I ever will.*

'But you too will be free to pursue other relationships.'

*One that is more than just fun...one where you love the man as much as he loves you.*

'I will never have another relationship with a man,' she said quietly, looking down at her hands, still clenched tightly together.

'You don't have to worry,' he said, wishing he could take her in his arms and reassure her. 'No one knows about us. No one will ever know. As far as all of Society is concerned you are still a chaste young woman who is above reproach. There is no reason why you can't enter into another relationship, one that could lead to marriage.'

*To a man you consider worthy of marriage, a condition that excludes me.*

'I don't wish to marry anyone else,' she murmured. 'I told you that when we first—well, when we first became lovers.'

Jackson closed his eyes briefly and drew in a deep breath. She still wanted to be his lover, but that was no longer enough for him. He could not weaken now. He had to be strong.

'That might change,' he said, pleased his controlled voice revealed nothing of his inner turmoil. 'Situations change. People change.'

*God knows I've changed since I met you.*

'Yes, I suppose I have changed. Knowing you has changed me,' she said, still staring down at her hands.

Her response mirrored his own feelings and he was curious to know what she meant, but he would not allow himself to get sidetracked. He needed to end this as quickly as possible before he waivered.

'And with those moralising ladies still on the rampage

we need to exercise more caution,' he continued. 'If our relationship became public it would destroy your reputation.'

'I don't care what they or anyone else thinks of me.'

'Well, if you don't care about it for your own sake, you should care about it for the sake of the school.' He really was a pompous ass. Who was he to sound so superior and judgemental? He had not resigned purely to save the school. It was so he did not have to see her again. And he was not calling off their relationship because he was worried the moralising ladies would find out. He was doing it for his own selfish reasons. It was all to protect himself, so he would not have to continue to feel this crushing pain every time he looked at her.

'You do understand, don't you, Emily?' he continued, sounding even more high and mighty. 'It would be best for the school. We don't want our behaviour to place the school in jeopardy.'

'Yes, I suppose you're right.'

Jackson hated himself for the way he was speaking to her. This was the woman he loved, the woman he had shared countless blissful afternoons with, the woman he had made love to, who he had held in his arms and shared his private innermost thoughts and feelings. Now he was ending their relationship as if it was something he cared little about, when he cared deeply. Too deeply. But it had to be done. And there was no point letting Emily know just how miserable he was.

She was a kind woman. That was one of the many reasons he loved her so. If Emily knew how much pain he was in he knew he would have her pity, but he did not want her pity. He wanted her love, and that was something he could never have.

He looked over at her as he made ready to leave, wondering how he was to say goodbye. Did he kiss her? No. Apart from the fact he was unsure how he would react if he once more felt the touch of her lips, they were in a public place. Anyone walking by could see them. A kiss on the hand? Surely that would not be misconstrued. But he did not trust himself. Even the touch of her skin might undermine his resolve.

Did he merely bow his head and wish her well? It was so formal and faintly ridiculous after all that they had shared. But he had to leave. He could not remain sitting here, staring at her for an eternity.

'Goodbye, then, Jackson,' she said, once again staring straight ahead.

He remained sitting still for a second or so, then climbed out and watched as the carriage drove out the gates, down the road and out of sight. He turned and walked towards his own carriage.

It was over. It was now time to get back to the life he had lived before he had met Lady Emily Beaumont, although right now he could no longer remember what that life had entailed.

Emily's mind and body remained numb as she drove home. She saw nothing of the chaotic traffic outside her carriage window. The passing houses, the shouts of drivers, the whinnies of horses were all a blur. All her mind was focused on was trying to digest what had just happened. She desperately tried to remember all that he had said, but the words kept whirling round in her head and refused to settle.

The only thing she knew for certain was that it was

over. Jackson didn't want her. He didn't want her in his life any more.

The carriage pulled up in front of her home. As if in a trance, she climbed out and looked up at the house, hardly recognising it. What did she do now? She had been expecting to attend a meeting, bathe in the praise of Mr Greaves and Jackson for saving the school and then celebrate that victory in private with Jackson. Then she would return home to her parents, her mind and body singing after an afternoon of bliss. She had even intended, if the time was right, to confess to him her true feelings and bare her soul. That was some consolation, she supposed. He had broken things off before she had completely humiliated herself and told a man who was now tired of her that she had done what she promised she would never do—she'd fallen in love with him.

She took a step up the path and stopped. If she went inside now, feeling as she did, her mother would know something was wrong. She was bound to ask, and Emily was incapable of thinking of a credible, yet false, reason to explain why she was so distressed.

'Please take me to Lady Amelia's home,' she told the carriage driver and climbed back inside the cab. As the editor of a successful women's magazine, Amelia was often at her business premises during the day, but Emily hoped she would be at home. If she wasn't, she would wait for her, she'd hide away until she had a chance to come to terms with this shocking news and was able to face the world, and her mother, again.

She was greeted by the footman who informed her that Lady Amelia was indeed at home today. Not waiting for the footman to announce her, she rushed down the hall-way to the drawing room.

'What is it? What's wrong? Is it the school?' Amelia asked, standing up from her desk and rushing towards Emily, her arms outstretched.

All Emily was capable of doing was shake her head.

'Is it Jackson?' she added, quietly.

Emily nodded. Just as Amelia encased her in her arms the tears she had been holding back flooded from her eyes. No longer numb, the full force of her feelings crashed down on her, making her weak as her friend led her to the nearest chair and held her as she cried herself out.

Her tears finally drying, she sat up and wiped her eyes.

'I'm so sorry,' Amelia said. 'Do you want to tell me what happened?'

Emily took in a few slow breaths, her hand on her heart as if that could reduce the intensity of the pain. 'He's finished with me.'

'Oh, no. I'm so sorry,' Amelia repeated.

'I don't know why I'm so upset. I knew it would happen one day.'

Amelia said nothing, but Emily was sure she knew what she was thinking.

'Yes, I know. I've been shown up as naïve and gullible, yet again. I've again set my sights on the wrong man. And this time I've been even more of an imbecile. I've actually fallen in love with a man I knew from the very start was wrong for me.'

Amelia continued to say nothing, merely lightly rubbed Emily's back.

'I, of all people, should have known better. I had thought Randall and Gideon were right for me, but I'd been wrong.

That had hurt, but I suspect it was more my pride being damaged that caused my pain. But this is different.' She placed her hand on her stomach to ease the pain. 'This is unbearable.'

Amelia wrapped an arm around her and Emily placed her head on her shoulder.

'And worse than that, I knew he was the wrong man for me, right from the start,' she continued. 'He never tried to deceive me about his true nature. That's the very reason why I set my sights on him. Because he was so wrong for me. I knew, or at least thought, I could never fall in love with such a man. I am such a fool.'

'You're not a fool, Emily, and you're certainly not the only woman who has fallen in love with the wrong man. The heart doesn't always do what the head commands.'

'But I really thought my head was in control,' Emily said, sitting up straighter and trying to make sense of how this had happened to her. 'Until it wasn't. Somehow, somewhere my heart took over and I stopped thinking rationally. I forgot who Jackson really was. I forgot what our relationship was really all about. It was all so illogical. Did I imagine it would go on for ever, even though I always knew it wouldn't? That to my mind is the very definition of a fool, someone who knows what is real but refuses to believe it.'

'No, that's the definition of someone who has fallen in love only to have their heart broken.'

'Well, I don't want to be a fool. I won't be a fool.'

Amelia held her top lip with her teeth, as if holding back the words she wanted to say. But there were no words that would convince Emily she was wrong. She had fallen for the wrong man, again, but she would get over that disappointment. Again.

She was a sensible woman, more than capable of over-coming hardships and putting them behind her. And that was exactly what she would do now. She would triumph over this adversity and become all the stronger for it.

'Well, thank you for our talk and all your good advice,' Emily said, making ready to leave. 'I will just have to get on with my life. It's not as if this is unexpected. It had to happen eventually. It's all a bit silly of me to take it so badly. I suppose it was because I wasn't expecting it to happen today. But I knew it had to happen one day and that's what I'd hoped for really. As Jackson said, we've had our fun. Now it's over and it's time to return to our real lives.'

She shrugged as if it were all that easy. 'I thought I was in love, but, well, I'm not the first woman to think she's in love. I'll get over it. Other women have got over heartache, and I will do the same.'

She nodded, determined that her statement would be true. 'And one thing I can say about Jackson, he might be a man who moves from one woman to another without a backward glance, but at least he is discreet. I suppose he's had to learn how to be.' She swallowed down those pesky tears that were threatening to fall. 'No one will ever know about what happened between us.'

Amelia looked at her with sad eyes, as if not convinced by her confident words.

'Don't worry, Amelia,' she said, patting her friend's hand in reassurance. 'I'm perfectly fine now. It was just the shock of it happening so suddenly when I was looking forward to spending more time with him. In fact, it's all for the best that it has finally happened. I really haven't been dedicating nearly as much time to the school as I would like. I can now throw myself into that worthy cause, heart and soul.'

She stood up, stuffed her sodden handkerchief back into her reticule and lifted her chin. 'Thank you so much for listening to all my prattling.'

'Perhaps you would like to come to afternoon tea tomorrow,' Amelia said gently, also standing and taking hold of both her hands. 'I'll invite Georgina and Irene.'

'Yes, that will be lovely. It will be so good to catch up with them and find out what they've been up to. We didn't have much time to really chat last time. I rather monopolised the conversation, I'm afraid.' She gave a small dismissive laugh, as if her confession that she had fallen in love with Jackson was a mere folly. 'Yes, I've been far too preoccupied lately and have neglected my friends.' Emily pulled her watch out of her reticule and frowned at it. 'But I really must be going. I have so much to do.'

Amelia escorted her to the door and out to her waiting carriage. 'If you want to talk, anytime, please don't hesitate,' Amelia said and kissed her lightly on the cheek. It was kind of her, but Emily could see no point in talking further about what had happened between her and Jackson. It was over. It was time to put all this behind her and focus on what was important in her life.

# Chapter Eighteen

Jackson had never been one to look back and he was determined not to start now. It was over, as he knew it one day would be. It was time to get back to enjoying his life in the manner he had done for all his adult life. Wine, women and song would replace worthy causes, one woman and sensual afternoons. No, forget the last one. He would not think about those afternoons he spent with Emily. He would forget all about her, as he was sure she would forget all about him, if she hadn't done so already.

Yes, it was definitely time to get back to those women, that wine and perhaps a bit of that tuneless singing, which sometimes followed when sufficient wine had been consumed.

To that end he headed to his club where a group of his friends appeared to still be where he left them, six or so months ago, propping up the bar, contemplating the night to come or reliving the previous night's revelries.

'Jacko,' came the jubilant cry from the assembled men.

'Long time no see,' Giles Winthrop said, pulling over a stool for Jackson. 'A little bird told me that you've been involved in some charity or other, something to do with fallen women.'

This elicited much raucous laughter from the men, back-slapping and the expected jokes about Jackson and women of ill repute. Jackson took it with as much good humour as he could, all the while thinking of Pretty Kitty and knowing she did not deserve to be the butt of these privileged men's humour.

'What have you got planned for tonight?' he asked once they'd exhausted all their jokes.

'First we're off to the Gaiety Theatre,' Giles said. 'The latest play finishes tonight so there should be a high old party afterwards. And plenty of chorus girls who will just be dying to show an earl, baron or viscount or two how to really have a good time.'

Once again this was followed by raucous laughter and jokes about chorus girls, most of which bore a similar theme to the jokes about fallen women. Were his friends always this predictable? Or was it because, unlike them, he was completely sober?

That was something easily remedied. He signalled to the steward, who picked up a brandy balloon and poured a generous amount, knowing exactly what Jackson's tipple was.

He downed it in one and signalled for a refill, hoping the ennui possessing him could be washed away in a tide of alcohol. That soon he'd develop his familiar enthusiasm for parties, chorus girls and women who wanted to show a viscount how to have a good time.

Once sufficient liquor had been consumed, the men climbed into a series of hansom cabs. Encouraging their drivers into a competition with promises of generous tips for the winner, they raced across town to the Gaiety Theatre, where the performance was coming to an end.

With much noise, a few men tripping over their chairs and guffaws of laughter as if this was a hilarious comedy act, the group took their seats in a reserved box. Once they'd settled, they looked down at the chorus girls dancing on the stage below.

'Look at how high those chits can get their legs,' one man said, causing more guffawing from the others and a few smutty jokes about the party to come.

Jackson sighed at the lack of respect for women who were merely doing the job they were paid to do, while his friends continued to laugh heartily around him. He really was becoming the sort of man he once despised, a judgemental bore who doesn't know how to enjoy himself. That really had to stop.

The performance finished, the men made their way round to the backstage, where they were welcomed by the same young ladies they'd seen dancing. Before long Jackson found himself at a raucous party in the back rooms of a nearby tavern, where there was indeed plenty of wine and women, with the singing provided by the performers, thank goodness, and not by Jackson and his friends.

'This really is a high old time,' a chorus girl said to him, sliding her hand around his waist and pressing her comely body into his. 'Isn't it?'

She was such a pretty young thing, with big blue eyes, a cheeky smile and the lithesome, strong body you'd expect from someone who made their living through dance. In other words, exactly the sort of young woman that always attracted him. And that look in her eye made it clear that she intended to celebrate the final performance by letting her hair down and going delightfully wild.

Yes, she was exactly his sort of woman. He placed his arm around her shoulder, and that cheeky smile became ever the more encouraging.

'Indeed it is,' he said, introducing himself.

'Pleased to meet you, Jackson,' she said. 'I'm Maggy.'

'A delightful name for a delightful young lady,' he said, surprised at how easily this all came back to him. 'And perhaps you and I could make tonight even more of a high old time, in private of course.'

'I imagine that could be arranged,' Maggy said with a quick, saucy wink.

With his arm draped over her shoulder they made their way towards the door. 'Are you in the chorus?' he asked, even though he knew the answer, but a smattering of polite conversation was surely required.

'Yes, but I'd love to be an actress. Unfortunately...' She shrugged then smiled up at him.

'Unfortunately what? What's stopping you? I think you'd make a fine actress. You're certainly pretty enough.'

She simpered slightly at the compliment. 'But I never did learn my letters and it's a bit hard to remember all them lines if you can't read.'

He stopped walking just as they reached the door. 'No, don't let that stop you—' His words were cut off by Giles, who crashed into him, his arms around two smiling chorus girls.

'Watch out for that one,' Giles said to Maggy, laughing at his own joke. 'We used to call him the three-minute man, because he could get most women out of their drawers in less than three minutes.'

Jackson rolled his eyes at his friend's attempt at bawdy humour, took Maggy's hand and led her back into the room towards a quieter area of the chaotic tavern.

'It's true,' Giles called out from across the noisy room. 'We timed him once.'

'That's quite some achievement,' she said, that saucy smile returning. 'I might not be able to read and write but I can tell time, so maybe we can put you to the test.' She frowned as she took in the small nook. 'Just not here, if you don't mind, you promised me somewhere private.'

'No, that's not why I brought you back here. I wanted to tell you about The Women's Education Institute in the East End. They provide lessons in reading and writing skills. Its free and the tutors are extremely kind and encouraging. If you learnt to read, I'm sure in no time at all you'd be out of the chorus line and a star in your own right.'

The young woman's cheeky smile disappeared and her face became serious. 'Honestly? Do you really think I could learn to read?'

'I know so. And I know that if you really put your mind to it, you could become the fine actress you want to be.'

She smiled at him, her eyes sparkling. 'Right. I'll go along tomorrow. Ta ever so much. I better get going so I can get a good night's sleep and get down there first thing in the morning.' With that she rushed out the door.

Jackson watched her go, a sense of satisfaction and achievement washing through him.

'What on earth did you say to scare that one off?' Giles said as he staggered over, his own companions also having disappeared. 'The way that one was looking at you I was sure she was in the bag.'

Jackson slapped his friend on the back. 'I have hopefully helped her achieve her dreams, and I must say it feels rather good.'

Giles frowned at him briefly then laughed. 'Well, there's plenty of others whose dreams you can also answer. These two girls said that they'd be happy to...' He looked around as if suddenly discovering he'd lost his companions. 'Where did they go?' Spotting them in the corner talking to a group of men he staggered off, a champagne bottle raised above his head, and burst into off-key singing.

The two young women joined in with his singing and some impromptu high-kick dancing, which Giles in his inebriated state unsuccessfully tried to replicate, much to the hilarity from everyone else in the heaving room.

This was exactly Jackson's type of place. These were exactly his type of people. So why was he staring at the large clock behind the bar and wondering when it would be all right for him to depart?

It was gone three o'clock. Surely that was enough mayhem for tonight. He'd made an effort. He'd indulged in the activities he used to enjoy. It hadn't been quite as much fun as he remembered, but perhaps he was just out of practice.

Tomorrow night he'd make even more of an effort to once again restore his reputation as a reveller, a man for whom no party was too wild, no indulgence too excessive.

After all, if he didn't do that, what else did he have?

Despite the confident words she had said to Amelia, and then repeated to Georgina and Irene at their afternoon tea, Emily had stayed away from the school for several days, nursing her wounds. But she could put it off no longer and today was the day she would take back her old life.

'Will you be shopping again this afternoon?' her mother asked as Emily stood at the front door while the maid helped her into her coat.

That simple question hit Emily so hard in the chest it took her breath away. She closed her eyes briefly then smiled at her mother. 'No, not today. I'll be visiting the school in the morning and I should be home for luncheon.'

'Oh, do you finally have enough gloves?'

Emily felt her eyes grow wide as her mother continued to smile at her. Was there a hidden meaning behind that innocent question? Did her mother really know how Emily was spending her afternoons? Was guilt making her overly suspicious?'

'Yes, I have sufficient gloves now.' Enough gloves to last me a lifetime, and each pair of gloves will be a painful reminder of where and why I bought them. Emily breathed in deeply and exhaled slowly. She would dispose of those gloves at the first opportunity. She most certainly did not want their presence undermining her determination to remain stoic, or her ability to put her time with Jackson firmly where it belonged, in the past.

'Perhaps there is something else you could shop for. Hats perhaps,' her mother added.

'I do not need to shop for anything,' she said louder than she meant, causing her mother to widen her eyes in surprise.

'Will Viscount Wickford be at the school today?'

'No,' Emily replied, suddenly wishing her mother would go back to discussing shopping. 'He is no longer involved with the school.' She swallowed down the lump that had formed in her throat.

'Such a shame. Men like the Viscount are a rare breed.'

Emily stared at her mother. Was she serious? 'Well, all I can say about that is thank goodness. The fewer rakes there are in the world the better.'

'There's nothing wrong with a man who knows how to enjoy himself,' her mother said, causing Emily to wonder if she had ever really known her mother. She had despised Randall Cochran for being a rake, now she was praising Jackson for the same behaviour.

'And I've never seen you happier than when the two of you were working together to make that school of yours a success,' her mother added, smiling at Emily. A rather self-satisfied smile that made Emily wary of what was to come next. 'It made you almost as happy as all those shopping expeditions did.'

Emily swallowed again. Her mother knew. Or at least she suspected her involvement with Jackson. Emily could only hope she did not know just how involved she had really become. If she did, she certainly would not be smiling.

'My dear,' her mother continued, dismissing the maid with a wave of her hand. 'Happiness is a rare commodity. Whatever has happened to make you stop shopping so regularly, I believe you should try and find a way to rekindle the desire to do so.' With that her mother patted her on the arm and walked up the hallway, leaving a stunned Emily staring at her retreating back.

With as much composure as she could muster following that bizarre conversation, she left the house and took the carriage to the school. Her new life was to start again, today. It was time to put all her troubles away, and bury herself in what she loved doing most; working hard for the benefit of others.

With that in mind, with her head held high and her shoulders firmly back, she walked from classroom to classroom to see where she was best needed. Each classroom was fully occupied in the task at hand, whether it was reading and writing lessons, classes training young women to become maids, kitchen staff, dressmakers or an array of other areas of employment. There was even a new class teaching young women how to use modern typewriters, the loud clacking of keys filling the air. And there was Kitty, sitting among the dexterous women. Was there no skill she was determined not to master?

She looked around the busy room and at the tutor, providing instruction to one struggling student.

No one needed Emily's help. That was all for the good, even if it did not satisfy Emily's need to be busy. She scanned the classroom one more time to see if there was something, anything, she could do. Kitty waved to her from the back of the class and signalled her over.

'What are you working on now, Kitty?' she asked, looking down at the confusing metal contraption with all its levers, rollers and ribbons.

'I'm typing out a business letter. This is actually rather fun. I think I prefer it to embroidery and sewing. I can see myself working in a nice warm office.' She smiled up at Emily.

'I'm very pleased to hear that,' she said, looking over Kitty's shoulder at the piece of paper poking out from the typewriter's roller. It was a letter from a fictitious lawyer to a client and looked rather professional.

'So, is everything all right with you, my lady?' Kitty asked.

'Why, yes, of course it is,' Emily responded, surprised that Kitty should enquire after her health.

'Well, you don't seem your usual self, and you have been looking ever so happy lately.'

'What? No, everything is fine.' Emily attempted to cover her surprise with a large smile. A reaction that only caused Kitty to glance at her sideways, eyebrows raised.

'Will the Viscount be gracing us with his presence today?'

Emily was sure she detected some hidden meaning in Kitty's words, but perhaps she was just being overly sensitive to the mention of Jackson's name. Just as she had with her mother's comments about shopping.

'I very much doubt it,' she said, keeping her voice as even as possible. 'He has informed Mr Greaves he will no longer be involved in the running of the school.' Good, her voice betrayed nothing of what she was feeling.

'That's a shame,' Kitty said, still giving her that strange sideways look. 'He's such a fine, upstanding gentleman, that one.'

Emily gritted her teeth together. She did not need a lecture from Kitty on Jackson's character.

'You'll meet none better,' Kitty continued. 'A real hero to my way of thinking.'

Emily gave a tight smile and nodded, while looking down at Kitty's typed letter as if fascinated by the legal terminology. 'Well, yes, I suppose he did act rather heroic on that evening he saved you.'

'I reckon he's not the only one he's saved.'

She turned her attention to Kitty, trying to decipher the meaning of her words. Everyone appeared to be making obscure, cryptic references today that she couldn't quite grasp. Kitty with her claims that Jackson is a saviour, and her mother's reference to her need to find happiness through shopping. Or was she reading more into their words than actually existed? Emily deemed it sensible to assume the latter.

'I wouldn't know,' she said, looking around the room at the other busy typists, as if intrigued by all the activity.

'I reckon any woman who had a man like him in her life would be silly to let him go,' Kitty said. 'She should fight tooth and nail to keep him.'

*She did know.*

Emily grasped the edge of the desk, her legs suddenly weak.

'Don't worry,' Kitty whispered. 'Your secret is safe with me, but I've been around long enough to know that look in a woman's eye when she's enamoured with a man, and a gentleman's eye to that matter, when he fancies a lady.'

Emily knew she should admonish Kitty and tell her that she had gone too far. Instead, she stared at Kitty, unable to talk, words flying around in her head and refusing to settle into sensible sentences.

'I also know what a woman looks like when she thinks she's lost her man. All I'm saying is, that one is definitely worth fighting for and you shouldn't just give up until you've won him.'

'It's not as easy as that,' Emily finally choked out.

'It never is, but if something is worth fighting for, it doesn't matter how hard it is, you just have to fight even harder and never give up.'

Emily looked around at the other students, who were engrossed in their work and paying them no heed.

'All I can say,' Kitty continued, 'is you deserve a good man in your life. One who makes you laugh and smile. You need a man who makes you happy. That musty old doctor never did it.'

Emily raised her eyebrows. Was there nothing this young woman missed?

'I saw the way that doctor looked at you when I visited the hospital, like you were a meal ticket. And I saw the way you looked at him.' She shook her head. 'It was nothing like the way you looked at the Viscount.' She sighed and smiled contentedly. 'I could tell you were in love.'

'It doesn't matter whether I was or I wasn't,' Emily said, lowering her voice. Kitty leant forward so she could hear. 'The Viscount was the one to end things, not me.'

'Well, sometimes men don't know what they want and it's up to us women to let them know. You need to show him that he is in love with you, even if he doesn't yet realise it.'

For Kitty it all seemed so simple, but she did not understand. Jackson did not want her. By now he had probably moved onto the next woman. Some other woman was making discreet visits to his flat at the Tanner Street Shopping Arcade. Some other woman was in his arms, in his bed, some other woman was experiencing what she so briefly experienced and would never experience again.

'I have to go,' she muttered to Kitty, rushing out the room before the tears started to fall and she made herself look ridiculous in front of the tutor and all these industrious students.

# Chapter Nineteen

Jackson was trying, really trying, but his nights were not going to plan. Each evening he set out with a renewed determination to enjoy himself to the full, and each morning he came home feeling as if it was all somehow pointless.

Every night followed the same pattern. There was gambling, there was plenty of wine and brandy, there were willing young women, everything a man could possibly want to ensure he had a memorable night. And yet his good humour was forced from the moment he arrived at his club, and each night had ended the same, with him returning to his bed in the small hours of the morning, alone and dispirited.

'You're losing your touch,' Giles informed him last night, or was it early this morning? 'All those good works have ruined you for having a good time,' he'd added, laughing uproariously as if he had made a hilarious joke.

It wasn't particularly funny, but was it right? He *would* rather spend his time helping to improve the lives of people like Pretty Kitty than carousing night after night with his old friends. And, damn it all, he'd much rather be doing so with Emily.

He'd asked Giles's chorus girlfriends about Maggy and was pleased to hear she had indeed signed up for reading lessons. She was reportedly so excited about what she was learning that she had convinced several other girls in the chorus to join as well. This caused Giles to roll his eyes, but it gave Jackson more satisfaction than anything else that had happened since he had ended his relationship with Emily.

He picked at the plate of food in front of him. It was closer to lunchtime than breakfast, but after a night on the tiles his first meal of the day was always a hearty breakfast. Cook claimed it was the best way for Jackson to get over the excesses of the night before and prepare himself for the night ahead. Usually, Jackson would agree, but unfortunately, once again he had no appetite. No appetite for food or for anything else it would seem.

He speared the bacon with his fork. Perhaps tonight would be different. Perhaps tonight his spirit would be revitalised. Perhaps tonight he might not have to push himself so hard to have the good time that used to come to him so naturally.

He'd arranged to meet Giles and the others at his club in the early evening, yet again, for another night of carousing. This time they planned to attend a party hosted by the Prince of Wales's latest mistress. Such parties had always been a highlight for any man determined to enjoy life to the full. Not only were they wild and raucous but they were often featured in the scandal sheets, which provided the added enjoyment of shocking his father.

He sighed deeply. What was wrong with him? Even the thought of shocking his father held no real appeal. Giles was right. All that good work had ruined him for having a good time. Or was it Lady Emily Beaumont who had ruined him for having a good time? Was it the memory of her face, her smile, not to mention her gorgeous body, that had changed him on such a fundamental level he no longer knew how to enjoy himself?

No, that wasn't right. He'd enjoyed himself when he'd been with Emily, more than he had realised was possible. There was a certain irony in what had happened, which he could find funny, if he didn't find it so tragic. He'd been horrified when he'd woken in the Hope Charity Hospital to find the do-gooding Lady Emily looking down at him. He'd worried he'd be subjected to moralising sermons about his wayward lifestyle. Never for a moment did he think she would destroy his ability to live a wayward lifestyle, not by sermons, but because he fell in love with her.

But he would not let her change him for ever. Nor would he let his unrequited love destroy the life he had lived before he met her. He was not the first man to experience a heartbreak, although this was the first time this particular man had experienced that particular affliction. But it would pass. It had to pass. Didn't it? All he had to do was try harder, live it up more recklessly and indulge himself even more excessively. Easy.

He quickly sliced up his bacon into small pieces as if to underline the strength of his feelings. From this moment on he would stop thinking about Emily and what they had shared. Yes, they'd had their fun, just as he'd had fun with numerous other women before her and would do the same with countless women in the future. She'd made it clear the extent of her feelings for him, which did not extend very far, and he would waste not a minute longer ruminating on what was or could have been.

He *would* go out again tonight. He *would* have a good time. He would drink, carouse and lose himself in the arms of some delightful young woman and he most certainly would not spend even a second pining over her.

Keeping that in mind through the day, and crushing down any thoughts of Emily every time they surfaced, he entered his club that night and plastered on his most joyful smile. He was determined to show the world that bonhomie he was famous for.

'So, are we up for painting the town red before we join His Majesty and his friends?' he asked, slapping Giles on the back with a hearty thump.

'That we are,' his friend replied with genuine happiness at seeing him. 'I've promised to take those two chorus girls along. They're so excited about meeting a member of the royal family, and I'm sure they'll be more than willing to show their gratitude.' He winked at Jackson then called out to the steward for more bottles of champagne to be opened. 'But first, let's celebrate the night to come.'

Corks were popped. As the stewards quickly poured the bubbling wine into glasses before it frothed down the sides of bottles, the assembled men let out a resounding cheer, as if it was an unexpected event, instead of what they did every night, night after night.

But Jackson would not think about that now. In fact, from this moment on, he would not be thinking. He would misbehave, he would frolic, he would revel, romp and roister.

And, hopefully, his antics would make it into the scandal sheets. Then he would have the satisfaction of not only shocking his father, but with any luck Lady Emily as well. Then she would know that he was well and truly over her and had not given the end of their time together a second thought.

* * *

Jackson had achieved everything he set out to achieve, at least the pounding in his head and his ferocious thirst suggested he had. Of the night before he had little recollection, which had to be a good sign, didn't it?

Just after midday he stumbled downstairs and slumped into a chair at the breakfast table, still dressed in his robe.

'The morning and the midday mail,' the footman said, removing a small pile of letters from his silver tray and placing them beside Jackson's plate. One bore his father's familiar handwriting. With a resigned sigh he picked up a knife and cut it open. It contained the usual information on the estate, but surprisingly no admonition on Jackson's behaviour. That was presumably because Jackson's antics had not made it into the scandal sheets recently. Hopefully whatever he got up to last night would be covered in salacious detail and that odd state of affairs would be put to rights.

The next bore the elegant handwriting of his solicitor. He quickly perused the legal jargon, only to be reassured that the state of his finances was predictably healthy.

He turned over the typewritten letter. It bore no address of the sender, so he cut it open and quickly perused its contents as he buttered his toast.

His knife clattered onto the plate as the full force of the vile words hit him.

*I am writing to inform you that I am disgusted to learn that Lady Emily Beaumont has been party to immoral practices involving yourself.*

*For an unmarried woman to indulge in such vices with a man who has no intention of making an hon-*

*est woman of her is the very definition of moral tur-
pitude.*

Jackson gripped the letter tightly, his thudding head-
ache gone, his raging thirst forgotten.

*I also wish to inform you of my intention of alert-
ing the board members of The Women's Education
Institute, who I am sure will immediately dismiss a
woman of such low character. I also intend to write
to her parents, who no doubt will deal with her immoral behaviour as they deem fit.*

Jackson shoved the offensive letter into the pocket of his
robe and rushed upstairs, yelling for his valet to help him
dress, immediately. Without bothering to shave, or wait for
his cravat to be tied properly, he rushed out of the house,
ignoring the footman attempting to hand him his hat and
gloves.

With no time to arrange for his own carriage he waved
down a passing hansom cab and gave him instructions to
take him to the Beaumonts' townhouse. As the cab drove
through the busy streets, far too slowly and cautiously in
Jackson's opinion, he tried to think what he would say to
Emily and her parents.

Nothing came to mind, apart from how sorry he was,
something that was less than useless under the circumstances.

The cab pulled up in front of her house. He jumped
down before it had come to a complete stop and threw some
money in the driver's direction.

'Thank you, guv,' the driver said. 'You'll be wanting

some change,' he called out as Jackson raced up the pathway and pounded on the door.

A footman opened the door and, before he could speak, Jackson pushed passed him, ran down the hallway into the drawing room and found Emily seated by the window, drinking a cup of tea and perusing a magazine.

He stood in the doorway, gasping to catch his breath, and stared at her. Had she always been this divinely beautiful? With the light streaming through the large sash windows, she was bathed in golden sunshine, giving her a radiance that was breathtaking. Everything about her seemed to glow—her chestnut hair, that soft, dewlike skin, those big brown eyes.

How could he not have fallen hopelessly in love with such a woman. He was only a man after all, a particularly weak man, and she was like a goddess. It was so obvious now that a woman like her could never love him the way he loved her. And it just went to show how intelligent she was that she had seen straight through him to his true character, and knew he was not for her.

'Jackson—I mean, Viscount Wickford, this is a surprise,' she said, standing up, her eyes large, suggesting this was more than a surprise. She was shocked.

Jackson remembered why he was here. It was not to admire Emily. It was not to wallow in self-pity over what he'd had and what he'd lost. It was to deal with the letter, its incendiary contents burning a hole in his pocket.

'I am so sorry, Emily,' he said, rushing over to her chair. He was about to take her hands to comfort her, then stopped abruptly, remembering he had no right to do so.

Instead, he stood before her, crushed under the weight of guilt and shame.

'I will of course inform the board that you were completely innocent. I shall tell them that I forced myself on you and then once I'd had my way with you, I blackmailed you into continuing to meet with me against your will. I'll say I threatened to blacken your name in Society unless you gave me what I wanted, but at all times you were completely innocent and completely unwilling. If that results in your parents prosecuting me, then so be it, but believe me, I will do everything in my power to make sure you are not punished for what I have done, what I should never have done.'

She frowned and shook her head as if trying to make sense of what he was saying.

'I am so, so sorry,' he repeated, knowing his words were ineffective, and there was nothing he could really do or say to undo this travesty.

'And I'm sorry too because I have no idea what you are talking about,' she said.

'The board, the threats, the accusations.' He fumbled into his pocket to pull out the letter. 'Here, this arrived this morning. I had assumed a similar one had been sent to you as well.'

She smoothed out the crumpled paper, read its contents and her hand flew to her mouth to cover a gasp.

'I'm so sorry,' he repeated ineffectively.

'Who? How? Why?' She gasped out. 'We were so careful. No one knew. I'm sure of it.'

'It hardly matters who, how or why. Someone saw us. Someone is planning on telling the board and now I have to make things right.'

She stared up at him, the offensive letter clasped in her hands.

'By telling everyone you forced me? By telling a lie?'

Jackson shrugged. 'Yes, of course.'

'But you didn't force me.'

'But I should not have let it happen. I know the consequences for women such as yourself who stray off the strict path laid down by Society.'

'As did I.'

'But, Emily, you don't understand. You'll be ruined. Society will shun you. You'll, well, you'll never be able to find a husband.'

She rolled her eyes, causing him to wonder if she realised just how serious this was.

'They're threatening to tell your parents. They will be scandalised,' he continued, desperate to make her understand. 'They're threatening to tell the board members. You'll never be able to do charity work again. Your life will be ruined and it's all my fault.'

'No, it's the fault of whoever wrote this appalling letter.' She turned it over. 'They don't even have the decency to sign it.'

He threw his hands up in the air. 'That hardly matters. It was probably one of those women from the Ladies for the Promotion of High Moral Standards.'

She frowned. 'Yes, except they wouldn't hesitate to sign it, and would not warn us of their intentions. They'd go straight to the board, and they wouldn't just want my resignation. They'd use this knowledge to have the school shut down.'

'I don't know, perhaps one of them is planning to blackmail us first.'

She turned the letter over, looking remarkably calm under the circumstances. 'If it was a blackmail letter surely it would say what they expect from you, so they don't reveal this information.' She shrugged. 'They'd ask for a large amount of money or something. And it's strange that a blackmailer would send it to you when it is my good name they are threatening. Surely they'd try and extort money out of me.'

He threw up his hands again in exasperation. None of that surely mattered. 'All that is as it may be, but we need to end this. So, I shall tell your parents immediately what I have done. Are they home?' He looked towards the door.

'No. And I believe we should think this through before you take any hasty action.'

She reread the letter. 'The writer hasn't told either my parents or the board members yet. I met with Mr Greaves earlier this morning and he made no comment about anything that is mentioned in this letter. He did, however, mention you.'

Jackson's stomach clenched tighter. 'Mr Greaves is a decent man. If he had been told, he would no doubt see this would all be my fault, not yours, and presumably did not wish to distress you, but the sooner I confess and put an end to this the better.'

'I don't believe that to be the case. Mr Greaves continued to sing your praises. He said, not for the first time, it was such a shame you had resigned from the school. He said he even intends to contact you to see if he could encourage you to change your mind.'

'He what? Well, he won't be thinking that once he hears about this.' He pointed at the offensive letter.

'Did you know that the school has invested in several typewriters and is teaching secretarial skills?'

'What? No.' And surely under the circumstances it would be of no interest to him.

She read the letter again and smiled.

Smiled? She actually smiled.

Had the shock of the letter caused her to lose her mind?

'There's only one person I'm acquainted with who knows how to use a typewriter.' She looked up at him, still with that incongruous smile. 'I think what we have here is the work of one Miss Kathryn Trotter.'

'What? Who?' he all but shouted.

'Also known as Pretty Kitty.'

'What? Who?' he repeated, his confusion growing with every word she said. 'Why on earth would Kitty want to threaten us, blackmail us and try and ruin your life?'

He looked to Emily, imploring her to make sense of something so senseless.

'Because she knew exactly how you would react. She is trying to prove a point to me. And it looks like she succeeded.'

# Chapter Twenty

'Point, what point?' Jackson said, pacing backwards and forwards as if trying to control his explosive energy.

Emily looked down at the letter in her hand, unsure how to answer that question without revealing too much.

'All I can say is I am confident she had no intention of threatening us or of blackmailing us, or even of going through with anything she said in the letter.'

He shook his head, his eyebrows drawn so close together they were almost touching. 'None of this is making any sense.'

Emily lightly scratched her forehead. She was going to have to tell him of her conversation with Kitty. She wished she did not have to, but given Jackson's obvious agitation, what choice did she have other than to put him out of his misery? 'What I suspect she is doing is a bit of match-making.'

'She's what?' He stopped his pacing and looked over at the letter in her hand. His confusion was justified. If you want to get two people back together it certainly was a strange way to go about it. But then, it had succeeded in a way, hadn't it?

She drew in a strength-giving breath, determined to get this over as quickly as possible so he could be on his way.

'I was talking to Kitty the other day and she is under the impression that you and I are more than just colleagues, that there has been, shall we say, a dalliance between us.'

'It seems Kitty is rather perceptive. Let's hope she's the only one,' he said, staggering over to the divan and sitting down. 'But why on earth would she send me such a letter? What on earth is she hoping to achieve? And what's all this about matchmaking?'

'She believes you to be a hero. She would know that if you believed me to be under threat you would immediately try and rescue me, just as you did with her.'

He continued frowning as if he could not understand Kitty's reasoning. But Emily knew Kitty was right. Jackson *was* an honourable man. He was a man who would do whatever it took to save a woman in distress, but that did not mean he loved her. He had taken a beating to save Kitty and she had been a complete stranger to him. Of course he would save a woman in distress, any woman.

'If that's true, then it means your reputation is safe,' he said slowly.

'Yes.'

'That's good then, I suppose. It means no one knows about what happened between us.'

'No one knows except Kitty, it would seem.'

'Yes, but if what you suspect is true, then she means you no harm.' He exhaled a low, loud sigh, looked up at her, then quickly stood, as if suddenly realising he was seated in the company of a woman who was still standing. That was a formality they had hitherto abandoned but it seemed such behaviour was no longer acceptable.

'So what exactly did Kitty say to you that made you realise the letter had to be from her?'

She took a seat, and indicated for him to sit, giving herself time to formulate how she was going to phrase this. 'As I said, she has a very high opinion of you and thinks you are a hero.'

He laughed dismissively. 'You save one street walker and suddenly your sullied reputation is redeemed and you're a hero.'

'You did save her from a terrible fate.'

He shrugged as if it were of no account.

'And you did just offer to confess to a crime you didn't commit, one that would surely have had dire consequences for you, all to save my reputation.'

He shrugged again.

'If my parents had decided to prosecute you could have been sent to jail. *Your* reputation would be sullied for ever.'

He gave another shrug as if that sacrifice was also of no account.

'I believe you have heroic qualities you prefer not to acknowledge.'

'I'm just relieved this will go no further, although I still can't for the life of me understand Kitty's thinking.'

'I suppose she didn't just want to prove to me what a hero you are, she also wanted to get us back together so we would talk and, perhaps, well, you know.' It was her turn to shrug, suddenly feeling shy in front of a man with whom she had shared so many intimacies, both physical and emotional.

'That we would become lovers again,' he added for her.

'Yes, I suppose so. Although I think she even believes that we could be more than that.' She gave a false laugh as if dismissing Kitty's romantic delusions. 'Perhaps she thought that you'd offer to make an honest woman of me, rather than offer to go to jail.'

He huffed out a dismissive laugh. 'Then Kitty doesn't know as much as she think she does. Did you not tell her you had no intention of marrying, and certainly a man such as me?'

'I may have alluded to that, but I don't think she believed me.'

'You should have spelt it out for her then and told her you didn't want any more from me than you'd already had. That all you'd ever wanted was some fun with a man you could never have any real feelings for. Then she would never have written that letter and caused us such distress.'

'Why would I say that?' Emily asked quietly.

He looked down at his hands, clasping his knees. 'I'm sorry. I have a somewhat embarrassing confession to make. I arrived at your house on the day you hosted the afternoon tea to save the school, after the moralising ladies had left, and overheard your conversation with your friends. So I know how you really feel about our relationship.'

Heat burst onto Emily's face. He had overheard her tell her friends she was in love with him and then he had immediately ended things.

'Is that why you said we should not see each other again?' she choked out.

'Yes.'

Emily's heart shattered into even smaller pieces.

'I suppose then it is me that should apologise to you,' she said, unable to control the small tremor in her voice. 'I know it was not what we agreed when we became lovers.' She looked down at her hands, gripped tightly together to stop them from shaking. 'I know I told you there would be no emotional involvement, but I promise you, I never had any intentions of not abiding by our agreement. I would never have made demands on you.'

He leant forward in his seat and stared at her, his forehead once again furrowed. 'Demands on me? Abiding by our agreement? What are you talking about?'

Did he really want her to spell it out? Could he not see that she was already humiliated enough? So much for being a hero. 'What I said to my friends. You know.'

'About me being someone with whom you just want to have fun? Someone who could never mean anything more to you than that? That you were just waiting for it to run its course and end?'

'No, the rest of it.'

'What rest of it? There was more? What you had said was hurtful enough, even if I did have to agree with the sentiment.'

He didn't know. He hadn't heard her tell her friends she had fallen in love with him. Relief swept through her. She had not completely humiliated herself in front of the man she loved, the man who had no feelings for her.

'So you might as well tell me the whole story. What else did you tell your friends? That you were better off without me in your life? That it had been a big mistake getting involved with a lowlife like me in the first place?'

'I said none of those things because none of them are true.'

'Perhaps you should have.'

'No, and you shouldn't think like that about yourself either. You are a good man even if you refuse to admit it. You saved Kitty. You wanted to save me. You started up a school that is helping a lot of women and will help countless more. And you've done all that without once wanting to take any credit, like so many other men would.'

Kitty's words came back to her. *'That one is definitely worth fighting for.'* She was right. But how do you fight for a man who doesn't want you? Perhaps she could start by being truthful. What was the worst that could happen? She had already been rejected by him. He was already lost to her. There was nothing worse that could happen.

'You only overheard the first part of what I was saying to my friends. When I was trying to convince them and myself that you meant nothing to me.'

His furrowed brow smoothed out as he raised his eyebrows in question.

'If you had stayed a bit longer you would have heard me tell them what I really felt,' she rushed on before she risked losing her nerve. 'You would have heard me confess that I had fallen in love with you.'

The words seemed to hang in the air as she held her breath and waited for his response.

'Did I just hear you correctly? Did you say you told your friends you were in love with me?'

She stared at the ground as if there was something fascinating on the carpet. 'Yes, but you were never supposed to hear. I know I promised you I would not fall in love with you, but, well, I failed.'

She looked up at him. 'But don't worry. I don't expect anything from you. Don't start acting all heroic and thinking you have to marry me or anything.'

'Oh, Emily, my love, my darling,' he said, smiling and slowly shaking his head. 'When I heard you telling your friends that you could never love me, I had to end our relationship because I could not bear to continue to see a woman I had fallen hopelessly in love with, all the while knowing she did not feel the same about me and never would.'

'What?' Emily spluttered. 'Love? You? Me?'

'Yes, love, you, me,' he said, crossing the room, taking her hands and lifting her to her feet.

'I love you, Emily Beaumont,' he said, and kissed her.

Was this really happening? Emily could hardly believe it to be true. But could her imagination really conjure up that familiar heady scent, the touch of his rough skin against her cheek, the feel of his muscles against her? No, this was reality, and it was so much better than any dream.

When he withdrew from her lips, he lightly kissed her on the forehead. She closed her eyes and sighed.

'You can't possibly know how happy you have made me,' he said.

'You're wrong.' She opened her eyes and looked up at him. 'I think I know exactly how happy you feel.'

'Emily, my love,' he said, gently stroking her forehead and pushing a stray lock of hair behind her ear. 'I never thought I'd have you in my arms again, and that thought was torture.'

'Yes, torture, for me too,' she said, amazed at how inarticulate his kisses had made her. 'So kiss me again and end this torture.'

He laughed lightly, but did as she commanded, his urgent lips finding hers.

Fire burned within her as his kiss deepened. He loved her, that had to mean he still wanted her for his lover. She kissed him back, releasing the fervid desire for him that she'd been denied over the painful days and nights of their separation.

He broke from her kiss and she wondered if he was thinking what she was; that they should lock the door so no one would enter, and fully satisfy their need for each other.

'As we have so much to thank Pretty Kitty for, perhaps we should invite her to our wedding,' he said, smiling down at her, the smile that always made her weak with desire.

'Yes, of course,' Emily said, sure she would agree to anything that would stop his talking, so those lips could return to hers.

'What?' she said, withdrawing from him as the intent of his words hit her.

'That is if you would do me the honour of becoming my wife.'

She looked into his eyes. Was he teasing her?

'Will you, Emily? Will you marry me?' he repeated.

Emily could only nod, seemingly incapable of forming words.

'I promise I will do everything in my power to make you happy, every single day of your life,' he continued as if she hadn't already given her agreement. 'I love you so much it is hard to believe that one man could possess so much love, and I need to share that love with you.'

She nodded again.

'If you will be my wife, I promise I will try to be a man worthy of you, worthy of a woman who is so good, so kind, so beautiful, so wonderful in every way.'

She nodded faster. 'Yes, I will marry you,' she said, finally finding her words. 'And you don't have to prove you are worthy of me, you have already proven that, again and again.' She smiled up at him. 'Although, if you really do want to prove your worth to me, you can kiss me again, right now.'

'With pleasure,' he said, his arms holding her closer as he kissed her long and deep. A kiss that expressed more eloquently than words ever could how much they loved each other.

# Epilogue

'I knew eventually you'd find the perfect man,' her mother said when she told her she was to wed Jackson, while her father merely smiled at them both benevolently.

'And now my little girl is going to marry for love, just as your father and I did,' she patted the corner of her eyes with her lace handkerchief.

Once again her mother had seen what it had taken Emily so long to see, that Jackson *was* perfect for her. The man she had once thought wrong in so many ways, but in the end he was exactly the right man for her. Her mother had been correct about Randall and Gideon and she had been right about Jackson.

'Thank you, Mother,' she said, squeezing her hand. 'And thank you for seeing Jackson's fine qualities even before I did.'

'I hope that means you're going to listen to me in the future.'

Emily shrugged, then smiled. 'Of course I will. Especially when you encourage me to do things like go shopping.'

Her mother arched her eyebrows, smiled slightly, but said nothing.

While her parents couldn't be happier, Jackson's father did not greet the news with such joyousness.

'Wonders will never cease,' he said, frowning at them over his newspaper. 'You've actually found a decent woman prepared to marry you.' He directed his frown at Emily as if unable to understand how she could possibly want to spend the rest of her life with his son.

'Yes, I found my hero and I'm never going to let him go,' she said, smiling up at Jackson while the old Duke looked on in disbelief.

'Seems she's a bit addled in the head,' he muttered before returning to his newspaper. 'You're made for each other.'

Jackson's expression turned dark at what had been intended as an insult, but Emily placed a restraining hand on his arm. She would not let that bitter man ruin their happiness.

'Yes, you're quite right, Your Grace,' Emily said, causing Jackson to look at her as if she was indeed addled in the head. 'We are made for each other, and if this is what addle-headed feels like then I hope I remain this way for the rest of my life.'

This caused Jackson to laugh, and the old Duke to huff and shake his newspaper as if wishing to be rid of them.

'You're right,' Jackson said, when they left the old man's presence. 'His constant criticisms used to annoy me, and even provoke me into acting in ever more outrageous ways, just to horrify him further, but now I can see he is merely an unhappy old man and I feel sorry for him. Perhaps if my parents had been able to marry for love, if they had found the happiness I have…' He paused and kissed her on the top of her head. 'Then he would not be so angry all the time.'

Emily smiled at her husband-to-be, admiring his compassion for someone who had treated him so unfairly. But he was right. Without love, his father had become bitter and angry, and she was ever more grateful she had found a man she could love with all her heart and who loved her in return.

Just as Emily had been a bridesmaid for her three friends, Amelia, Irene and Georgina accompanied her up the aisle on her happy day. Emily could hardly contain her excitement throughout the wedding ceremony. She was about to become Jackson's wife. They would be spending the rest of their lives together. There would be no more subterfuge, no more hiding, they could love each other openly whenever and wherever they wanted.

And, as agreed, they invited Kitty to the wedding. Jackson even mentioned her in his speech at the wedding breakfast, and thanked her for bringing them together in the first place, and for her somewhat unusual way of bringing them back together when a terrible misunderstanding had nearly driven them apart.

They also had Kitty to thank for suggesting they hold some more of those fancy balls so they could open more schools. That was exactly what they intended to do. The success of The Women's Education Institute had shown them just how great the need was for such places for young women. Plans were already in place for another school in London, and Jackson and Emily could see no reason why this model could not be reproduced throughout England. All it took was dedication and hard work, something the two of them were eagerly anticipating.

The board members of the school and hospital, and many of the staff, also attended. Everyone was universally overjoyed by the union, although Jackson's friends still found it hard to believe that two people who had seemed so wrong for each other made such a happy couple.

'Being in love is the best feeling in the world,' she over-heard Jackson telling his disbelieving friend Giles during the ball following the wedding breakfast. 'When you fall in love yourself, you'll understand what I'm talking about. Emily has changed me and made me the man that deep down I always wanted to be. She has made me see what's important in life.'

The friend merely shook his head, presumably agreeing with the old Duke that love made you addle-headed.

'It changes a woman as well,' she said, sliding her arm around his waist. 'It makes her see what is important.'

'And what is really important is you and me, and our future together,' he said, leaning down and kissing his wife.

\* \* \* \* \*

*If you loved this story,*
*be sure to catch up with the rest of the*
*Rebellious Young Ladies miniseries*

Lady Amelia's Scandalous Secret
Miss Fairfax's Notorious Duke
Miss Georgina's Marriage Dilemma

*And why not check out Eva Shepherd's*
*other brilliant Harlequin Historical romances?*
*Including her Those Roguish Rosemonts miniseries*

A Dance to Save the Debutante
Tempting the Sensible Lady Violet
Falling for the Forbidden Duke